Blind Man's Bluff

A CANDLE ISLAND COZY

Blind Man's Bluff

MISS GUIDED

Sadie & Sophie Cuffe

FIVE STAR
A part of Gale, Cengage Learning

GALE
CENGAGE Learning

Farmington Hills, Mich • San Francisco • New York • Waterville, Maine
Meriden, Conn • Mason, Ohio • Chicago

GALE
CENGAGE Learning®

All scripture quotations, unless otherwise noted, are taken from the King James Bible.
Five Star™ Publishing, a part of Cengage Learning, Inc.

LIBRARY OF CONGRESS CATALOGING-IN-PUBLICATION DATA

Names: Cuffe, Sadie, author. | Cuffe, Sophie, author.
Title: Blind man's bluff : miss guided / Sadie & Sophie Cuffe.
Description: First edition. | Waterville, Maine : Five Star Publishing, 2017. | Series: A Candle Island Cozy ; book 1
Identifiers: LCCN 2016040457 (print) | LCCN 2016052151 (ebook) | ISBN 9781432832568 (hardback) | ISBN 1432832565 (hardcover) | ISBN 9781432834609 (ebook) | ISBN 1432834606 (ebook) | ISBN 9781432832452 (ebook) | ISBN 143283245X (ebook)
Subjects: | BISAC: FICTION / Mystery & Detective / Women Sleuths. | FICTION / Christian / General. | GSAFD: Christian fiction. | Mystery fiction.
Classification: LCC PS3603.U39 B57 2017 (print) | LCC PS3603.U39 (ebook) | DDC 813/.6—dc23
LC record available at https://lccn.loc.gov/2016040457

First Edition. First Printing: January 2017
Find us on Facebook– https://www.facebook.com/FiveStarCengage
Visit our website– http://www.gale.cengage.com/fivestar/
Contact Five Star™ Publishing at FiveStar@cengage.com

Printed in the United States of America
1 2 3 4 5 6 7 21 20 19 18 17

To our fifth-grade teacher, Agatha Hatch, who inspired us to be our best selves (sometimes through intimidation, but always with kindness) and was our lifelong encourager and supporter. And to teachers everywhere, in our family and in yours, who always give the best of themselves.

ACKNOWLEDGEMENTS

To our church families and friends in the many Maine coastal island communities of Vinalhaven, North Haven, Swans Island, Arrowsic, Five Islands, Georgetown, Islesboro, Deer Isle, Isle au Haut, and Deer Island (NB) and Campobello (NB), Canada. Our lives are so much richer because of our island connections.

To Terry Burns, Hartline Literary Agency (retired).

To our Lord and Savior Jesus Christ without Whom there would be no words, no music, and no happy endings.

Prologue

I sat up in the dark, heart thundering like the hooves of a Kentucky Derby winner. A second later I collapsed back into the pillow, the grumble of actual thunder barely audible over the din of rain pounding on the roof. I glanced at the clock radio; no display—timeless. The power was out and any minute now I'd need to get up and make sure the bucket under the unstoppable leak by the chimney was doing its job. I hunkered down under the blankets, willing my mind and pulse into that dopey sleepwalking state where I could do what had to be done without any brain activity involved.

I felt for the flashlight on the nightstand, my hand knocking into the phone just as it jangled. One ring, then silence. I picked it up anyway and fumbled it to my ear. Silent but surprisingly not dead, the dial tone buzzed the message. That must've been what woke me up—a lightning strike and the ringing jolt on the end of the line. I replaced the receiver and in one of those weird instances, it rang while my hand was still on it.

"Hello?" All I could hear was my own breathing. "If anyone is there, I'm sorry I can't hear you." I hung up the phone and switched on the flashlight, shooting the beam on the wall clock. One-fifteen. Ugh. The darkness and rude honesty of the wee hours ahead poured over me like a bucket of tar. The minutes between one and four a.m. have a brutality like no others.

I was awake and there was no help for it. I grabbed the flannel shirt at the foot of the bed and slipped it on. The worn wood floor was cool under my bare feet. The cup of raspberry tea I promised myself after checking the usual suspect spots of the house wasn't enough incentive to banish my bummed-out spirits. Perhaps I'd can it for the night and cook something. Why pretend to sleep when you can make something hot and gooey and . . .

Hello . . . why am I up at this vile hour? No electricity. Electric range. The joke was on me. At least I didn't have to exert any willpower over midnight snacking.

I shined the flashlight around the corners of the bedroom, searching for slippers, ignoring the dust bunnies and their larger-than-life shadows. Being awake was bad enough, getting wet feet was adding insult to injury. The phone went off again, although I hadn't seen a flash. I automatically lifted it to my ear. Expecting nothing, I said, "Hello?"

"I know who you are and what you did. You won't get away with it."

"What?" I mentally scrambled to absorb the words. Obviously my brain wasn't as awake as I thought. "Who—?"

"Don't pretend you don't know."

"Who is this?" The line went dead. I stared into the receiver, scowling as if I could guilt it into giving up the name of the culprit. The voice was raspy and unfamiliar, but the words were pure Hollywood. Some kid on a dare. If they called again I'd give them the devil.

I hung up and watched the phone. Feeling foolish after thirty seconds, I shook off my self-righteous peeve and resumed the search for slippers. I found them by the bedroom door and had just shoved my feet in when the telephone rang. I let it ring seven times, but the caller had more patience than I. On the eighth ring I hauled it to my ear. "Hello?" I used my sternest teacher voice. "Does your mother know what you're up to this morning?" Heavy breathing answered. "Look, I have a brother who has asthma so I sympathize with the breathing problem. If you're that bad off, hang up the phone and get your inhaler or go to the ER."

The caller inhaled sharply; no exhale, but I shared in that held breath. Was I being incredibly naïve and stupid about this? Maybe it was a weirdo outside my window! I sighed and got rid of the pent-up breath and the delusions of a woman alone at the end of a rural lane in the middle of the night in a torrential rain storm.

"You think you're so smart!" The voice vibrated with malice. "You're not, you know. Accidents can happen to a person. Accidents like falling off a cliff and drowning." The threat ended in a sob.

"Hey . . . hey, it's okay," another voice soothed, muffled by the wailing. Then it sliced through my ear sharp as a knife, "What is *wrong* with you? Who do you think you are, harassing a poor—" *Click.*

The callers cut the connection. Before I could listen to my better judgment, I hung up and quickly dialed the call-return number. A gust of wind hit the east side of the house with a Louisville Slugger wallop and the line went dead. It figures, and maybe it was for the best.

Chapter One

"Hey, Gwen, wait up!"

I turned toward the familiar hail and smiled through the blowing mist as Randy Osbourne trolled alongside me, sticking his head out the passenger window of his white station wagon. He pulled in to the curb and idled.

"I don't see how you can drive that way and not end up with your back in a pretzel by the time you've finished your route," I said to the grinning mailman.

"Just like yoga, only I do it with stamps and a steering wheel," he said. "Thought I'd save you a trek down that muddy lane of yours."

"Thanks."

"Some weather, huh? More like April Fool's than Memorial Day weekend. Makes you wonder if summer has any plans to show up this year or not." His cheery voice muffled when he twisted over the seat and thumbed through the sorted box of mail in the back.

I turned my gaze down Bookerton's Main Street. The fog covering the town shifted, unveiling the hazy green of maples and oaks lining the sidewalk. The faded storefronts hovered ghostly in the drizzle. Not a soul in sight. A seagull wheeled overhead, crying for company before it disappeared into the low cloud deck.

I shivered and hugged my jacket close to ward off the chill of gloomy weather and not enough sleep.

"Here ya go." Randy thrust a packet of mail in my direction, forcing my mind back into focus. A gust of wind off the ocean pelted my back with drops. The morning drizzle turned up the volume into a downpour.

"Stay dry!" he called, and ducked his head turtle-like under the shelter of the car roof. The vehicle was moving away before his words, "See ya at church," settled in my ears.

The rain funneled down my sleeve, seeped into the cuff of my sweater, and blurred the address on the top letter. I dashed down the street and bolted into Ted's Barber Shop. The smell of shampoo and hair gel, and the whine of clippers hit me in a warm, moist wave.

"Miss McPhail!" Trevor Carson lifted the clippers off his client's head, but they droned on while he fixed me with that wide, blue-eyed Carson stare, unchanged from the day he'd entered my kindergarten class so many years ago.

"Son, pay attention," his father, Ted, said. The buzz of the clippers stopped, the only sound the drip of my jacket on the doormat. Four sets of eyes met mine.

"Do you mind if I hang out in here for a few minutes?" I asked.

"Sure, sure." Trevor took my coat. "There're some magazines over there."

"I'm fine." I tried to forestall the attention, but his father joined us.

"Coming down like hoe handles and broomsticks." Ted glared out the window at the gray street. "It can quit anytime. Ain't like we didn't get enough last night."

"Isn't," Trevor murmured, echoing my thoughts. He caught my eye, gave a little grin, and shrugged. "The water was running over Lower Main Street at three this morning," he said. "You should've seen it, Miss Mack, just like Niagara."

"Tidal surge," Ted said. "It's fine now." He gestured toward the short row of seventies-style chairs. "Have a seat. Can I get you some coffee?" He hovered, and I noticed Trevor shifting from one foot to the other, as he had when he confessed to pushing Johnny Jones on the playground for teasing Brian Orr, or to taking Cheryl Grover's orange marker every day. Did he have something on his conscience—maybe a prank call to his former teacher?

Obviously I hadn't been the only one up too early this morning. The cloud of suspicion vanished before it could materialize. No way was he my midnight caller. I couldn't wrap my head around it being any of my past students. Though I could think of a handful that had run amok as juvenile delinquents, I wouldn't believe any one of them would sink so low as to harass their former kindergarten teacher. In New York City or LA, sure, but not in Bookerton. Besides, the second call hadn't fit with a prank mentality; at least I didn't think so. It was probably as simple as a wrong number or a fouled-up connection due to the stormy weather. Whichever it was, I felt sorry for whoever belonged to the tortured soul at the other end of the line, but what could I do about it?

My power and phone were still out and, though I felt like a wimp, I was rather glad of it. I'd probably never know the whys and wherefores of this one. I shook my head to clear away the unsettling nag from last night. If I didn't let it go, I'd soon become a paranoid old fusspot, and the Carson men were doing enough fussing for everyone.

I flicked my gaze to the two men seated in the barber chairs. Jason Boudreau's eyes met mine, watching my reflection in the mirror from Trevor's station. "Don't let me interrupt," I said, "I'm sure it'll let up soon."

A snort came from the elderly man enthroned in Ted's barber chair. "I wouldn't count on it, Gwen. More than likely we're in for an all-day soaker." Alfred Gaines added his squint to the visual barrage. He was doing a bang-up imitation of Mr. Magoo, except for the deep grooves of disapproval outlining his mouth. He laughed, but the grooves stayed put. "Pretty soon you'll need a boat to get back to that house of yours."

"Or a sub," Ted added.

"Yeah, you're right," I said. I walked past father and son and eased into a red vinyl chair. I gave the men my best stern schoolteacher nod, but not even Trevor responded by getting back to business. I looked down at the mail in my hand and ran my thumb over the sodden address. Glastonburg Summer Institute—the letter I'd been expecting for the past month. I curled my fingers into my palms, itching to rip it open and begin packing.

His Coke-bottle glasses lying out of reach on the counter, Alfred talked on to the empty doorway. "Don't get out your way too often anymore, Gwen. Me and the missus stay pretty close to town these days." His deep voice had gravel in it now, but the old preacher's tone was rock solid. "We'll have to come out and visit you this next week. You and Janet can talk about the garden, and I can have some of that sweet bread of yours." This time his grin lifted his jowls enough to cover up the concern I'd glimpsed.

I gave him a smile he couldn't see, but it was enough to elicit a response from Ted. He turned back to Alfred and picked up a comb.

"Are you coming to see us play Blynn River High next Tuesday, Miss Mack?" Trevor asked. "It's a home game and I'm pitching."

"I wouldn't miss it." I bent toward him and whispered, "I think Mr. Boudreau's falling asleep in his chair."

Trevor did a quick take over his shoulder only to see my fellow teacher chuckling at us. He turned back and touched my arm. "If you need anything, you just holler," he whispered. "Mr. Boudreau can wait." My former student strolled back to the chair as if he owned the joint. "Mr. Boudreau, could you please keep your head still?"

Jason Boudreau swiveled back to face the mirror and raised a reflected eyebrow at me. I gave him a polite smile and bowed my head to the news in my lap. I shut out the buzz and the chitchat and tore off the end of the envelope. The fact that it wasn't thick hit me the moment I pulled out the single sheet of paper. No housing registration form, no schedule, only a "Dear Gwen" letter.

Worse, a "Dear Ms." letter. I put my pet peeve of PC issues and texting aside and scanned the missive.

Dear Ms. McPhail:

Thank you for your interest in serving as an instructor for the arts program this summer. In the past, the Glastonburg Summer Institute has been privileged to attract the country's most gifted and talented musicians who come to share their intellect and craft with our students. This honored tradition continues in our current slate of teaching professionals for this session.

Due to the return of many of last year's professors, we regret to inform you the position you applied for has been filled. If you would care to reapply in the future, we would be pleased to . . . blah—blah—blah—blah—blah—

"Ahhh!" I jumped out of my skin and back into reality when Jason touched my shoulder.

"Sorry, Gwen, I didn't mean to startle you."

I looked up into brown eyes sorrier than the scolded Poky Little Puppy. "Oh, I must've been daydreaming." I shot to my feet, dismayed to catch the other members of the shop staring.

Good old Jason grabbed my coat from the rack and turned me toward the door. "It hasn't let up a bit, but I thought we could grab a muffin and tea at the bakery." He barely waited for me to thread my arms into my jacket before he propelled me out the door.

"Bye and thanks," I called. I crammed the mail into my pocket and flipped up my hood as my colleague hustled me through the drenching rain across the street to Sarah's Smalltown Bakery.

The sinful fragrance of hot bread and doughnuts added ten pounds with my first indrawn breath. I didn't care. "What'll you have?" Jason settled us at a small table by the window. "I'm buying."

"Good Morning, Miss Mack. Hi, Mr. Boudreau. What can I get you?" Cheryl Grover was there when I looked up. That girl had an unnerving way of always popping up out of thin air, but I couldn't be concerned with my former student's idiosyncrasies right now. I hastily ordered before I could talk myself out of the self-indulgence. "Raspberry tea and a jelly doughnut."

I barely waited for Jason to order and Cheryl to leave before I turned on my companion. "What's up?" I asked. "Come on," I said to his suddenly solemn face. "You didn't think I'd notice all the sympathy oozing off you guys at Ted's? It was thicker than the mud in my driveway."

Jason sighed and covered my hand with his long fingers. "It's not official," he said, "but I heard Principal Boyle finagled a spot at Glastonburg this summer for his wife. She'll be teaching three two-week sessions on folk music. Sound familiar?"

My colleague clammed up while Cheryl delivered our order. I quickly withdrew my hand at our young waitress's wink in my direction. "Thank you, Cheryl." I briskly placed the napkin on my lap. She nodded and disappeared. "And you know this how?" I stirred my tea while my other hand clenched the life out of the napkin.

"I heard it in the barbershop." Jason shook his head. "And what you hear in the barbershop is always true. Almost always," he added at my skeptical snort. "They say Principal Boyle's cousin was appointed to the institute's board and he pulled strings." He leaned forward; I shifted back in my seat and took a bite of doughnut. "I wish I could confront him. Principal Boyle has such a manipulative personality. It's not fair. You should be principal at Brier Elementary. You've earned it, the kids adore you, and I—"

I held up a sticky hand to ward off what was coming. "Principal Boyle does a great job with the kids and the parents. I don't want all those headaches."

"I know." Jason eased back in his chair and took a sip of coffee, never taking his eyes off me. "As I said, it isn't official, but if it turns out to be true, I was thinking we could make lemons out of lemonade."

"I think you mean lemonade out of lemons."

He shrugged and his words tumbled out faster. "I could give you a hand with that fixer-upper of yours this summer, maybe put on that sun porch you've always wanted. I'm a handy guy with a hammer and saw."

"Thanks." I fingered the letters in my jacket pocket. I didn't want to spill the official news just yet and encourage a closer confidence. I'd go home, have another cup of tea, sort out my life in private, and make some plans.

The bell above the door jangled and in stepped Steve and Lois Boyle. Lois hit me with a gloating smile. Whoever said, "If you want God to laugh just tell him *your* plans," was right on target with my life today. Obviously God had something big brewing here and, with a slip of the tongue, I could very easily slide into an obnoxious place that might feel so good and self-righteous right now.

So I said a quick prayer to keep my tongue sweet and my head on square. "It's official," I said in a low voice. "I got the letter from the institute today." I stood and pasted a small smile on my face. "Congratulations, Lois." I stepped forward and gave her a quick hug. "I heard you're teaching at Glastonburg this summer."

I moved back and she preened. Steve Boyle cleared his throat. Jason attached himself to my side. "Yes, I'm *so* looking forward to it," Lois said.

"I'll bet you are," Jason said. "It's quite a feather in your cap, being chosen out of all the other qualified applicants. A rare opportunity, wouldn't you agree, Steve?"

"Definitely." Steve put an arm around his wife's waist. "I see your mother at the far table, Dear. We shouldn't keep her waiting. Nice to see you, Gwen, Jason."

I nodded.

"I'll tell you all about it." Lois ignored her husband. "I'm not only teaching, but I'll be taking some private lessons from jazz musician Rudy Thoms and classical pianist Kerry Andersen. I can't wait to hobnob with all the other professors; so much talent and creativity in one place. It's going to be beyond wonderful. We should get together and talk, Gwen."

"Let's do that." My smile turned to clenched teeth. I prayed the enamel fence would hold. "It sounds like a once-in-a-lifetime experience."

"Honey, we really should go." Steve gently pulled her away. "See you Tuesday."

"Ta-ta." Lois waved her languid hand over her shoulder.

"I could—" Jason fumed.

I dragged him back to our table. "No you couldn't." I smiled. "You want to keep your teaching job and so do I. Besides, you're way too nice. Let Lois have her moment."

"I'd be glad to, if her moment wasn't the one she's stolen from you."

"There'll be another moment for me. Better things in store." I took another bite of the doughnut and glanced at the clock above the counter.

"Sure," Jason said. "When God closes a door and all that, but . . ."

I mentally filled in *but sometimes getting to that next open door, it's heck in the hallway.* I should've stayed home but I needed to buy some caulking for the leaks in my roof. Was my companion tuning in on my thoughts at last? I was getting a headache.

Jason rubbed his temples, then looked up with a grin. "What do you say we blow this town? We could hit the road right now and go to the beach, make a day of it."

Nope. Totally clueless. "Have you checked the weather lately?"

"Okay, so let's go to the city, take in a museum, the book store, and then have dinner."

He reached across the tabletop and I chose that moment to pick up my napkin and wipe the sugar off my lips. "It sounds nice, Jason, but I've got a million things on my to-do list today."

"I could help you with that. I'm a handy guy to have around, you know."

"I know, but I wouldn't be much company."

"That's exactly my point," he persisted. I glanced at the clock again, mentally squirming in my seat. "I can take your mind off everything." The bell above the door dinged boxing-match style. Jason had me on the ropes and he wasn't about to stop plugging away until I lost the battle.

"I'm sure you could, but—"

"Auntie!" I was enveloped from behind by cold, wet arms draped around my neck. They felt wonderful. *Rescued!* I spun in the chair and grinned at my niece. "We were just coming out to visit you, but we had to stop so Dalton could get some 'real' coffee," Tasha said.

"What a nice surprise," I said. "Jason, you remember my niece, Tasha."

Jason sighed, but he smiled. "Of course. Please have a seat."

He stood and Tasha slipped into the chair beside me. "You've grown up."

"I'm a nurse now," Tasha said. "Or I *was.*"

I sent her a sharp look, but Jason had the floor. "It's been a few years, but I can't forget that time you and your brother pelted those horrible little green apples at my car, and me, when I drove up the lane to visit your aunt. Do you remember?"

"We used slingshots." Tasha grinned wickedly. "Auntie helped us make them."

I gave her a none-too-gentle nudge with my sneaker under the table and she laughed. "I tried to raise them right," I said as her fiancé arrived at the table with two coffees, "but, as you can see, she hasn't changed."

"Ah, don't listen to Gwen," Tasha said. "I've put all my wayward childish pranks behind me, haven't I, Dalton." She put a possessive hand on Dalton's sleeve. "This is my fiancé, Dalton Madison." Pride added a husky tone to her voice.

Jason stood and the men shook hands. "You're a lucky man," Jason said. "A beautiful woman, just like her aunt."

"Yes," Dalton agreed quickly.

I ignored Jason's gobbledygook, focused, instead, on my ongoing reading of my future nephew-in-law's character. He was the twenty-first century version of Pierce Brosnan, only with a football-player physique—dark and handsome with carefully tousled hair and perfectly distributed one-day beard stubble on his bullish jaw and neck. I should buy him a decent razor for a wedding present.

"It's nice to meet you. Please, don't let us interrupt. Natasha and I were just passing through on our way to Hanover's Point. We can't stay long, so there's no need to change your plans." Dalton remained standing and sipped his coffee while gazing over Jason's shoulder at the freedom of the road outside.

"We can stay for a bit," Tasha said. "There's no sense hurrying to Gates's beach house in weather like this."

"I don't expect you to stay," I said. "If you've got plans, go on. We'll catch up later." I sounded just like Dalton. *Ugh.*

Tasha scowled and shook her head, not liking the comparison any better than I, it appeared. "We're not in a rush. Gates is giving a party before he and Dalton go out to California on business. People will be coming and going all the time. It'll last for hours; trust me."

Dalton set his empty coffee mug on the table. "We really can't afford to be late, Tash." He bent down and shot me a toothpaste-ad smile before touching my niece's cheek with a manicured finger. "I need to make a couple of calls. That'll give you two a chance to chat. Be back in a bit."

We all watched the tall young man in the blue blazer stroll over to the restroom and disappear inside.

"Well, I ought to be going," Jason said. "Always nice to see you, Tasha."

"See you at church," I said when he lingered too long at the table fussing with his jacket.

"I'll give you a call later, Gwen." He sauntered to the counter to pay Cheryl.

"He seems . . ." Tasha began.

I glowered at the twinkle in her eye. "Don't say it."

"How long has Jason Boudreau been angling for a date?" Tasha got her thick, honey-colored hair from me and, sadly, her persistent nature as well.

"Too long." I couldn't stop the chuckle that came out to join her laugh.

"It's sad, really." Tasha watched Jason hunch his shoulders against the rain as he jogged past the window and out of sight. "He's a nice guy."

"This from the girl who used to pelt him with apples and put burdocks in his coat pocket."

"I forgot about the burdocks!"

"*He* hasn't. When you were younger, you and Nate hated him."

"He was too smarmy. But what did we know, we were just kids."

"That's true, but it doesn't matter. Jason's just a friend."

"You sound exactly like Nate. He'll introduce me to a new friend of his and preface it with 'Meet not-my-girlfriend, Whoever.' "

"And who is the current 'Whoever'? Nate usually calls now and again, but he's not answering e-mails or phone messages. He was supposed to be here last month to help me fix the chimney leak and stay awhile until I left for—"

"I know." The freckles on Tasha's cheeks disappeared, eclipsed by the red tinge that crept in whenever she was uncomfortable. "He's not coming. Actually that's why I came today. He asked me to stop by and tell you."

"Ah."

"I shouldn't be stuck doing his dirty work," Tasha said.

"But you are, so spill it."

"He's becoming a whitewater rafting guide so he can work on the Blynn River this summer. Whoever's parents own a rafting business."

"Fair enough." I was oddly disappointed by the defection of my ne'er-do-well nephew. "And how are things with you? What's this about you not being a nurse anymore?"

"Well, I'm still a nurse, of course," Tasha retorted, then toned it down a bit when she caught my eye. "Dalton . . . uh . . . we both felt it would be better if I gave up my job at the hospital, just while we're getting ready for the wedding. Actually I'm enjoying the flexibility and the time off."

"And how's the wedding coming?"

"Good," Tasha said. "Dalton's mother is really making—*has*

made—most of the arrangements. And that's fine with me. She knows who to call and what's best. She's booked the church and the reception at their club, then we jet off to the French Riviera and Monaco for our honeymoon. It's all set. I don't have to lift a finger."

"Wow." I stopped before I said anything else. "I just got a letter from the Glastonburg Institute." A safer topic for us than her leave of common sense and this huge wedding to the rich and richer.

"You'll be able to get off for the wedding, won't you?" Tasha demanded. "I can't get married without my only blood-aunt there."

"Not a problem." I hauled the soggy mail out of my pocket and deposited it on the table. "I'm not going."

"Oh *no*! You've been looking forward to this forever. What happened? You and your guitar were made for that job."

"Apparently not." I congratulated myself at sounding nonchalant.

Tasha snatched the letter from the pile, sending an official looking envelope spinning over to stop in front of me. "I can't believe it!" She flung down the paper. "What a bunch of snobs. You're too good for them. Something better will come along."

"Yes." I studied the unfamiliar address on the envelope in front of me.

"Something better already?" She picked up the unopened letter. "Who's Harcourt, Branch, and Goodenow?"

"I don't know," I said. "Let's find out. Open it."

Tasha carefully slit the envelope with a long, perfectly manicured nail. She was taking on more of Dalton's world each time I saw her. I wanted to grab hold of that hand, as I'd done when she was a child, and pull her away from the danger. But was it danger, or merely the fuddy-duddy worries of a middle-aged spinster? Dalton was wealthy, responsible, but oh-soworldly, and last time we got together I caught a glimpse of a selfish child hidden under his gold-plated polo shirt. I folded my hands to stop them from reaching out to interfere.

"Huh? Who's Vance Norman Jones?" Tasha handed me the letter.

"I don't know." I wrinkled my brow. "Jones? It doesn't ring a bell."

She laughed and tweaked the paper out of my fingers. "Whoever he is, he left you his estate on Candle Island. Can you *believe* it? You probably *can* believe it. God sends down rain, then gives you a bucket that overflows with showers of blessing. See? I *did* learn a few things during all those summer holidays with you."

"What?" Dalton was back. He swiveled a chair around and straddled it, looking over Tasha's shoulder.

"Uncle Jonesy!" I snapped my fingers. "He and Daddy had a business together buying old boats and refinishing them."

"I thought Grandpa was a marine electrician at the naval base," Tasha said.

"He was." I closed my eyes, trying to remember the wiry young man who'd bunked in my brothers' room so long ago. "I was only four, maybe five. Your grandfather and Uncle Jonesy did this as a sideline. Uncle Evan, Uncle Neil, and your father were old enough to help out some, too. It only lasted a year or so. Your grandfather got tapped to go on sea trials for the Navy, and Gram thought he was spreading himself too thin. I was too young to know the whys and wherefores, but I remember my job was to put a little flag on the stern of the boats when they were finished."

"What happened to Jonesy?" Dalton asked.

I looked over, surprised to see him intently studying the letter. I reached out and gently took it back. "He must've died."

"Obviously," came the sarcastic reply. "I mean, did he take

over the boat business from your father?"

"He could've. I don't know." I bit my fingertip, trying to recall. "If he did, he moved operations elsewhere."

"Yeah, to Portside Shipyard, and then he branched out to Candle Island Yacht Company," Dalton said. "Some of the guys at the club have vintage Vance Jones yachts. In fact, Ellingsford does. You met him, Tash."

Tasha shook her head.

"Royce Ellingsford. Come on, he's the guy who invited us to sail with him to Nantucket this fall when we get back from our honeymoon. He won the Stinson Reach race five years running, sailing in a Vance Jones yacht. You have to remember when he came to our table at the club."

"Oh, sure. Nice man." At Dalton's pained expression she added, "Larger than life."

"That's an understatement," Dalton said. "Gates and I are hoping to bring him on board with a money making venture we're developing, but now, if you own the shipyard and the yacht company . . . what a piece of luck!"

I swallowed hard, tearing my eyes away from the diamond-chip stare he leveled on the paper in my hand. "There's no such thing as luck. God is *not* in the fairy-tale business of sprinkling capricious pixie dust on anyone. Besides, this doesn't mention anything about owning a business. I imagine it's just a little piece of furniture or something." I sounded like a prattling old woman.

"No way." Dalton sprang to his feet and paced behind me to resume his study of my letter. "It's real estate. It *has* to be."

"You can't know that," Tasha said.

"Only one way to find out," Dalton said. "We'll follow you home, Gwen, and you can call this attorney."

"It's Saturday," I protested. "And a holiday weekend."

"With the fees they get, it doesn't matter," Dalton said. "I know how these guys operate. I can place the call for you, if you'd like."

"No, that's okay." I rose from my seat to put some distance between us.

"I thought you wanted to go over to Gates's place." Tasha came and stood beside me.

"You said it yourself." Dalton grinned. "If we're a little late it's no big deal."

I practically ran down the street to my car, glancing over my shoulder to see Dalton already seated in his SUV. Tasha looked small as she peered through the rainy windshield of the passenger's side.

"Hasn't anybody heard of privacy?" I muttered. I got into my car and tromped on the gas, the roof repair forgotten. There was no place to hide with the SUV bumper hogging all the scenery in my rearview mirror, but I did have twenty minutes of praying time before we'd arrive at home and I determined to make good use of it.

By the time I pulled over to the side of the road to park, I felt ready. God was in control. I just needed to let myself be guided by Him, not pulled along by some hotshot who, at this very moment, wheeled into the end of my driveway and ran over the teepee barrier of shovel and rake I'd placed there.

"It's too muddy to go up the lane," I shouted. The driver's-side window edged down and I slogged over. "We have to walk in."

"No need," Dalton insisted. "This has four-wheel-all-wheel drive. It'll make it. Hop in."

"We can walk up," I heard Tasha say.

"You've got to be kidding!"

"She's not." I leaned into the open window, scattering rain on Dalton's sleeve. "The ruts are as deep as the Grand Canyon. I wouldn't want you to get your vehicle all messy. Why don't you go on to the party and I'll talk to you later?"

"Oh no." Dalton killed the engine. "This is fine. I was just thinking of you, Gwen." I stepped back quickly when he opened the door, vaulted out of the driver's seat, and took my arm. "Watch your step."

"Right back at you." I glanced down at his Italian loafers, then over at his fiancée struggling through the mud. I took off up the well-worn trail that wound through a dark, dripping forest of firs. Soon Dalton's helping hand fell away as the trail narrowed between two boulders. A few moments later I popped out through the lilacs bordering the back garden and hurried with my entourage across the lawn to the sagging porch.

"Come in and I'll put the kettle on." I flung my sodden jacket on the coat tree and led the way to the kitchen. "Have a seat." My companions looked as bedraggled as I felt. "On second thought, Dalton, maybe you could start us a fire."

"There's firewood on the porch." Tasha headed outside. "I'll get it."

I frowned, and a second later Dalton caught Tasha's arm. "No, I'll do it," he said. "You stay here with Gwen and dry off." As soon as he disappeared I picked up the phone. I could've kissed the receiver when the comforting dial tone came to my ear. Service was back and, if I was quick, I could sidestep Mr. McGreedy-in-law and his cell phone. I hurriedly punched in the number I'd memorized from the lawyer's letter. Tasha stood staring out the window while I left a message on their machine.

Chapter Two

I lifted my face to the raw salt spray as the car ferry chugged by Murdoch Island with its rusted quarry crane poking up through the tumbled giant granite slabs. I turned from the rail and watched the mainland. The mustards and colonial blues of the dollhouse-sized tourist shops of Hanover Point resembled a Wysocki puzzle. They slid from view as we rounded the head of the island.

"We're almost there, Miss McPhail." Mr. Blevins, of Harcourt, Branch, and Goodenow, was at my shoulder à la Jiminy Cricket. The little man was adept at chirping pertinent facts; a good fit for his job, but he wasn't a natural conversationalist.

He didn't need to be. The young man at my other elbow was doing enough talking for all of us. I felt like a Gwen sandwich. "Did I tell you I came out here once as a kid?" Dalton asked.

"Yes." I heard Tasha from her nearby vigil leaning over the rail, but her next words were pulled under by the throb of the engines.

Dalton barely paused for breath. "The Ellingsfords have a cottage on the lee side of the island, and they invited our family out for the Fourth of July one year when I was about ten. It's a beautiful place. I remember thinking that someday I wanted to own a place on Candle Island. This seems like kismet." His eyes glowed as he looked into mine. I turned slowly toward the rail, but instead of looking out to sea, I studied my niece's profile. If not for the breeze whipping her hair, she could've been made of

Murdoch Island granite.

"It's Gwen's moment." Tasha's voice strained in the rising wind. My chattering squirrel niece had been dismally quiet since that day two weeks ago when we'd first discovered Jonesy's bequest to me. Except for Dalton's dripping tongue hanging out and lips smacking in anticipation of "my moment," as Tasha had called it, I was actually glad the couple had insisted on tagging along. I needed time with Tasha. This maiden voyage out to view my newly acquired cottage was meant to be shared with family. I eased away from the men and closer to my girl.

"We're family," Dalton said. I jerked around to look at him and met those gleaming movie-star teeth. "I'm glad we could be here to keep you company, Gwen."

"I am, too." I touched Tasha's forearm. "It's always more fun to share the journey with those I love."

Tasha smiled at me but looked rather green around the gills. "We're almost there," I said. The ferry bobbed around a tiny rocky isle tufted with a spruce cap. "You gonna make it?" She gave a slight nod. The boat rounded a craggy point and nosed in toward a harbor. I could see three vehicles lined up at the shore, waiting.

"We wouldn't have missed this, would we, Tash!" Dalton came up behind us. He inserted his body between us and put his arms around both our shoulders. A wave of eau-de-Dalton enveloped me, in spite of the wind. I was sure it was an expensive manly fragrance; my father would've called it fancy man's toilet water—something even the dog wouldn't drink. I smiled at the memory, looking up into the big cheerful face of my nephew-to-be, reminding myself I shouldn't judge a casserole by its topping, or a man by his personal potpourri.

"Well, I do appreciate the company and the fact that you postponed your trip to California to be here, Dalton," I said. "It was very thoughtful."

"I can't have my Auntie Gwen going into uncharted waters all alone," he said.

"Yes."

I was thankful Mr. Blevins felt the need to announce our arrival. "We ought to get in the car," he said. "Perhaps I should drive, Mr. Madison, if you'll permit me."

"By all means." Dalton steered us toward the SUV and opened the back door for Tasha and me before he slipped into the passenger's seat. "I'll ride shotgun in case you need help with any of the driving systems."

"Thank you." Mr. Blevins checked the dashboard thoroughly before he buckled up. "I'm quite familiar with this type of vehicle. I recently purchased a similar model for backpacking in the mountains."

I glanced up at his statement to find him smirking at me via the rearview mirror. Perhaps Mr. Blevins was Davy Crockett under those George Burns glasses and Brooks Brothers suit. Just one of many surprises popping up like firecrackers in front of me this summer.

"The Jones cottage is on the far side of the island," he continued. The ferry jarred to a stop, the ramp clanked down, and the young crew woman beckoned us forward. "Not too long of a drive from Coveside, that's the name of this little village here at the landing." He nodded his head while pulling the car up the road from the shore and continued inching through the town's narrow street. "As you can see, it has amenities; a small but well-stocked grocery store, the church, school, the town pier, even a little library, I understand."

I swiveled my head around to take in the cluster of sturdy buildings as we crept by. Standard coastal island fare, but I studied the austere brown church with its elaborate stained-glass windows. Then my eyes caught and held on the native-stone building settled between two old captain's homes, one complete with a widow's walk. The gold leaf sign above the heavy wooden door proclaimed McMahan Memorial Library, and begged me to tell the driver to stop, but I kept silent. It wouldn't do to even fantasy window shop here. This was not my home. This was not my library.

I blinked myself back to reality and flicked my eyes to safer territory—people-watching. A couple with two young children in strollers waved. An older man with a wild, white mop of hair and a face as craggy as the island shore glowered at me as I returned their wave.

"Some of the natives don't look too friendly," Tasha said.

"Mostly folks out here are neighborly in their way," Mr. Blevins said, "but they're a close-knit community. Traditionally they don't take to us mainlanders, what they call 'those from away.' " He halted at a stop sign and turned his head to look directly at me. "Just thought you ought to know, Miss McPhail. They'll be polite enough, and even help you out if you're in trouble; but, for the most part, if you weren't born here, you'll always be an outsider."

"Understood," I said, and he gave me a little grin before turning his attention back to the road.

"That's old school," Dalton said, his long arm resting on the back of the driver's seat to pull all of us into his conversation bubble. "This is the twenty-first century. Not many of the old diehards left. What with the internet, cell phones, and wireless everything, there's nobody who embraces that archaic way of thinking anymore. It's a global community now. No matter where you are or who you are, there's no getting away from it. Even in Africa or China, we're all connected."

I nodded politely at his one-man-band recital and focused past his head to the small slot of changing scenery beyond the windshield. We'd gone around a sharp curve and were now crawling past a group of houses huddled in a valley. The tiny village was out of sight of the shore, but the piles of buoys and stacks of lobster traps in their yards bespoke of a centuries-old lifestyle, the kind Dalton was convinced no longer defined a culture.

Mr. Blevins carefully negotiated a series of switchbacks and eased up a long hill. We crested the rise and the panorama of ocean shining like splintered glass in the June sun was enough to take even Dalton's breath away.

Taking a track to the right marked "Blind Man's Bluff PVT LN," Mr. Blevins broke the silence. "This is the Jones estate, or, more accurately, your part of it, Miss McPhail." The vehicle continued along past gnarled and twisted spruce that stood sentinel on the rocky cliffs of the shore. The gravel road veered downhill to a small, weathered, shingle cottage with a glassed-in porch. It fronted a private beach narrowed by the high tide to a slivered pathway of smooth rocks.

I could barely breathe. I was looking at a dream I hadn't known I had; yet, in my heart, I felt as if I were coming home. God had read the blueprints of my soul and this is what He'd built for me. "It's perfect," I whispered. Tasha grabbed my hand and squeezed it.

"This isn't it." Mr. Blevins stopped the SUV so he could again turn to face me with that studious, trustworthy expression. "This belongs to Vance Jones's widow and their son. It was the original family home."

"Oh certainly." I felt greedy and small. "I just assumed—" I stopped before I talked myself into the unattractive outcome of the "when one assumes" cliché. *Even if it's just a shack it'll be a lovely place to pitch a tent or put a picnic table,* I silently chided my new awareness of my selfish self. *Thank you, Lord, for whatever the gift and wherever You're guiding me to today.* I mentally affixed the picture of myself having summer picnics on these windswept cliffs, but, as Mr. Blevins proceeded forward, I'm ashamed to say my heart was tugged back toward the simple cottage by the shore.

I couldn't stop myself from glancing out the rear window as the car climbed a steep grade. Purple, indigo, pink, and magenta lupines spilled like paint over the back slope tumbling down to the cottage, waving good-bye in the breeze.

"As we discussed, Miss McPhail, I've hired someone to take care of the property for you." Mr. Blevins's words, and the car virtually stopping as we neared the top of the grade, pulled me back to my destination. "Mr. Stinson Scott agreed to take you on. I met with him myself. He has excellent references, retired Coast Guard, a local man. He's now a caretaker and troubleshooter for several properties on the island. I think you'll find him reliable and trustworthy. He's supposed to meet us here."

"Here" appeared suddenly, filling the windshield with a massive wall of brick and glass. "Ha! Ha!" The glee in Dalton's exclamation and whistle of admiration elicited a rare chuckle from Mr. Blevins.

"Yes," Mr. Blevins said. "It's quite a sight. Mr. Vance Jones designed it himself. It was built right after he sold a custom yacht to the Getty family. What do you think, Miss McPhail?"

Mr. Blevins tooled around the circular drive and parked the SUV in front of wide granite steps. I craned my neck to look up at the monstrosity of modern architecture. "It's huge," I said, feeling very small.

"Eight bedrooms, each with its own bath. A banquet room, conservatory, library—"

"Let's take a look." Dalton ejected from his seat and opened my door, leaving Mr. Blevins blinking at me through his round lenses.

I got out slowly and studied the white columns guarding the portico; the formal landscape of junipers, spiral dwarf Alberta spruce, and yews all trimmed to a whisker; the sheer height of overpowering brick. "It's awfully tall," I said. Tasha came around the SUV and slipped her arm into mine.

"A full three stories and a half. From the third floor study you can see the mainland." Mr. Blevins joined us. "I believe Mr. Jones had a telescope in the room expressly for that purpose."

We walked toward the mansion. "This is unbelievable," Dalton said.

I silently agreed. It was too much for me to take in all at once. I tapped the head of a homely lion statue guarding the bottom step. I wanted to sit down beside it and howl.

"You're here." The voice was deep, the delivery slow, as if the speaker tasted each word before allowing it to leave his mouth. The man coming down the steps to meet us was tall and sure. His dark-green shirt was flannel, his jeans slightly worn but clean. A blue Candle Island Fire Department ball cap hid his hair and shaded his narrowed eyes.

"Mr. Scott." Mr. Blevins shook his hand and made the introductions all around.

"Quite a place," Dalton said as soon as the polite murmured greetings were over.

"And you are?" Mr. Scott asked.

"Dalton—"

"Madison. I caught the name the first time around," Mr. Scott continued. "You're not a McPhail."

"I'm engaged to Natasha McPhail, Gwen's niece." Dalton stepped back, wrapped an arm around Tasha's waist and drew her forward.

"They'll be living here with you?" Mr. Scott asked.

"Oh no," I said. The words came harsh as a crow's caw. I cleared my throat and tried to speak as slowly as the caretaker. "I don't think anyone will be living here, at least not a McPhail."

"Then you'll be needing me as permanent caretaker?" Mr. Scott continued fixing me with a disapproving blue stare.

"What Gwen means is, no one will be living here year round," Dalton said. "It'll be a summer home."

"Dalton," Tasha protested.

"Think of it, Gwen," Dalton pressed on, and I could see why he was such a mover and shaker in his father's investment business. "We could have the wedding here. It would be a blast."

"Dalton, come on. Your mother has the wedding all planned and scheduled at the club," Tasha said. "It's a done deal."

"Mother doesn't know about this place. When she sees it, she'll flip."

"Well, maybe we ought to see it ourselves before we decide to invite the entire population of mainland China for an overnight." Tasha echoed my thoughts.

"Right, right," Dalton agreed, squashing the sarcasm under his enthusiasm. "Lead the way, Mr. Blevins."

I let the group go in and turned to face the sea. From this promontory there wasn't the slightest sign of the little cottage below. The view of the ocean was partially obscured by evergreens, but the glimpses of sparkling waters between the branches seared my eyes with blinding sunlight. I could feel the immense presence of the house looming at my back.

"He died over there."

The deep voice dropped in my ear, sinking cold as a rock tossed into the waves below us.

"I beg your pardon?" I knew very well what he was saying.

"I saw you staring at the bluff," Mr. Scott said. "Lots of folks have come around to have a look. It's a thirty-foot drop at low tide."

"Uncle Jonesy fell? Mr. Blevins said he had an accident, but I didn't know he—"

"Uncle Jonesy went over the edge."

Mr. Scott said the name with just enough inflection that I could picture the twist of his lips. I turned to face him. "Did you know Vance Jones well, Mr. Scott?"

"Everybody knew Vance. He was my cousin."

"Oh. I'm sorry for your loss."

Mr. Scott nodded. "I didn't say I liked him. Don't you want to see what he left you?"

"Not particularly." I glanced once again at the third-story windows. "I'm not much of a castle fan."

Mr. Scott laughed and I looked up in surprise. The stern face returned in an instant. I thought he'd regretted the outburst, but his next words carried slightly less chill than before. "I take it you're not the princess type?"

"You need to ask?"

"Dalton seems to fancy himself a prince." Mr. Scott took off his cap and looked over to the atrium where my three companions were beckoning through the glass. His close-cropped hair was a surprise, a deep rust with flecks of gray throughout. *Is that called salt and paprika?* I smiled at the thought. I wanted to ask *What happened to your freckles,* but stopped myself when I felt his eyes come back to study me.

"Well, Mr. Scott, I guess I can't put it off any longer. Shall we?"

He put his hat on and placed a strong hand on the small of my back.

"Perhaps you should lead us through the portcullis," I said as we topped the steps and stopped at the oversized front door.

"Oh no, you're the lady of the manor; I'm just the hired help. Lead on." Mr. Scott opened the door. "By the way, it's called a frontispiece." I glanced back as he followed me inside the cool interior, his face no longer friendly and his voice a frigid ten below zero.

Through every room of the mansion, I was more aware of Mr. Scott's dour presence than the mahogany wainscoting in the study, or the marble fireplace in the library, or the exotic orchids in the conservatory. I arrived back at the portico, oh, excuse me, Mr. Scott, frontispiece, feeling lost. I hated the house with its in-your-face opulence, and the caretaker hated me.

"What did you think, Miss McPhail?" Mr. Blevins's eyes shown brighter than a Fourth of July sparkler.

"It certainly is roomy," I said, "but it's rather like a museum. Had the family lived here long before Uncle Jonesy had his accident?"

"Oh yes," Mr. Blevins said. "This house is twenty years old, at least the main part of it. Mr. Jones added the conservatory and the back deck more recently."

"Ah." I didn't want to appear ungracious. "I've never seen anything like it."

"It's quite a house," Dalton said.

"I can't believe anybody actually lives like this," Tasha said. I smiled at her bewilderment that mirrored my own. Of all my nieces and nephews, Natasha and I had a special connection, as if she were my own daughter.

"Anybody is us, now, Tash," Dalton said.

"Yes, well." Mr. Blevins cleared his throat. "I must be back on the mainland for a two o'clock appointment." He took my hand and gently but firmly guided me to one side. "It's been my pleasure to be of service to you, Miss McPhail. Here are your keys to your new life."

"I'm not sure I want to leave my old one." The keys weighed heavily in my palm.

"You already have," Mr. Blevins said softly. "But in the short time I've known you, I've glimpsed that rare quality of what my grandmother called willow stubbornness." I raised my eyebrows and he patted my hand. "You'll find the right course, the balance of old and new; I know it. And if you need any help, legal or whatnot, I hope you'll give me a call." He tucked his card into my hand, then turned to the others as he glanced at his watch. "Mr. Scott, would you mind driving me to the ferry landing?"

"You might be better off to have Dalton drive you over. My truck's been acting up," Mr. Scott said. "I haven't had time to look at it, what with all this morning's hoopla."

Mr. Blevins nodded. "Mr. Madison, would you mind?"

"Sure, sure," Dalton agreed. "I'll be back in a few."

"Right," Tasha said. "Oh, Dalton," she called as the two men went out the door. "Why don't you pick us up something at the grocery store for dinner."

"Like what?"

"Whatever."

"Something easy to tide us over," I said, and stepped through the door into Dalton's impatience. "Just sandwich stuff will be fine for now." I took a twenty out of my wallet and handed it to the young man. "We can go on a comprehensive shopping trip later. Don't worry," I said as he looked past me into the mansion. "This'll all still be here when you get back."

"Right." His gleaming grin came out like the sun from behind a cloud.

Tasha came to stand beside me on the windy steps and we watched them go. "Well, Auntie, what do we do now?"

"I don't know. Is it just me, or is this an albatross?"

"Don't worry about having the wedding here. I'm going to talk Dalton out of it."

I shrugged. "You're welcome to have your wedding here, if you like."

"I know that, but it's so . . ."

"Creepy?" I supplied.

A snort in the doorway made me spin around. It seemed Mr. Scott was in no hurry to fix his truck. "You mean to tell me you think this place is haunted?" He came and stood beside me.

"The things you folks from away come up with; I can't believe it."

"Of course not," I retorted. "I don't believe in all that foolishness, Mr. Scott. I meant creepy in an over-the-top luxuries way. It's indecent, all this money wasted on material things."

"They're your material things, creepy or not," Mr. Scott said.

"Surely not all of them," I argued. "All the furnishings, the full china cabinet, the plants and books must belong to Uncle Jonesy's widow."

"I noticed that, too," Tasha said. "They probably need a little time to come to grips with all that's happened before they can move out their stuff."

"They've come to grips with it and they've moved on, trust me," Mr. Scott said. "This is all yours. They don't want it."

"But surely they must want *some* of it," I protested.

"Where would they put it? You saw the house they moved into down the road. The entire cottage would fit into your library. Besides, this was all Uncle Jonesy's stuff; his wife, Dot, and son, Ron, never saw any use of it."

His lip curled over the *Uncle* reference and I tried to rein in my rising temper. "Mr. Scott, do you have a problem with me, or are you simply baiting me for the fun of it?" I ignored Tasha's chuckle.

"Not at all." He spread his palms wide. "I only work here."

"You mentioned a truck repair, so we'll leave you to it," I said. "Come on, Tasha, let's you and I go for a walk."

"Before you leave, I need to show you how to arm the security system. I've programmed a new code for the new owner, but if you'd like you can change it to something with a sequence of numbers you might remember, like your niece's birthday or their wedding date."

"Mr. Scott." I hated myself for letting his condescension niggle under my skin. "I'm perfectly capable of remembering the numbers you've chosen. They'll be fine. However, I don't believe we need to lock up the whole place while we're out here in the dooryard. We're only going for a short walk. Let's go, Tasha."

"In a place this size, you never know who's lurking around." His voice followed us down the steps and across the lawn.

I simply waved my hand and continued to march toward a well-worn trail through a sparse growth of twisted spruce. We walked briskly, without talking, for several minutes, then stopped when we emerged onto the barren rocks. The waves broke on the cliff face with dizzying intensity. I put out my arm to keep Tasha back from the edge. She laughed. "I'm not six years old anymore, Auntie."

"I know. Old habit."

"Isn't it beautiful up here?" Tasha said. "It's like we're the only two people in the world."

"Yes." I followed her gaze out over the restless sea, dotted with smudges of islands in the distance, but couldn't stop from looking down at our feet. Was this where Uncle Jonesy had fallen to his death? I could feel the pull of vertigo and stepped back quickly.

Tasha grabbed my hand. "Are you all right, Auntie?"

"I'm fine."

"You ought to be careful. Blind Man's Bluff is a dangerous place. Lots of shipwrecks on these rocks." Mr. Scott's voice behind us startled me. As I jerked my head around, Tasha pulled me back, causing us both to stumble over a wide uneven split in the ledge. Mr. Scott grabbed my free arm in a bruising grip. I pitched toward him and Tasha twisted away from me. Her hand was yanked from mine and she cried out.

"Are you okay, Tasha?" I ignored the green flannel so near my cheek I could sense its softness. I pulled away, but he was around me in a flash, helping Tasha to her feet.

"Ow!" Tasha's ankle turned and she immediately bent her knee, shifting all her weight to her left foot. I put my arm around her for support.

"Like I said, a dangerous place." Mr. Scott flanked Tasha on her other side. "Looks like you got your foot stuck in that crack and twisted your ankle when you went down. Might've even sprained it. A sprain's more painful than a break."

"Don't tell me you're a doctor?" I said.

"No, but I'll take a look if you want." He ignored my sarcasm. "I know a little first aid."

We lowered Tasha to sit on a nearby rock while Mr. Scott probed the ankle with sure but gentle hands. "It's already swelling," he said. "Probably not broken, but you should have it x-rayed to be sure. I'll take you to the clinic." He helped Tasha to her feet and scowled at me.

I supported Tasha's other side and we awkwardly pulled in opposite directions.

"My truck's this way," he said.

"I thought it was on the fritz," I said as we shuffled in step away from the ledges.

"It's running rough but it'll get us where we need to go."

Chapter Three

"Scotty."

I looked up from my magazine to see a stocky mountain of a man coming toward us. He moved with grace in spite of his size. His short-sleeved Hawaiian shirt, blond hair, and California surfer-dude tan clashed with the stethoscope hanging around his neck and the keen, intelligent hazel eyes leveled at us.

He pumped my escort's hand and bent over to take mine. "I'm Sledge Knox," he said. "This is our first x-ray of the day, so it may be awhile before we get pictures of Tasha's ankle. The power quit during that thunderstorm last night, put some of our systems on the blink. Not to worry; it happens all the time. We'll get the kinks worked out soon, but she says you don't have to wait."

"Oh that's all right." I rose and looked down the short hallway.

"Really, there's no need." Sledge grinned. "I'll see she gets something good for lunch and bring her home when she's finished."

"I don't want to put you out, Mr. Knox."

"You'll be doing me a favor," he whispered. "Besides, I have to make a few calls out your way so it's no big deal."

"Thanks, Sledge," Mr. Scott said.

Sledge nodded and was gone down the hall in a blur of red hibiscus, yellow parrots, and tie-dyed blue sky.

"A colorful young man," I said, and settled back into the leatherette chair.

"He's a gentleman of the first order, teaches Sunday School, the real deal," Mr. Scott said. "Tasha will be perfectly safe with him."

"Oh, I have no doubt."

"Sure you do." Mr. Scott looked down on me and I shot to my feet. "Why else are we still here? Did I mention he's a doctor?"

"Sledge?"

"Nickname. His official title's Angus Bruce Knox, M.D., but around here he's been Sledge since he was a kid."

"Like Scotty?"

"Yeah." The hint of a smile twitched his stern lips. "Shall we go find some lunch, Miss McPhail?"

"It's Gwen, since I was a kid," I said. "Lunch would be nice."

His hand on my back guided me out of the clinic. "Walk or drive? It's not far."

"Walk, please." He matched his stride to mine. The wind gusted at our backs and I noticed his hand had slipped away. "I'd like to see more of the island."

"You can live here your whole life and never see it all."

"Spoken like a man who loves his home," I said. "Do you live nearby?"

"On Faraday's Mistake, about a half-mile that way." He pointed down a narrow dirt road to the left when we walked by.

"That's an intriguing name," I replied. "It must have a story like Blind Man's Bluff."

"Why would you say that?" he asked. When I looked up into his face, he quickly glanced over my head at the village spread below us, the water sparkling behind it. *He died over there.* His lips were set in a stern line, but I could still hear that drop-dead statement he made when we first arrived at the mansion. Uncle Jonesy's so-called accident, my mysterious midnight caller, Blind Man's Bluff, it all added up to . . .

"Well, on that bluff we could see the beauty for miles, yet you told us it's been a disastrous blind spot for many ships," I said. His eyes avoided mine. "It's rather an oxymoron, don't you think? And now, with Vance Jones falling to his death there, it seems even more an ominous, yet beautiful, place. Are they certain he died?"

That got his attention. Impatient blue eyes bore into mine. "Why would you ask that?"

"I mean, did they recover the body? What if he faked his own death?"

"And why would he do that?"

"I don't know, but it happens," I said. "Someone decides to trade in their current set of problems or discontent for a new life. They leave their truck at the airport and fly away, or hop a freighter to Mozambique, assume a new identity, and disappear."

"Mozambique? And you know this because . . . ?" Scotty raised a rusty eyebrow at me, his face inscrutable.

"It happens on the news every day," I said. "Well, maybe not *every* day, but more often than you might think."

"Not in Vance Jones's case." Scotty swept his arm toward a group of buildings set out on the point overlooking Coveside. "That's Candle Island Yacht Company; *that's* Vance Jones."

"Just because a man's successful doesn't mean he's problem-free or happy." I squinted, studying the large, blue-and-white buildings in the distance. I saw an ant-sized worker on a forklift unloading lumber from a truck. "Does his son run the business now?"

"Ron's there for the time being, but Vance is still calling the shots." Scotty sounded like he was already grinding an axe.

"You disapprove," I said. "Does Ron share his father's gift for boat building?"

"Did anyone ever tell you, you ask too many questions?"

I laughed. "How else am I going to find answers? I encourage my students to ask questions about everything. It's the best way to learn and discover."

"Huh. You might want to keep your questions under your hat out here on the island." Scotty took my arm and gently trolled me down the hill to the main street. I hadn't realized we'd stopped walking at some point during our conversation.

"I'm not wearing a hat," I countered.

"Here." He put his ball cap on my head.

"Oh, no; I'm not a hat person." I stopped our forward motion and touched the bill of the cap to flip it off.

"Relax." Scotty covered my hand. "It goes fine with what you're wearing."

I jerked my hand away from his and faced him. "I don't recall asking for your fashion statement."

"You didn't." His glower no doubt mirrored my own. "It's a metaphor. Keep it on to remind yourself to keep a lid on the questions. Friendly advice." He held up his palms as if washing his hands of me. "You want folks to accept you, let *them* do the asking. We've been spotted; come on."

His hand exerted gentle pressure on my back, but I refused to move. "Advice from a stranger is fraught with—"

"Danger. Yeah, yeah, I know." He finished the old ditty with a grim smile. "But advice from your caretaker? That's another story. I'll let you find a rhyme for that one, Teacher."

You are not my caretaker, self-appointed or otherwise. I clenched my teeth, debating the wisdom of letting the retort fly, but God provided a way for me to escape temptation when a raised voice overrode our conversation.

"Young Stin! Been lookin' high and low for you! Where you been hidin'?" The shout was full of snarl and bark.

I looked down the street to the picnic tables set up behind a trailer take-out. A whimsical sign with a mussel in a sou'wester—or maybe it was a clam with anorexia and tanning issues—declared *Barb's Lunch Box—best clam roll in Coveside.* Some avid gourmet had graffitied "in the entire world." In spite of the four-star rating, I thought I'd stay away from the clams.

To the left of the sign an old man was on his feet, one hand held high, beckoning our way. I recognized him as the white haired, angry non-waver we passed earlier, when we drove through town with Mr. Blevins. It seemed he was still upset about something, or someone.

"I should've packed peanut butter and jelly," my escort muttered, then looked at me. "We've got to go, Miss McPhail. We did come down here to eat lunch, remember? You can manage that, can't you?"

"Yes." Other diners stared in our direction. "I'll endeavor to keep my ears open and my mouth occupied with . . ." I stopped in front of the take-out window. "A BLT without the T." The girl at the window nodded and smiled.

Out of the corner of my eye I watched the old man approach. He charged at us like a bull, in spite of the age reflected in his weathered face and gnarled hands. Another older man stood up from the picnic tables and leaned in our direction, eager to catch every word. I was aware of the less obvious interest of some of the other lunch crowd as well. Let them get an eyeful; I was simply a middle-aged school teacher, as ordinary as peanut butter and jelly, as my companion had said, yet I was glad I had on a chic outfit instead of my usual backyard jeans and t-shirt.

"Young Stin." The older man frowned through me at Scotty. "You were s'posed to go fishin' with me today."

"That's tomorrow, Grampa," Scotty said.

"I was up at four thirty waitin' for you to show up."

"You always get up at four thirty."

"Nope. Woulda slept in today if I'da known you had no intention of keepin' your word. Pitiful waste of a day."

"I told you last night I had to work." Scotty's words came even slower than usual. He ran a hand through his short hair.

Both men looked down at me. "And who are you?" the older gentleman demanded.

"She's the one who lives in Vance's new house," Scotty said.

Scotty's grandfather stepped closer and looked down his beak with eagle-eye fierceness. "Ah," he said. "You're wearin' my grandson's old hat."

"Didn't want her to get too much sun." Scotty turned and picked up our order from the window.

"What's the matter; can't you speak for yourself?" The old man continued his scrutiny.

I laughed. Scotty spun around and glared at his grandfather. "Yes, I can," I said before my caretaker opened his mouth for me. "The hat's to remind me not to talk too much."

"Ah." The old man broke into a saw-toothed grin. "A woman should be seen and not heard? Hogwash!" He jabbed a knobby finger at Scotty. "No wonder you ain't married, Young Stin. Some of the archaic ideas in that head of yours!" He turned his gaze to me. "You come sit by me. Beautiful women usually don't have much up here." The old gent tapped his temple. "Don't have much of anything interestin' to say because they've had no need to cultivate their brains. You look like a woman who has plenty of interestin' things to say."

"Thanks, I think." I laughed as he led the way to the picnic table.

I hung back, waiting for Scotty to move. His work boots appeared to be rooted to the ground. "We'd better get this over with." He threw a pointed look at his hat on my head. I followed his grandfather over to the picnic table, sat down, took the cap off, and set it beside me on the bench.

"So you're Vance's heiress." The other man at the table had a deep raspy voice and a smoker's cough. His moustache was neatly trimmed and he held himself soldier straight, but his dark eyes were sunken and rimmed with raccoon bruises. He was shorter than I, with a horseshoe fringe of gray hair around a sunburned scalp. *Should I offer him Scotty's hat?* It wasn't doing me any good.

"Actually, I'm Gwen."

"Dr. Douglas Beckett." He shook my hand before he sat down heavily. "You're not what I expected."

"I beg your pardon?" I said. Scotty slid onto the bench next to the doctor and rocked the table. I glanced at him but he was glaring at my seatmate.

"Don't look at *me,*" his grandfather said. "Doug's right." He grinned and bit off the end of his hotdog.

"I expected you to be more . . ." Dr. Beckett tilted his head to the side and squinted across the table, framing me up for what, I dared not ask. "Flamboyant."

"Sorry to disappoint."

"Yeah, it's a shame," Dr. Beckett agreed.

"She's not staying," Scotty said.

The doctor coughed like the engine in Scotty's truck. He grabbed his napkin and bent forward. From my view, the top of his head and tips of his ears turned a fuzzy crimson, deepening with each spasm.

"Not stayin'?" Scotty's grandfather echoed. "Why not? What's wrong with our island?"

"Shouldn't we help him?" I gestured across the table.

"He'll be fine," Scotty's grandfather said. "Don't dodge the question."

Dr. Beckett's fingers clutched mine, pinching off my circulation, but I could feel the tremors pass from his soul to mine.

"You all right, Doc?" Scotty gave him a gentle thump on the back. Dr. Beckett nodded, looked across at me, his watering eyes burning into mine.

Poor man; if these were his friends, I hated to think how he'd fare among enemies.

"Come on, Doug," Scotty's grandfather said. "You're not helpin'."

"Right, Stin," he said on a gasp. "Why aren't you staying?"

"What's the matter with our island?" Old Stin repeated.

"Nothing. Nothing at all. It's perfect, but I don't belong here," I said. "I'm sure you understand." I looked straight at Scotty.

"Well *I* sure as shootin' don't understand." Old Stin knocked my forearm with his bony elbow, breaking contact with the doctor.

"I don't belong in that mausoleum." I turned to the older man. "I don't know why in the world Vance Jones left it to me. I haven't seen or heard from him in over forty years. The place should've gone to his widow, not me."

"Rats!" Dr. Beckett muttered. "I'm beginning to like you. Didn't want to do that." He stood and spun away from the table. I watched him stalk over to the next table and sit down beside a stout woman with Peter Pan–short hair that glinted maroon in the noonday sun.

"Sorry." I took refuge in my sandwich.

The gentleman at my side had polished off his hotdog and leaned on his elbow, watching me. "Never mind Doug," he said. "He's lost his sense of humor, now he's gotten older. Just wait'll he's ninety-two. A sense of humor's all you got left; nothin' else works anymore."

"Wow," I said.

"Don't say it," Scotty warned.

"I was going to say you've got a wonderful sense of humor, Mr. Scott."

The old gentleman hooted. Dr. Beckett shot us a dark look from over his shoulder. His new dining companion stared at me. Her face had more lines than the Declaration of Independence, but her eyes shone out of the careworn mask like the Statue of Liberty's torch. I nodded and she glowered. I smiled politely and broke eye contact.

"Call me Stin," my seatmate offered.

"*Old* Stin," Scotty said.

"That's Vance's widow." Old Stin nodded to the woman glaring at us.

"Dot Jones," Scotty said. He rose and gathered up the lunch trash.

"You probably ought to meet her." Old Stin clutched my arm and hauled me to my feet.

"I don't know . . ."

"I do." Scotty scowled at his grandfather. Except for the forty-year age span, I was caught in the crossfire of mirrored stubborn streaks. "You're the other woman." Scotty rounded the table and put a firm hand on my shoulder. He reached behind me with his free hand and scooped up the cap in a stranglehold.

"What?" I shook my head. "This is absurd. I most certainly am not the other *anything.* I'm simply a woman. I'll straighten this out right now."

"No you won't," Scotty said.

Old Stin chortled, let go of me, crossed his arms, and leaned back, enjoying the show.

I shook free of Scotty's heavy hand and stepped out from the table. Glancing over the small yard, I gave my prim teacher nod to the gallery of tourists, fisher folk, and teens before spinning on my heel and coming face to face with my caretaker.

"I'm glad you saw reason," he said.

"I thought it might help if you or your grandfather made the introductions," I said. "Get us started off on the right foot, since we're neighbors."

"I thought you said you weren't stayin'." Old Stin stuck his craggy face so close to mine I could smell the dab of mustard lodged at the corner of his lips. "As I recall, you said you didn't belong here, didn't want the—"

"Don't start," Scotty warned. "You know, if the Titanic had turned around, it never would've hit that iceberg."

"Are you speaking to your grandfather, or me?" I asked. The iceberg gaze he leveled at me kindled into blue flame. I pushed on. "I believe the iceberg hit the Titanic, rather than the other way around."

"You would. Come on, then." Scotty put the hat on his head. "I might as well wear this; it's not doing you any good." He drew me toward Dr. Beckett and his dining companion. "There's only one-tenth of an iceberg floating above water, so I'd advise you to watch out for the ninety percent you can't see, not that it'll do any good."

"Point taken," I said softly, but his slow, deep tones overrode my words so I wasn't sure he heard.

"Hey, Dot," he said. "I'd like to introduce you to Gwen McPhail. Gwen, this is my cousin, Dot."

"I'm pleased to meet you." I offered my hand. "My father worked with your husband when I was very young."

Dot Jones stared at my hand as if it were a piece of week-old road trash. For an awkward moment, I kept it there. My arm dropped to my side when her hate-filled gaze lifted to my face; then the cloudy, light eyes burned through me like the July sun through morning fog.

"I was hoping we might get together for tea and talk about this whole mess," I said. Dot jerked from her seat and marched away. "Obviously, there's been some mistake," I said to her stiff back. The maroon hair flipped up in the breeze off the water, exposing an angry scar on the back of her neck.

"That went well," Scotty said.

"You warned me." My companion's face was calm as the sea, except for the raised eyebrows that skimmed the band of his cap like gulls in flight. "If she won't speak to me, maybe you could talk to her."

"Me?" Scotty's ruddy brows rose higher on disbelief to hide up under his hat.

"You're her cousin. I just want her to know I'm going to talk to the lawyer and see what I need to do to give her back her house."

"Just like that?" Dr. Beckett's sarcasm drew my attention like a road flare.

"Just like that."

"You've only been here less than a day," the doctor argued.

I looked at my watch the way I did when my students begged to have five more minutes on the playground. "Actually I've been here about three hours and forty-five minutes, but who's counting?" I said, and grinned at his bulldog expression. "Vance Jones's house was hate-at-first-sight for me. Your island is beautiful, but, like I said before, I don't belong here. Dot Jones does."

"Might not be as easy as you think," Old Stin said. He stepped past and leaned on the picnic table, aware of his audience and in no hurry to rush his comments. His eyes twinkled in his leathered face, betraying the laconic tone. "Vance was good at tyin' people up in knots, and I 'magine he's set it up so he can pull strings and jerk folks around from the grave, eh, Doc?"

"Doesn't matter," I said. "There's always a way to do the right thing."

Either the doctor and Scotty were allergic to the fried-grease smell roiling off the lunch wagon, or they were simply allergic to the black-and-white concept of truth. Their snorts joined together, barraging me with cynicism. I stepped closer to Old

Stin. "Whatever's been done, it doesn't mean I can't undo it."

"Goin' up against Goliath," Old Stin said with a conspiratorial grin, and patted my arm with his knobby fingers. "You got any island blood in you?"

"I don't believe so," I said.

"Who are your people?" The old man's eyes danced like a monkey at the circus.

"Woods, Durrells, and McMahans."

"McMahan." Old Stin pounded his fist on the table. "I shoulda seen it. You got the McMahan chin, stubborn as Emerson's Rock. Can you see it, Doc?"

I was tempted to turn the backside of my profile to all of them, but I didn't want to hurt this sweet, crusty man who just might be my only friend on the island.

"Prob'ly Lemmie's tribe. Lemuel McMahan left here when I was a young fella; had a fence post–sized chip on his shoulder and a swarm of hornets at his heels. He was accused of stealin' lobster traps and boat motors; lit out after dark, pilfered Ralphie Jones's boat to do it. No one ever heard from him again . . . until now."

"I hear every family has its share of black sheep and horse thieves." Scotty's low voice rumbled in my ear.

"Very funny," I said, but I couldn't stop the tug of a smile. I was regretting my decision to leave Candle Island so quickly.

"I'll talk to Dot," the doctor said. He pushed up from the table and closed his eyes for a second. "I'll let you know." His dark eyes opened and pleaded with mine. "You aren't leaving tonight, are you?"

"No. I'll put out the word before I leave the island," I said. "I wouldn't want to stain the family reputation further by following in Great-Grampa Lemmie's wake."

Chapter Four

I wandered into the library, my footfalls swallowed up in the spongy carpet. It was springy, like walking on moss, but sucking like muck at my ankles, giving me the feeling of being pulled underground. The color was all wrong, too. A neutral cream color, which was pretty in its way, but it didn't say "I'm a magic carpet and I'll take you places." It huffed out, "I'm rich and I'll seduce you," with every careful step I took.

I tiptoed through the stacks, running my fingers over the buttery leather spines of the books. So many words, ancient and modern; so much knowledge on these shelves, yet it appeared Vance Jones wasn't an avid reader. The books were in mint condition, a beautiful collection, just like the Remington sculptures in the conservatory and the Wyeths hanging on the walls. This could've been a seductive place, with its carved-maple bookshelves, its wonders of words, antique globe, and the collected replicas of Model T's and vehicles I'd never known existed, in their hermetically sealed glass case running the length of the far wall, but the entire room was cold; a museum piece, a show place.

Who was this man with a taste for fine art and good books? A stranger ill remembered whom no one grieved or missed, yet who had so generously remembered a little girl from his past. Nothing made any sense, the people I'd met today in particular. I wasn't imagining the level of disgust in Scotty's remarks, or the glee in Old Stin's voice in their comments about Vance

Jones's manipulating ways.

In the bright light of day, I'd convinced myself the crank phone call was a mistake, one that hadn't been repeated. I'd pretended to put it out of my mind. Yet now it was roaring back like a stormy gale. Here I was living on the cliff where a man had gone over the edge and died. *I know who you are and what you did. You won't get away with it. Accidents can happen to a person. Accidents like falling off a cliff and drowning.*

The hate-filled words knocked around my skull. There was someone out there who didn't believe Vance's death was an accident; someone besides me; someone who apparently knew of my inheritance before I'd even been informed of it.

I wearily rubbed my forehead and looked out the window. The summer sun splashed over the brick walls of my prison. The yard far below was Fenway-Park green and manicured to perfection. No mud, no mess. I clenched my hands into fists, itching to jump into my old jeans, dig up those formal shrubs, and put in wild beach roses and daisies. "And what would you think of that, Young Stinson Scott?"

There was no answer, of course, from the expert on icebergs, who'd disappeared as soon as he dropped me at the door. He was definitely ninety percent mystery.

Our walk to the clinic and subsequent drive back to this mausoleum had been like an ocean voyage. The conversation rolled in gentle waves of island lore and lulls of easy silence. Scotty steered the talk toward comments about the wildflowers, shells, and trees, and I'd let him take the rudder, for now. Even though he'd clammed up about anything personal after I made my date with the doctor, I couldn't deny a pleasant warm curl inside that generated from his polite small talk.

A flash of light bounced through the window and struck me. I blinked at the glare and, when I opened my eyes, it was gone. Squinting toward the twisted path through the spruces, I spied movement that was gone as soon as I glimpsed it, leaving me to wonder if it was a figment of my imagination.

The distraction was a welcome one. I hurried out of the library and up the stairs to Vance's private retreat. The study was as opulent as the rest of the house, except awards hung in place of fine art. I barely glanced at the framed accolades, and, for the moment, dismissed the trophy display in favor of the battered easy chair, the scratched wooden school teacher's desk, and the general mess of yacht blueprints, files, and magazines that gave the room character and a purposeful air. My eyes skimmed over the evidence of a life interrupted, the state-of-the-art laptop gathering dust, the telescope positioned blindly at the far wall of glass.

Feeling like a peeping Tom, or Thomasina, I slipped over to the extravagant apparatus, closed one eye, and gingerly peered into the instrument, wondering, as I did so, if I dared touch any of the knobs to adjust the focus. The picture bloomed in a burst of clarity and color in front of my eye. I blinked at the brilliance, my eyelashes colliding with the rubber ocular piece, forcing my eye to stay open. A dark-haired woman and a stocky man in a familiar blue ball cap stood on the ledges of Blind Man's Bluff. As I watched, the couple dragged a wooden chest to the edge of the cliff.

The woman's head jerked up and she turned toward the house. For an instant I had the strangest feeling she was looking at me, but then the reason for her attention zoomed into focus. The same blue cap, soft-green, flannel shirt, well-worn jeans, and a slight rolling swagger heralded Scotty's appearance in my porthole view. As he grabbed the other man's shoulder, the stocky guy kicked the wooden chest toward the precipice. The woman dropped to her knees and shoved it over, just as Scotty lunged and yanked her back from the edge.

Like watching a modern silent movie, I saw the threesome

face off, body language bowstring taut, mouths wide and mobile. Scotty leaned into the noiseless argument, rigid as steel, while the other guy moved his arms so much I thought he might sprout wings and take off. The huge gestures abruptly stopped; he wrapped his arm around the woman's shoulders and the couple disappeared down the trail. Scotty stood sentinel straight, staring out to sea.

"Auntie! Are you here?" I jumped at Tasha's faint call, nearly upsetting the telescope. I shot out a shaky hand to steady the tripod, then dashed out of the room and shut the door with a less than discreet slam. I clattered down the stairs and met Tasha head-on at the second floor gallery. Sledge was a step behind her, a brightly colored wall of solid muscle.

"Hi." I puffed out the greeting. *Nothing like a guilty conscience to bring on a self-induced stroke.* My heart pulsed in my brain, hammering the sides of my skull.

"Are you all right?" Tasha gripped my forearm.

"I'm fine." I held my breath to appear calm. Not a good idea. I drew in a great gulp and continued on the exhale, "I guess I need to up my workout if I'm going to climb these stairs without having a heart attack. I'm getting too old for this."

"You are not old!" Tasha protested.

"Tell that to my gray hairs."

"I'm sure Brother Nate was responsible for each and every one; they have nothing to do with age."

"Right. Thanks for the thought." I pasted on a shaky smile.

The scene I'd just witnessed bothered me more than it should. I didn't know these folks. What they did was none of my business. I ran impatient fingers through my bangs, half expecting the feel of Scotty's metaphorical cap on my head that should remind me to mind my own business, hat or no hat. I looked at Tasha, leaning on crutches, then over my niece's head at the stalwart young doctor. "How's the ankle?"

Sledge smiled, and I could feel his calm, capable, confidence beam on me like a beacon, but he never said a word. He waited.

"It's a sprain," Tasha said. "Not even a bad one. I just have to stay off it for awhile."

"Well, then, let's go down on the deck, put our feet up, and have a cold drink," I suggested.

"Sounds good to me." Sledge finally spoke, but I felt he'd been a part of the conversation all along. "Take it slow and easy on the stairs until you get used to the crutches, Nurse."

"Yes, Doctor." Tasha laughed and led us quickly down to the first level.

"Show-off," I muttered in her ear when we hit the marble chessboard floor of what I called the throne room, due to its cavernous wasted space and the location of a cranberry-velvet upholstered monstrosity set upon a carpeted dais in front of a dark hunting tapestry. "Did you two get any lunch?"

"Leftover pizza at the clinic." My niece grinned.

"I tried to take her out, but she insisted I work instead of slacking off," Sledge said. He opened the French doors, then hustled up some high-priced lounge chairs from the far end of the deck.

"Go ahead and sit," I said. "Make sure the patient behaves herself and I'll see what's in the fridge."

"My aunt thinks she's a comedienne," I heard Tasha say. Their burst of laughter followed me on my hike through the length of the house to the kitchen, bolstering my spirits. It seemed the trip to the island clinic had cured Tasha of her Dalton-itis. No telling how long it would last.

I pushed through the double doors and was assaulted by yards of gleaming stainless-steel appliances and cold, black granite countertops. I hardly remembered touring this room with Mr. Blevins. Obviously it'd been too much to take in and my mind was still blown.

I gingerly opened the gargantuan refrigerator expecting to find a wizzled lemon wedge, a moldy piece of cheese, and a bottle of imported water. Instead, a display of juice, milk, lemonade, water, and soda stood in neat array on the top shelf. Below it sat a variety of cheeses, including Swiss, my favorite, deli meats, a whole roasted chicken, strawberries, lettuce, and salad fixings. I closed the door and leaned against it, suddenly remembering Dalton. How could I have forgotten my nephew-to-be?

"Dalton?" I strode toward the walk-in pantry that could swallow my entire kitchen back home and still have plenty of room for the Bookerton High School band. The longing to be sitting at my own dear little kitchen table washed over me. In a flood of homesickness, I imagined myself leaning my elbows on my homemade red gingham tablecloth, sipping raspberry iced tea, my nails plugged with moist soil, my fingers tinged with the spicy scent of nasturtiums. *What ails me? I'll be going home soon enough.*

"Dalton?" I called again.

"Yeah?"

I spun around and there he was, marching into the kitchen, carrying one meager grocery bag. "I got a few things, but let's just say I've seen fresher items in the dumpster behind my apartment building. We need to stock up on the mainland."

"Oh, well, thanks for going to the market," I said in a rush. "But I have to apologize." I brushed past him and opened the refrigerator à la Vanna White. "I should've looked before I sent you on a fool's errand."

"No problem." Dalton flashed his trademark gleam of teeth. He reached into the fridge and grabbed a bottled water. "It gave me a chance to get the lay of the land or, should I say, the island."

The refrigerator door closed with a hushed whoosh as I

studied the suave young man. The cool, stainless-steel backdrop was a perfect foil for him but, as he leaned back and swigged the water, I glimpsed a glutton.

Fighting my constant dislike for this new addition to the family, I smiled. "Did you meet anyone interesting in town?" I thought of Old Stin.

"Just a bunch of locals, but I did run into Ron Jones leaving the boatyard. A stroke of luck, actually."

This boy with his reliance on luck! I mentally shook my head and it coincided with the bonging of the antique mantel clock in the adjacent dining room. "Oh my, I had no idea it was so late," I said aloud, my brain doing the mental arithmetic. Where had Dalton been for the past three hours? "What took so long?"

"Oh, I got tied up."

The remark was too offhand, too glib, too quick; and my teacher radar was too hypersensitive to let the lie pass. "Oh? Did Ron Jones invite you to tea?"

"Hardly." Dalton hedged. "As I said, he was leaving the boatyard. He was in a hurry, so we barely spoke. He pointed me toward the head designer, Les Bigelow. Nice guy; doesn't think much of Ron."

"It seems odd that this Les person would run down the boss to a total stranger."

"I know Les." Dalton's grin made his handsome face look like a conceited, overfed wolf. "I've been talking to him about designing a yacht for my father. He gave me a tour of the place. Quite impressive and, under the right management, Candle Island Yacht could be a major player."

"Maybe you can tell that to Ron Jones the next time we see him."

"Ron Jones is *not* Candle Island Yacht." Dalton capped his empty water bottle. He flipped it in the air, caught it, then, deciding it was so much fun, he did it again and again and again. His habits were becoming more disturbing than poor little Tony Strout's craving for wax. I still had his tooth prints in most of the crayons in my desk drawer at school. But Tony was five years old.

"There must be a bin for returnables in this galaxy of cupboards." I snagged the busy bottle.

"Oh, sure, sure." Dalton systematically flipped open doors as if it were a game of hide-and-seek. It was hide-and-seek all right, and I was determined to find out what this man was hiding behind his day-old stubble, flashy grin, and nervous energy.

"What did you mean when you said Ron Jones is not Candle Island Yacht Company?" I tossed the empty in the bin and Dalton smirked.

One of my student teachers once drew me a cartoon where a kindergarten teacher, bearing an uncanny likeness to me, was portrayed as a cowgirl, a star on her ten-gallon hat, her bandoliers filled with markers, a box of tissues in her holster. She was singing with a guitar strapped around her neck, while lassoing a child from a playground stampede and pulling him hand-over-hand toward a little desk. Not a flattering comparison, but not totally without merit, either. I wasn't leaving this conversational rodeo without a satisfactory answer, even if I had to hogtie him and drag it out of him.

"It's common knowledge, at least at the boatyard." Dalton went back to the refrigerator and pulled out the chicken. "Do you mind?" He set the bird on the counter.

"Be my guest; you must be hungry." I rifled in the cupboard for a plate; no homey, day-to-day kitchenware in this joint, only fine china. I placed the plate in front of him and smiled sweetly as he dismembered the bird. "You were saying?"

"Ron didn't inherit the boatyards outright," Dalton said between bites of drumstick. "The way I understand it, he has to stick to certain stipulations his father set up in the will. If he doesn't, bye-bye Ronnie Boy, and someone else inherits the whole enchilada." His eyes glowed and the look he gave me was akin to Pavlov's dog.

"Oh, no." I shook my head.

Dalton chuckled. "Actually, I don't know the whole deal; there're a lot of bogus rumors flying around down there among the rank-and-file, but I'm sure our friend Mr. Blevins could shed some light on the situation. It might not be a bad idea for you to give him a call."

"I thought you might need a hand."

I started at Sledge's friendly entrance into the room. I hadn't known I needed the cavalry, but sent up a silent *thank You* for the Divine intervention.

"Sledge, uh, Dr. Angus Knox, isn't it?"

"Sledge is fine." He grinned. The young doctor obviously had more class than I when it came to the petty need to take Dalton down a peg.

Mentally chastised, I began again. "Sledge, I'd like you to meet Dalton Madison. Sledge, Dalton. Dalton, this is Sledge. He's the one who fixed up Tasha's ankle."

Dalton's dark eyebrows lowered into a unibrow, but he smiled and said, "Hey, nice to meet you. What's this about Tash?"

"Oh, I forgot." Whether I was losing it from old age or brain overload due to my weighty inheritance, the phrase was becoming too true. "You weren't here when Tasha and I took a walk and she twisted her ankle."

"Nothing serious; I was glad to take care of it," Sledge said, but with those few words, the temperature in the kitchen shot up. They were an odd contrast—Dalton, every inch the privileged yacht-club scion; Sledge, easily mistaken for a beach bum—but it was their faces that held my attention. Sledge was openly assessing Dalton, while my nephew-to-be didn't bother to hide his boredom.

Dalton wiped his greasy hands on the towel by the sink. "Well, I guess I ought to go see the damage. If you'll excuse me." He brushed past Sledge.

"She's out on the back deck," Sledge said. "Would you like me to take you?"

"I can find my way," Dalton said. "Don't let us keep you from your other patients." The swinging door punctuated his subtle snub.

"I was just about to bring out those cold drinks I promised," I said, quickly covering the chicken and putting it back in the refrigerator. "I hope you're still planning on staying."

"Oh yeah." Sledge's grin was back in place. He swept the counter free of the pile of chicken bones, deposited them in the trash, and washed his hands before insisting on carrying out the drink tray. I preceded him outside. *I could get used to having this young man around.*

Dalton sat on the end of Tasha's lounger, murmuring endearments, her ankle gently propped on his lap, the poster boy for caring fiancés worldwide.

I did my best stewardess imitation, passing out lemonade and iced tea, before allowing Sledge to place the tray on a nearby table and escort me to the seat next to Tasha. As I sat in the proffered wicker, I sensed he'd given up his place; whether in deference to me, or propriety for Tasha, I wasn't sure. He leaned on the railing, sipping tea, a silent observer.

"I was telling Tash, I want to take her on a drive out to Mulroon's Point this afternoon." Dalton's voice was brisk.

"And where's that?" I asked.

"No need to worry, Auntie. I'll have her back safe and sound by curfew." Dalton chuckled.

Tasha had the good sense to give him a swat on the arm, but it was too playful to carry the message of my thoughts.

"Abuse," he teased. "Better wait on that stuff until we're

married or I might reconsider."

"Oh, aren't you awful." Tasha laughed.

I couldn't take any more of the syrupy show, and neither could Sledge. "Well, I ought to be going." The young doctor pushed away from the railing. "See if Doc Beckett needs me. If you need anything, Nurse, just call." His eyes twinkled. "It was nice to meet all of you, and I'm sure I'll see you around the island." He pivoted over the side of the deck and jogged around the house.

"Bye," Tasha and I called.

"He's a nice guy," I said.

"I called Mother while I was in Coveside." Dalton ignored Sledge's absence, which wasn't surprising, since he'd ignored his presence. "She told me the Ellingsfords are giving an Independence Day bash in honor of our engagement. Isn't that cool?"

"Really? Wow." Tasha smiled but didn't sound thrilled.

"Mother thought she'd come over on the third and get a feel for the place."

"Sure; there's plenty of room for everyone," I said. "Your dad and brother are more than welcome to come and stay as well."

"Thanks, but I can RSVP for them. Davis won't show up until it's absolutely necessary. Weddings give him the heebie-jeebies. He's probably scheduled extra therapy so he can make it through mine without a psychotic break. Dad'll take a raincheck. He's up to his eyeballs wrapping up transactions so he can have extra time off in August for the wedding."

"I guess it's all settled," I said.

"I'm not so sure," Tasha said. "I think we should—"

"No worries," Dalton cut in.

I wanted to take him aside, as I did Jill Gaines when she elbowed into the recess line, and tell him, "No cuts." But I kept still, for the time being.

"If your ankle's still healing, I'll have Mother bring a wheelchair for the party; and, you know, Tash, if you can't walk down the aisle, I'll carry you to the altar myself." Dalton gently placed her legs to the side, rose to his feet, and carefully swept her up in his arms. "See?" He laughed. "No problem." Tasha's laugh joined his. "Princess, your carriage awaits."

"Do you want to come, Auntie?" Tasha called out over his shoulder as Dalton opened the French door.

"No, no thank you." I quickly stood. "You two go on and have a good time. I've got plenty to do."

I wandered out the frontispiece and watched the SUV drive away with Tasha's head stuck out the window yelling, "Dalton's taking me out for dinner. Don't wait up!"

"Thanks for the tip," I muttered, and stomped down the stairs. I automatically turned to the foundation plantings, treading through fluffed mulch. With each step, the heady smell of fermenting bark chips and earth lightened my foul mood. I ran my hand over the top of the neatly cropped juniper, thinking of Trevor and his visits every spring to my classroom to show off his yearly buzz cut and urge me to run my palm over his freshly shorn head. "Like a tennis ball, Miss Mac," I quoted the barber's son.

"Talking to the plants, or yourself?" Scotty's slow drawl didn't startle me. A smile tugged at my lips and I turned to face him. He was pushing a wheelbarrow across the lawn.

"Just the man I wanted to see."

"That doesn't sound good." He stopped his forward progress. "Do the shrubs need tweaking?"

"Tweaking out of the ground, maybe." This caused his rusty brows to disappear into his cap. His usually calm features instantly settled back into place. I laughed. "I was just kidding! I'm not going to be staying here, so I don't have to like the landscaping."

"You don't like the house. You don't like the landscaping." The trace of a smile appeared. "You're a hard one to please."

"I'm not used to living in a perfect environment."

"A fish out of water. I know the feeling." He took off his cap and ran his large hand over his eyes. He looked tired and stressed, in spite of his casual pose. *Signs of a soul that needs to come clean.* He put his cap on and strode over to the other side of the juniper. "You said you wanted to talk to me?"

"Yes. I was wondering if you'd take a walk with me to Blind Man's Bluff," I said. "After what happened to Tasha today, I didn't want to go over there all alone."

"Sure." He took my hand in his and guided me out of the rough mulch onto the manicured lawn.

"Don't let me keep you from your work." I gestured toward the tool-laden wheelbarrow. "We can walk at your convenience."

"You aren't keeping me from my work, since I work for you." He released my hand now that we were on level ground. The statement didn't set well.

"Well, then, let's go."

I cut across the driveway with my best hiking stride, but he was at my side when I entered the winding trail to the cliff. We didn't speak until we broke out into the sun-drenched expanse of ledge, sky, and sea. The wind tugged at my hair and fluttered the sleeves of my blouse.

Scotty stood close, his arms folded. Though right beside me, his face looked a million miles away as he squinted over the bright water. It was no stretch of my imagination to picture him in uniform standing on the deck of a Coast Guard ship.

I looked away to the horizon, then down at the thunder of waves breaking below us. I inched closer to the precipice to get a better view. Scotty firmly gripped my arm.

"I just want a good look at the rocks below."

"Be careful." His voice raised a notch from his usual low

tones. "Ledges like this are a lot like toddlers and five-gallon buckets."

"What?"

"You start to bend out to look over the cliff and, before you know it, the drop and the water act as a magnet pulling you off balance and you're following your head down into the water. No toddler moments on my watch."

"Okay; how about if I sit and inch over to the edge?" He nodded but didn't let go of my arm. We went down on our knees in tandem, then I inched forward and planted my seat on the edge of Blind Man's Bluff. I was confident my rear anchor was weighty enough to offset any brain poundage, more's the pity. Hunching my shoulders, I gazed down at the hypnotism of the waves foaming and pulsing on the jagged rocks below. "Do you come out here often?" I asked.

"Depends on the weather."

"How about today?"

"Yeah, I like to eat my lunch out here sometimes. Nice place to be alone and do some thinking."

"You ate lunch with me today." I could feel his blue eyes glaring at my face, but I continued to stare at the beating surf far below our dangling sneakers.

"And your point is?"

I should've known better than to beat around the bushes. This was a man who only operated on the direct approach to life. "Do you suppose there's any sign of that chest you and your friends threw overboard earlier?" I asked. "What was in it?"

Chapter Five

His grip tightened on my forearm. Then his hand slipped down to my wrist before coming to rest, palm pressing on the narrow gap of rock between us. He no longer touched me, but his withdrawal was more than physical. It was my turn to look at his profile, but he stared steadfast across the ocean, in no hurry to respond to my question.

I thought my patience was exceptional, having been stretched and tested by kindergartners for twenty-five years, but I was no match for the old man of the sea. I began to grow moss and could take it no longer. "I just happened to be in Vance's study looking through the spyglass," I finally said. "I couldn't help but notice the crowd on the cliff."

"It's called a telescope."

"In this case, I guess it *was* a spyglass." I hoped to prod him into looking at me. "I unintentionally spied a crime, and now . . . ?"

"Now." Scotty's narrowed gaze pinned me to the ledge. "You're jumping to conclusions."

"That could be dangerous, given my present position."

"You are the most misguided woman I've ever met." He drew up his long legs and levered to his feet.

"Should you be standing this close to the edge?"

"I'm fine." He reached for my hand. "Come along, Miss Guided."

I let him help me to my feet and lead me back from the sheer drop. "I never would've taken you for a comedian, Mr. Scott."

"Funny," he said. "Nor I, you. If you'll excuse me, I need to get back to work."

I didn't move and was secretly pleased when he held his ground, waiting for me to precede him. If he could wait for the icebergs to melt, so could I.

"Okay." He planted his hands on his hips. "You're never going to find any trace of that chest, not that it's any of your business. It's a twenty-six-foot drop between high and low tide here, some of the most extreme tides in the world. There's also a good current down there that'd carry any remains out to sea."

"Next stop France."

"More likely Nova Scotia."

"I was making a joke."

"I know." His sense of humor was gone.

I craned my neck for one more look. Not close enough to see to the wave drenched rocks, I got only a view of sun and shadow on the cliff face. I thought of Vance, and the chest incident took a back seat in my brain. "I wonder why Vance was out here all alone." I looked up into Scotty's stern, ruddy face.

"Look at the path," he said. "He came here every day. When he was younger, he used to stand right here and shout over the water, 'I'm the King of Candle Island!' I must've heard him do it at least a dozen times. Probably he still did it, for all I know or care. Ego trip; the lord of the island, lording it over the rest of us."

"What do you mean?"

"If you let us go back to the house, I'll tell you."

"About the chest?"

"Don't push it." He took my elbow.

A little ground gained was something, so I gave ground and stepped beside him. He didn't speak until we were almost to the trees. Typical, but I figured the wait would be worth it.

"Vance was in the prime and pride of life." Scotty stopped at the entrance to the dark path, the roots exposed from constant use. When he spoke, his tone was impersonal, as if he were reading the phone book. "He had everything going his way: a couple of big contracts for the boatyards; he'd just bought a new sports car. He was trying to buy up more land. He was riding high."

"It seems strange that he'd fall over the cliff."

"Don't tell me you're still hung up on Vance faking his death and skipping to the mainland." He looked down his nose at me. "Forget about that."

If he thought to intimidate me, the effect was lost due to the non-aristocratic character of the nose itself, having obviously been broken at some point in the past. "No; I was referring to the fact that he was obviously familiar with this place. After years of coming here day after day, would he be so careless? He doesn't sound like the type to fall victim to one of your toddler moments."

"You didn't know Vance." He stared past my shoulder to the bare ledge of Blind Man's Bluff, and I wondered what he saw. I turned my head, but there was nothing there, maybe because I couldn't see the past.

"Look what happened to Tasha this morning," Scotty said. "Same thing likely happened to Vance—a slip, but there was no one to grab him when he lost his balance."

"Did he have a twisted ankle? I mean, was there an autopsy?"

His gaze flew back to mine. "You're sure you're a kindergarten teacher?"

"Absolutely."

Scotty took a deep breath and took off his hat.

"You aren't going to put that on my head, are you?"

"I'd consider it, if I thought it'd do any good, but I know better. Enough questions for now, huh?" He held up his hands in surrender.

"About the chest."

He took my hand and I let him lead me through the trees at a fast clip. "I don't know what you think you saw, but it had nothing to do with—" He stopped walking and talking. "It had nothing to do with Vance's death."

"You were going to say it had nothing to do with Vance."

"I was." He bit his lower lip. "I don't know exactly what was in the chest, but I *do* know it wasn't a crime. If I tell you who threw it over, will you promise to let it drop?"

I closed my eyes and weighed the request. If I agreed, I wouldn't sleep tonight.

"Curiosity killed the cat," he murmured.

"Satisfaction brought her back." I opened my eyes. "I can't agree to your terms."

He nodded. "The offer's open, should you change your mind." He gave me a small grin. His head jerked toward the house. My gaze followed his just as a white car pulled into the drive. "You've got company," he said, the grin gone.

"I should imagine whoever it is might be here to see you. No one knows me."

"Oh, no; everyone on the island knows you."

I nodded. "Of course. I hope I'm either killing the rumors or living up to them."

As we strolled across the lawn, the car doors opened. "Smashing them all to pieces," Scotty said.

I recognized the bald pate of Dr. Beckett just before the other man raised his hand and hailed us. "Mr. Scott," he said. "Just the man I wanted to see."

"I'll leave you to your visitors." I headed toward the side door, only to be intercepted by both men.

"I'd hoped to meet you as well." The visitor stuck out a hand in my direction. He was wearing a white, short-sleeved shirt and a tie. If I hadn't already met Sledge and Dr. Beckett in their island attire, I'd have taken him for a medical type.

I shook his hand, softer than my own, and, on close inspection, determined him to be either an insurance salesman or . . .

"I'm Pastor John Hersey," he said.

"Gwen McPhail. Nice to meet you."

"I came to ask Mr. Scott if he'd do the Responsive Reading and the Scripture this Sunday," Pastor Hersey said.

"My privilege, Pastor," Scotty said. "I'll see you then. If you'll excuse me, I promised Dot I'd drop by and take a look at her kitchen sink. That old plumbing is a disaster waiting to happen. I'll need to go in the house and get some tools in the basement."

"Be my guest; it's open," I said.

He ignored my questioning look. All business, he stepped past to the side door. I saw him try the handle, then swiftly punch in the security code and disappear inside. Odd. I was certain I hadn't turned on the security system when I left the house. And why was he suddenly asking my permission to get tools? *I'm missing something.*

"Ms. McPhail." John Hersey claimed my attention and I reluctantly gave it to him. "I wanted to invite you and your family to church on Sunday. It's a warm family group; I know you'd feel welcome."

"Thank you, Pastor; I look forward to it." I smiled. "I had wanted to come if I was still on the island, and it looks as if I'll be here a little longer than I originally planned. Can I offer you an iced tea or an afternoon snack?"

John Hersey patted his flat stomach. "Not today, thank you. When I'm out on visits, I find island hospitality so gracious, I must've put on five pounds in the three weeks I've been here."

"Perhaps another time," I said.

"Exactly my thoughts, Ms. McPhail. I look forward to it."

"We're on our way to visit a sick friend," Dr. Beckett said.

I'd felt his looming presence at my side during the exchange. When he hadn't spoken to me directly, I wondered if we were back to square one in his low assessment of my character.

"We just came from Dot Jones's place," he continued. His light touch on my arm drew my eyes to his face, sagging and gray. The gravity of his look pulled me into his battered heart. "I set up a time with her for our visit. You should know she wasn't keen on it, so I suggested we come here. Tomorrow at two o'clock okay?"

"That's fine," I said. "And thank you for helping me out."

"Just so you know, I'm not so keen on it myself, but something has to be done." Dr. Beckett walked away and got into the car.

"I hope you'll overlook Douglas's candor," the pastor said. "He's got a lot on his mind."

"There's no need for you to apologize for him; I appreciate hearing the truth." It sounded like a prim school teacher reprimand, and I suppose it was. I was of the firm opinion that everyone has a right to speak for themselves, and others had no business trying to put their interpretation on the content. "Thank you for stopping by," I said in a softer tone, and walked with him to the car. "What time is church?"

"Ten thirty." Douglas Beckett's voice was barely a whisper and ended in a volley of coughs. "Let's go, John," he gasped.

"Tell Dot she's welcome to bring her son tomorrow," I called after them. The doctor's head jerked up and down, but I wasn't sure if it was from the coughing spasms or an indication of my message received.

I stood for a moment looking down the empty drive, then I tilted my head back to gaze at the mansion towering above me. It eclipsed the afternoon sun, and the sheer weight of it hit me. What was I to do with the rest of this day and the next? For one of the few times in my life, I felt lonely.

"You're getting old; just get on with it," I murmured. "And talking to yourself is the first sign." I trudged into the house and found my way to the kitchen. I rattled around in the cupboards and pantry, and finally settled on a Dutch oven for a mixing bowl. All these gadgets and gewgaws, and not a decent bowl or wooden spoon in the place. Perhaps Dot took her personal baking things with her; I certainly would have. Or maybe I just couldn't find anything in this glorified coliseum.

I did find enough ingredients and makeshift baking tools to tide me over. I sprinkled yeast in the warm water, added honey and breathed in the homey scent. As I dumped in the flour and stirred the dough, my mind worked on the happenings of the day and the island people I'd met. In my prayers of the last couple of weeks, I hadn't a clue of what to expect here, and anything my mind had conjured up had been blown away like feathers before these strong opinions, personalities, and my own growing suspicions.

I pressed my palms into the soft dough, kneading it a bit roughly as Mr. Blevins's words from this morning echoed in my ear. "Here are your keys to your new life."

Standing here, I knew he was right—my life would never be the same. Not because of the inheritance, which wasn't mine to keep, but something life changing had happened between yesterday and today. Whether it started with the midnight phone call, Lois Boyle's seizure of the Glastonburg Institute job, the letter informing me of Vance Jones's bequest, Tasha and Dalton's upcoming wedding, or meeting Sledge and Scotty, Old Stin and Dr. Beckett, it didn't matter. I suspected it was all of that and more.

I'd already gotten into the habit of including these dear folk in my micro prayers that sent minute-sized praises, intercessions, and requests to God throughout the day. My life in Bookerton seemed like a far-away dream and, yet, this place was the stuff of Brigadoon and castles in the air.

I couldn't think about going back to my old life right now, so, as I set the bread dough to rise, I set my thoughts on my benefactor. I roamed through the massive rooms, feeling like a minnow in an ocean. No personal photos, no cozy touches—like a beautiful, whitewashed tomb full of a dead man's bones. The Scripture verse from Matthew twenty-three popped into my head just as the sun went behind a cloud, as if shadowing God's words.

I poked my head in the library, but the cold room repelled me. Instead, I took to the stairs, puffing when I reached the third floor. This had to be good for those thighs and nether regions that needed firming, if I didn't die of a heart attack on this huge stair-master monster.

Tiptoeing into the study, I pulled back the desk chair and sat down, the accompanying creak loud enough to wake the dead. I leaned on the desk top, wondering about the man who used to sit here. I stared at the blown-up picture by the phone. It was of Vance with some kind of huge trophy fish. I wondered if the photo was enlarged to make the fish bigger. Holding the frame, I tried to evoke a memory to say I recognized him, but I couldn't. There was nothing familiar. His wiry build and swept-back gray hair didn't exude the barracuda image the island folk claimed he had.

I squinted at the lean face hidden behind expensive shades, a deep tan, and his grimacing smile. "Why?" I asked him. I needed to know why. Why had Vance Jones left this all to me? It made absolutely no sense. My brothers' memories of "Uncle Jonesy" were as sketchy as my own. My parents, God rest their souls, might've been able to shed some light on this weird state of affairs, but I had a feeling they would've been as stymied as I.

I spun around in the chair, ignoring the protest of old wood and metal, and hitched it forward to the work counter along the back wall. My eyes darted over a partially folded blueprint of a yacht. I caught Les Bigelow's name on the design, as well as the client's ID of Samuel St. Laurent, III. I completed the fold and set it aside, then shuffled through a slush pile of inventory, invoices, and, as far as I could tell, some sort of work-for-hire contract paperwork.

I wasn't interested in the boatyard; Dalton had enough rabid curiosity in that sphere for all of us. I swatted away the pesky thought of my over-eager nephew-in-law and laid my palms on the cleared counter. *No laptop.*

In the back of my mind, I'd come in here to check out the computer and look into Vance's E-go—the combined tidbits of notes, e-mails, blogs, sites, and research that could paint a personality. Someone had beat me to it . . . or wanted to keep me from it. *Scotty.* Who else would have access to this place? The memory of him punching in the security code for the house bothered me. And why had he suddenly felt the need to formally ask permission to enter and get his tools?

I didn't have any answers as I pushed back from the work bench and scooted across the floor in the wheeled office chair. Feet curled on the legs, I coasted to the window. I stopped in front of the telescope, tilting the eyepiece down to accommodate my laziness.

When I looked through at this level, it afforded a blue circle of summer sky—nothing interesting there; not like the trio I'd spied on the cliff earlier. What were the chances the telescope would be perfectly positioned and focused on the spot where Vance had fallen to his death? I let go of the telescope and leaned back. Had someone watched Vance make his daily trek to Blind Man's Bluff the day he died? How would anyone know if he'd fallen off the cliff . . . or was pushed, perhaps?

My thoughts wound in ever tightening circles to the core of

my mental discontent. Vance Jones's death was suspicious. I couldn't settle on the exact reason, but my restless mind always came back to Scotty. I couldn't conceive of him committing murder, and I didn't want to believe he was capable of accidentally killing someone, but he knew more about what had happened on Blind Man's Bluff than mere hearsay. He was hiding something, or covering for someone. The knowledge sat on my heart like a pincushion, needling it so I couldn't let the matter rest. God had brought me here for His own reasons, and I prayed for the wisdom to understand His purpose for the good of us all.

My eyes roamed the walls, searching for answers in the collection of awards and trophies that surrounded the desk like the fortress defenses of a king. From his high-school diploma to numerous yacht-racing trophies, he obviously wasn't one to skip any accolade, no matter how long ago it was given. There were several photos over the years of iron man, biathlon, and triathlon competitions.

I'd never thought of Vance as an avid athlete, but it fit with his reputation as a competitive bully. I stopped in front of a montage of photos taken recently. Vance stood at the forefront, holding a small trophy for his age category. In the blurred background other competitors were embracing. Where was the buddy with his arm around Vance's shoulders, sharing in the victory? I quickly skimmed over the lifetime collection of achievements—nowhere was there an award, trophy, or photo where Vance shared the spotlight with anyone. Surely the person, his wife or son, had been there behind the camera. I raised my eyes to heaven trying to sort out the dangling tangled thought.

I caught the hands on the clock and went clattering out of the study and down the stairs. At the kitchen, I passed on the bottled water and pulled the iced tea with sugar and lemon out of the refrigerator. It was important to keep up my calorie intake after all that stair climbing and mental gymnastics. I took a sinful sip and closed my eyes. A second later, I heard the front door open and called out, "I'm making flat bread for supper. I thought we'd have chef salad and eat out on the deck."

"I didn't expect an invitation." The deep, slow tones preceded Scotty through the swinging kitchen doors.

"Oh!" I looked down at the mound of risen dough to collect my thoughts. "I thought you were Tasha and Dalton, home early."

"No such luck."

"There's no such thing as luck," I said. "Good, bad, or otherwise. I hope you'll stay for supper, Mr. Scott. I presume I have you to thank for the full larder and well-stocked refrigerator." I set down the glass of tea and rooted for a skillet.

He nodded. "Mr. Blevins and I didn't want you to go hungry, Miss McPhail."

I ignored his reciprocal flip formality. "It's wonderful, but why didn't you tell us before I sent Dalton down to the market?"

"He needed to do something constructive besides dreaming up ways to spend your inheritance."

"Ah." I put an iron skillet on the stove and punched down the bread.

"Nice right hook," my companion said. "I'll be glad to stay and make the salads."

"I can't promise anything."

"Can we compromise?" Scotty grinned.

"I think so," I said. "I'll stick to geography, history, and mathematics."

"Sounds fair." He leaned into the refrigerator and pulled out salad fixings.

I finished shaping a circle and placed the dough in the hot pan. "You seem to know your way around the place; how long have you worked here?"

Scotty's blue eyes narrowed and his face contorted as if I'd stepped on his toe.

"Geography, history, and mathematics."

"Ah, I should've known better."

His pained facial expression disappeared. "I do know my way around, and I'm familiar with hazard buoys and their orange diamonds. If I'm negotiating this hazard correctly, I'd say your rising interest in this situation isn't healthy, and it could make for a stormy friendship." He folded his arms across his chest and inclined his head to me. "I'll stick to navigation, tides, and the weather. It should make for an interesting meal."

Chapter Six

I lay in bed, listening to the wind gusts smacking into the house. It brought back that night in May when I mistakenly thought my weird phone call was a miscommunication brought on by the storm. Now I knew it was a shadow hanging over me, the harbinger of a different kind of storm. I didn't understand it yet, but I needed to, and this was the time and place to discover the truth.

I felt a lifetime away from my home, as if I'd been dropped down on an alien planet with only a future and no past. But this planet felt so much like coming home, I wondered if I'd feel like an alien when I returned to my old digs.

The fact that this place didn't shudder and creak like my ancient dwelling was a testament to its construction, but it had its own share of noises, and they weren't good vibrations. I'd chosen the smallest of the bedrooms and the one furthest from all Vance's techno gadgets humming with the white noise of electronics guzzling electricity.

Alone in this palace, after Scotty's pleasantly abrasive company, I couldn't settle anywhere. I'd switched on the big flat-screen TV, listened to the Bose, even walked three miles on the treadmill, not burning nearly as many calories as I felt I had. I was jumpy as a cat in dog obedience school.

I'd lain awake for the past two hours, listening for Tasha and Dalton's return. Now, with Tasha's soft laughter at the door as she slipped inside the bedroom, maybe I could relax. "Did you have a good time tonight?" I asked.

"Oh yeah," my niece whispered, the bed dipping as she sat beside me. "We cruised around the whole island. This is going to sound goofy, but it's almost like a magical place. I can't really explain it. It's more like a feeling, a heart tug. Everywhere I looked it's so incredibly beautiful, even the ordinary little houses. And their flower gardens—little splashes of color in old boats and boots and even toilets." She gave a little laugh, warm and comforting in the dark. "I wish you'd come with us. I saw lots of flamingoes, you'd've loved it."

"I'm glad you had a good time."

"We ate lobster at the Pier restaurant and watched all the little lights come on around the harbor." Tasha's voice grew softer still. "Then we took a romantic starlight walk on the beach at Mulroon's Point and the moon rose almost red out of the ocean."

"I'm thinking it's a good thing I didn't tag along. Might've killed the mood."

"Auntie!" Tasha gave me a quick peck on the cheek. "Tomorrow we'll do something special together," she promised, ending the sentence in a yawn.

"We'll see."

"We'll see," Tasha parroted. "Good night, sleep tight, don't let the bedbugs bite." I joined in, reciting the old bedtime rhyme from childhood. She rose from the side of the bed and slipped away into the darkness to the matching twin bed on the other wall. "I'm glad we came here, Auntie," she said. "It's what you'd call a cozy place. See you in the morning."

"Night, night." It was a cozy place—not Vance's glorified digs, but this island. I'd only seen a small piece of it, but I knew exactly what my niece meant. It was a comfortable haven, and somehow we'd come home—home to a sanctuary I hadn't known existed and wouldn't have believed I needed.

I squinched my pillow in half, tipping my head back on it to release the tension in my neck. The memory of Dot Jones's shingled cottage by the sea shimmered behind my closed eyelids. I'd only had a couple of glimpses of the place, but my soul yearned for it. It was shameful. I'd tried not to look when Scotty had driven me here after lunch, but I couldn't resist a quick peek. Just as well God gave me this ugly monstrosity instead. He'd made it so easy to do the right thing and give it all back to Dot.

Tasha's gentle snoring rose from the other bed, reminding me of all those camping trips we'd taken together when she was a kid. That girl could sleep and snore anywhere! She wasn't her auntie's little tomboy anymore. I had to respect that and let her go. I tried to conjure up an image of her future with Dalton, but the mental exercise was anything but restful.

Turning on my side, twisting up in the bedclothes like a mummy, I sat up and flapped the covers. It was a cool, raw night for summer. Needles of rain drove into the glass above my head. I settled back in bed, punched the pillow, and left a fist print. It was made out of some kind of NASA space age gunk that kept sucking the shape out of my head like a foam plaster mold. I was pretty sure my hair would pay the price by morning. I could try to fall asleep lying on my stomach, but horrified visions of smothering in my pillow stopped me. I'd recently tried to outlaw sleeping on my stomach, because it only led to rigor mortis of the major body parts overnight.

When you can't sleep, don't count sheep, talk to the Shepherd. I forced my eyes closed and tried to pray. I certainly had a long enough list with my doubts about Tasha's upcoming marriage; my concern for her errant brother, Nate; my worries over Scotty's possible involvement in Vance's death; and my own instant attraction to this island.

I awoke with a start. The room was utterly black. I blinked

repeatedly, wondering if I'd gone blind. I sat up slowly and caught the gleam of starlight out the window. The summer storm must've passed quickly. A snort, and what I used to call her motorboat start, signaled a rest-filled night for the still snoring Tasha.

I lay still and strained to hear any foreign sounds in the sleeping house. Whatever had awakened me must've been internal. I'd most likely only been asleep for an hour. I'd gotten used to this sleepless phase of my life, but some nights were more frustrating than others. I hardly wanted to greet the morning with bed head and raccoon eyes but, alas, such is the curse of this more-than-middle-aged woman.

I turned toward the nightstand to check the time. The display was dark. I smiled. It was a relief to have a nighttime mission I was used to, instead of playing human tornado with the sheets. I flung off the covers and slipped out of bed. The wind must've knocked out the power. A sound hadn't disturbed me; absence of sound had. I patted the end of the bedstead and found my father's big old flannel shirt that doubled as a robe and, on bare feet, felt my way to the door.

As soon as I stepped into the hall, the blue glow from a nightlight illuminated the corridor. The clicks and hums of Vance's contraptions, clocks, and appliances began again, filling the house with their low-level buzz. Too much noise, not enough noise, too much noise; I was on an insomniac's merry-go-round of my own making. Disgusted, I shuffled down the stairs. Night lights lit the landings and ground floor like a 747 landing strip. I shivered. *It's as drafty as O'Hare airport.*

I hesitated for a moment, closing my eyes, willing my brain to float, but it just wasn't going to happen. I trudged back upstairs, yanked on jeans and a sweatshirt, draped the oversized flannel shirt on my shoulders, clacked around on the dresser for my reading glasses, and tiptoed out the door to the music of Tasha's symphony of sleep.

I hoped her ankle would be much better in the morning, but at least it wasn't keeping her up tonight. I turned left at the bottom of the stairs and followed the footlights to the library at the back of the house. Night-light number thirteen—I couldn't resist counting—bathed the entrance in a ghostly blue.

I hated to turn on the big overhead light, probably a throwback to my mother's fetish of not using up unnecessary electricity in the middle of the night. I found a green banker's-type reading lamp next to an easy chair and switched it on. The small rectangle of light held just enough illumination to allow me to read the titles of a handful of books on the nearest shelf with a manageable amount of squinting. I picked out a volume by Robert P. Tristam Coffin, surprised but pleased to discover Vance and I shared a delight for vintage New England poetry.

Settling into the chair, I was glad I'd grabbed Dad's old shirt and I wrapped it closer around me, hunching my shoulders against the chill. Pulling my knees up into the overstuffed seat in my cocoon of light, I settled in and opened the book. The tender spine crackled and I stopped. Gingerly, I leafed through the pages, reassessing my estimation of Vance's taste in reading. The book was old, but not dog-eared and beloved like my copy. The realization brought forth a forlorn view of my benefactor. To surround oneself with lovely things, but to never experience the contentment that came from appreciating God as the Giver of these gifts, was tragic.

Maybe he'd loved his life. I had no firsthand knowledge that he hadn't, yet his house wasn't a happy place. My sigh filled the library. I shook off the melancholy thought and immersed myself in the book. Looking in the index, I turned to "This Is My Country," one of my favorite poems. The page opened automatically, a folded sheet of paper marking the spot.

I adjusted my reading glasses on my nose and unfolded the

paper. Handwritten scrawl in black pen revealed a personal letter. My eyes jumped to the bottom and fastened on the bold signature of Douglas Beckett, highly legible, especially for a doctor.

The book sagged into my lap. I carefully shut it and placed it on the side table, then leaned closer to the light.

The words jumped out at me. *Inoperable Mesothelioma, only months to live, get your affairs in order, spend the precious little time left to you healing your family so you can die in peace.* Short and brutally frank, it fit with what I'd experienced in my brief acquaintance with Dr. Beckett. The letter had no date. How long had Vance known he was dying, and who else had known?

I refolded the letter and stared at the paper in my hands. Had Vance sat here contemplating his past or his future? Was this the reason I'd been mentioned in the will? None of the twirling thoughts in my head stuck together to make a bit of sense. They were all leading up to the biggie. I didn't want to think it, but, like the Titanic and the iceberg, I couldn't stop in time. Had Vance thrown himself over Blind Man's Bluff because he couldn't bear the devastating news?

I carefully replaced the letter in the book and gently closed the leaves of poetry. I had no clear idea what to do with my discovery, but, for now, I'd leave it in Vance's hiding place.

I shelved the book in the stacks, tapping it in just so, then inching it out a wee bit, fiddling and fussing until it made a continuous seam with its literary neighbors. Finally satisfied at its undisturbed unremarkability, I switched off the reading light and slipped out of the room. A cup of raspberry tea with honey might warm me up—the thought was cheery enough to propel me down the runway lights to the kitchen.

I turned on the tea kettle and stared out the window at the Big Dipper hanging low in the sky. What if the person who took the computer helped themselves to the book of poetry? Surely the odds must be one in a million that someone would come along and select that particular book to read; but hadn't I just done so? Should I take that chance? It wasn't my letter to keep, and yet I felt an urgency to look after it and bring it to light at the proper time. When that time might be, I had no idea, but I had faith God would reveal it in His own good time. I dialed the kettle down on low and headed back to the library.

Skirting the foot of the stairs, a beam of light skipped through the arched window, kissing my toes before it disappeared. Rushing to the pane, I spotted the light bobbing across the lawn. Its forward progress slowed, then stopped at the corner of the house. I stood for several moments, forehead pressed against the cool glass, waiting for what, I didn't know. The light dipped and dimmed, then shown like a tiny beacon once more.

Before I could talk myself out of it, I marched to the frontispiece, punched in the alarm code, and sidled out the huge front door. My eyes already accustomed to the dark, I pressed close to the damp bricks. The pungent scent of bark mulch rose, as did my heart rate, with every spongy, sneaky step. I made it to the corner of the house, held my breath, and slowly stuck my nose out. The light flicked up and hit me in the eyes.

"What are you doing out here in the middle of the night?" The slow voice was laced with exasperation.

My heart flip-flopped. I stepped into the spotlight, blinking. "I believe I should be asking you the same question."

"You first."

I stepped closer, the cool, wet grass quickening my tread. "I came out to see who was lurking about on the lawn," I said. "Of course, I can't see a thing with that thousand-watt bulb in my eyes."

"Oh, excuse me." Scotty removed the headlamp. It shone on our toes, mine bare, his boot-clad, for a moment before he switched it off. I didn't have to see his face to picture the expression. He wasn't holding back on the sarcasm at this hour.

"Why do you have a shovel?" I asked.

"I was making sure the cellar drain was unclogged, what with the downpour."

"The storm's past. Why didn't you wait until daylight?"

"Didn't want the basement to flood and interfere with you doing laundry."

"Ah."

"You don't believe me."

"I do," I replied. "I'm just astounded by your dedication to your job. What about the other properties you look after?"

"They're fine." The bark of a laugh was very like his grandfather's. "I wanted to make sure everything was secure around here with the power outage. The security system might've blinked and need to be reset; happens occasionally. You should all be safe inside; no need to be out here prancing around in your bare feet in the dark, looking for prowlers. That's how people get hurt."

The prancing part got under my skin in a hurry, like a splinter from an old stick in the mud. "Surely I'm safe out here in the dooryard," I said. "I've gone out after dark many times to see what was going on around my own home on the mainland, and it's as isolated as this place. It's part and parcel of being a responsible homeowner."

"Ah." The reply opened the floodgates. "That's why you have a caretaker. You call him if you have concerns and he comes over and does whatever troubleshooting is necessary, because he knows the territory and is less likely to do something foolish." His headlamp switched on; he planted the spade in the lawn, then stepped closer.

I felt the now familiar hand on my back, but I was still stinging from the foolish remark and wasn't about to be escorted inside like a ninny.

A scream, savage enough to freeze the blood, rent the still, moist night. I reached out and clutched Scotty's arm, solid and strong. So much for fearless independence! He pulled me close, my back leaning into his chest. His body tense, I could feel his head swivel, alertness radiating from every pore. The light bounced over the bricks, then pierced the darkness of the back lawn.

We stood frozen together for a second. A low growl rumbled from the back-deck area, followed by a caterwauling aria that could've made it on the Broadway stage production of—

"Cats!" Scotty spat out the word. "I *hate* cats!"

I let out a huge sigh, unaware I'd been holding my breath. His arm fell away and he put a little distance between us, but the warmth of his hand returned to my back. I was getting used to the feeling and liking it entirely too much for my own good.

A moment ago I'd been itching to argue, and now the yowling of a stray cat had taken the starch out of my stiff-necked pride. *Be humble or you'll stumble*—but there's stumbling and then there's spunk. I like to think I know how to walk that line and, when I cross over, God's always there to show me the error of my arrogance.

"I like cats," I said, the statement punctuated by a string of inhuman screams.

"I'll take care of this." Scotty grabbed the shovel and I grabbed his arm as we took off toward the back of the house. The beam of light flashed over a tussle of movement, then caught and held malevolent, glowing, green eyes. The eyes narrowed as the huge black-and-white cat thumbed his nose, or the cat equivalent—twitched his tail—at us, then charged the large terracotta pot sitting next to the wall, hair bristling, growling and spitting.

The answering war cry was more cry than war, as the pot

rocked and the fur flew.

"It's that stupid cat of Dot's! Thinks he still lives here and rules the roost. Watch out!" Scotty stepped up on the deck with me still hitching alongside. Before he could wade into the fight, I rushed forward, clapping my hands.

The black-and-white hissed and bounded away over the rail and into the darkness. A second later a scrap of gray and white charged from behind the clay fortress, leaped onto the railing, and yowled a long, yodeling rebel cry.

"Scat!" Scotty said. The scrawny cat sat down and began licking his paw.

"Git!" my companion persisted.

I put out my hand to stop Scotty's advance on the pitiful pet. The cat gave us a wary look but held his seat. "Wait, I think he's hurt."

"Oh, don't tell me you're falling for that . . . that bag of bones."

"That other cat outweighed him by ten pounds." I edged closer to our midnight visitor. "Look at all that fur on the deck. He could be injured."

"Ha! He's got you going. He knows exactly what he's doing, smug as a weasel in a henhouse! Looks more like a weasel than a weasel. He's the homeliest excuse for a cat I've ever seen." Scotty stood still, his arms now folded across his chest, waiting for me.

"Does he belong to someone?"

Scotty shrugged. "Not to me."

"I figured that out, oh cat-hating one." I tried to keep my voice sweet for the cat's benefit. "I meant, do you recognize him?"

"It might be a her." I gave him a sideways glower as I sidled nearer my quarry. "I don't make a habit of hanging out with other people's pets, but, no, I haven't seen him before. I recognized Fluffy, but this guy looks like a stray."

"That big bully's named Fluffy?"

"He's all fur; a pampered paper tiger."

I reached out to the stray. His wet nose pressed my knuckle and his skinny body erupted into a throaty purr.

"Great, he sounds like a chainsaw," Scotty said. I stroked its head with a gentle finger and the chainsaw purr upped to full throttle. "The least he could've done is run off and defend his new territory. Show a little manly pride, Boy."

I laughed and, gathering up the half-grown kitten in my arms, walked to the door. "Do you mind?" I gestured with my chin toward the alarm.

"Probably crawling with fleas, ticks, and West Nile." Scotty opened the door and flipped the light switch.

"I'll risk it," I said. "Would you like to come in for a cup of tea? The kettle's on."

"I'd better get back to work." I was startled by the gruffness of his reply. He stepped through the opening but paused before he shut the French door. "There's some cat food in the pantry, part of Fluffy's old stash. 'Night."

" 'Night." I watched the light sway across the lawn like a giant firefly. He didn't return to the corner where I'd first tracked him, but trudged on down the driveway and the light dipped out of sight.

"Something's going on with him," I said. The cat purred and nuzzled my hand. "And I'm going to find out what it is, mark my words."

Chapter Seven

I woke with a snort, the morning sun striking me warmly across the cheek. After my midnight tea I'd stretched out for a few moments in the recliner and obviously gotten over my bout of insomnia. I rubbed my bleary eyes, suddenly sitting up straight. I pulled the handle on the recliner and shot out of the chair. The room spun. I clutched the arm of the chair, hoping to get my sea legs under me before I hit the deck.

All the while I searched the living room. No sign of the cat. I couldn't call him The Cat, poor thing. Last night he, and it was a he—thank you very much Mr. Scott—had snuggled close to my side, West Nile, fleas, and all, and fallen asleep purring his brains out. Obviously his purring was the purr-fect God-sent antidote to my own restlessness as we'd shared our forty winks together.

Now I stepped into the next room on unsteady legs, Scotty's cat phobias blossoming into my own concerns. I scanned the expensive oriental rugs on the parquet floor. No sign of damage or of the little mischief maker. The cat was used to being outside; what did he know about polite behavior and proper use of indoor bathroom facilities? He had to be around here somewhere, but "here" was akin to the Mall of America. "Here, Kitty, Kitty."

"Are you looking for this guy?"

I jumped out of my skin, then back in again, and turned to face my sneaky niece. Tasha laughed. "Sorry. I barged through the kitchen door with my crutches. I thought for sure you heard me come out."

I sighed and grinned. "That's one way to get the old heart started in the morning. How's the ankle?"

"Much better."

I reached over and stroked the cat lounging over her shoulders like a limp spaghetti noodle.

"Where'd he come from?" Tasha laid her cheek on the live fur collar.

"You didn't hear that awful cat fight last night?"

"No; Vance's house is basically soundproof, I think."

Being a good aunt, I didn't add, *how could you possibly hear over the snoring?* "Probably." I held out my hands and the cat oozed into my arms. His purring intensified. "I'm thinking of naming him—"

"Mason," my niece cut in. "He reminds me of Mason, that little cat you used to have when we were kids. Remember how he'd lie around my shoulders and purr? I called him my mink stole. I loved that cat."

I gave the animal in my arms a thorough perusal. With short gray hair, mismatched white socks that needed a trip through the washer, a white wishbone on his bony chest, and a lopsided white mustache and goatee, he wasn't classically handsome. I supposed he was like Mason inasmuch as both animals were cats.

"I thought I'd call him Purry." It wasn't exactly Shakespeare but a rose by any other name fit well. I'd thought about it as he lay beside me last night, purring even in his sleep.

"Perfect," Tasha said. "Purry Mason. You're a love bug, aren't you?" She leaned in and rubbed noses with the newly christened pet.

"Who's a love bug?" Dalton's rough, sleepy voice joined in the conversation.

"The cat." Tasha scooped Purry Mason from my arms, put him on her shoulder, and followed her fiancé into the kitchen. I tagged along behind. "Auntie found a stray last night. Isn't he precious?"

Dalton's "yeah" was more of a grunt as his head disappeared into the refrigerator.

"I'm taking Mr. Mason outside to do his business," I said.

Tasha leaned back on the counter and passed off the cat. "Dalton and I will make something for breakfast," she announced.

Dalton was swilling orange juice out of the carton. "I'll see if I can find some decent coffee and get a brew going," he managed between gulps.

I nodded, picked up the cat bowl I'd fixed last night, and darted into the pantry. I scored another tin of Fluffy's gourmet stash and hustled out to the deck. "Don't get used to this menu." I set the cat on the deck. He waited, sitting as regally as an Egyptian prince while I opened the can. As soon as the beef and gravy plopped into the bowl, he gave up putting on airs and bunted my hands out of the way. "You're not a rich kitty." The cat purred and plowed his whiskers into breakfast.

"You'll never convince him." Scotty swung up on the deck, the shovel still in his hand. "From the looks of things, he's moved in for life."

"I hope so." I watched the little cat sit on his haunches and lick his wishbone chest.

"You aren't going to go crazy on me and fill this house with a hundred stray cats, are you?"

"I'm getting to the age where I could fit the profile."

"Are you kidding? I don't give any credence to profiling. Never happen." He leaned down and the cat rubbed against his work-roughened hand. "Hey, Cat."

"His name's Purry Mason."

Scotty groaned and rolled his eyes. "In the light of day he's even a sorrier excuse for a cat than he was last night."

"He's young and has lots of potential."

"Spoken like a true kindergarten teacher."

Tired of our small talk, the cat slipped past Scotty's boot and pranced across the lawn.

"I hope he won't wander away."

"No way. Even with the insulting name, he'll be back for dinner; I'd stake my life on it."

I gestured toward the shovel. "Have you been digging drains all night?"

For an instant, a shadow clouded his clear, blue gaze, but it was gone before I could interpret the emotion or its cause. "I thought I'd take your advice and tackle it in the light of day. I'll square it away first thing so you can do the laundry." He swung off the deck with a mock salute.

"Wait!" He stopped mid-stride. "Would you come to tea this afternoon with Dr. Beckett and Dot Jones? It's at two."

"I'm not much for tea."

"I'll make sure there's something you can eat," I said. "It'd be a huge favor to me, and you can help speed up the process of giving Dot back her house."

"I'll think about it if I get done with the drains in time. Don't want to hold up the washing crew." He touched the bill of his cap and disappeared around the corner of the house.

What was the man's fixation with washing clothes? I glanced down at my sleep rumpled jeans and flannel shirt and my cheeks burned. I didn't bother to reach up and pat my hair—that ship had sailed. No wonder the guy was hinting about laundry!

I rested my elbows on the deck rail and breathed in the morning air tinged with the tangy aroma of salt eau de mud flats. If I was going to stay here for a few more days, I'd need more clothes.

The scent of coffee joined the freshening breeze. Dalton stepped through the French doors and strolled to my side. "I would've brought you out a cup, but Tash said you're not a coffee drinker. She said you bring your own tea supply with you when you travel."

He ducked his head, an affectation I'd noticed on the ferry crossing. I was reminded of a turtle tucking his neck in, then pointing his nose in the air as if caught between a decision to pull his head inside or thrust it out.

"Have tea will travel," I quipped. "You can't always find good raspberry tea; I imagine it's sort of like your taste for good coffee."

He nodded, the turtle move gone. Perhaps he was just a little shy, like Cody Simmonds who pulled his shirt up over his head whenever an adult spoke with him. I hoped Dalton would lose the recently acquired tic and get comfortable in his skin, but I suspected it would disappear when I gave up the mansion and put an end to his greedy fantasies.

Dalton turned his back to the view and leaned against the railing. "I can't wait for Mother to see this."

"Yes, I'm looking forward to meeting her."

"I'm taking off for the mainland today. I've got a couple things I need to do; then I'll be back with her in a few days."

"Sounds good." If I only walked from the bedroom to the kitchen, maybe the house would stay clean for my guests. I didn't want to think about vacuuming all those rooms. "I was going to ask Tasha to pick up some clothes for me at home, if you don't mind."

"Actually." Dalton drew the word out and took a leisurely swallow of coffee. "I thought Tash should stay here. Stay off the ankle and rest."

"Good idea."

"But I'd be happy to pick up whatever stuff you need."

Dalton drained the last of his coffee and stretched.

I like to think I'm a modern woman, but not modern enough to picture Dalton going through my dresser drawer. "I'll give Pearl a call," I said, thinking aloud. I glanced over and caught his questioning stare. "She's a friend, actually one of the teachers I work with. I'm sure she'll pack a suitcase for me and leave it at Ted's Barbershop. That way you won't have to drive out of the way to the house. You can just make a two-second pickup in Bookerton."

"Sounds good. You can count on me."

I hoped it was true as we sat at the kitchen breakfast bar eating French toast fifteen minutes later. I watched the affectionate byplay between the two, almost lulled into complacency until Dalton thrust back his stool. "I better get moving if I'm going to make the ferry."

"I'll be ready in five minutes." Tasha forked one more bite into her mouth, leaving a half slice uneaten. She collected his empty plate and limped over to the sink with the dirty dishes.

"You don't need to do that." I rose with my own plate in hand. "You did the cooking; I'll take care of the cleanup."

"We can help." Tasha looked at Dalton. "It'll only take a few minutes. The ferry doesn't leave for another forty-five minutes; there's plenty of time."

Dalton stepped close and draped his arms around Tasha's shoulders. "I thought you could stay with Auntie Gwen," he murmured in her ear. "I'm just going to be hassling a few things out with Gates. You'd be bored to tears. This'll give you two a chance to hang out, and it'll be good for you to stay off your ankle. Get it healed up in time for the party."

Tasha's lips curved in a smile. She whispered in his ear, they kissed, and Dalton grinned.

"Do you want me to drive you down to the ferry landing?" I asked.

"Oh, that's right." He ran a hand through his moussed hair, which, I was astonished to see, didn't hurt the style I called "dorsal-fin fish look" a bit. "You won't have a vehicle if I take the SUV, but I need wheels to—"

"It's fine," I interrupted. "We've got everything we need right here."

"Yeah, and that Scotty guy that works here can always run errands for you. I'll be back before you know it, Babe." He was out the door to freedom without a backward glance.

I got on the phone to Pearl, just in case Dalton made his swing through Bookerton later today. Pearl caught me up on the news: of Lois Boyle's picture in the paper soaking up the ambience of the Glastonburg Summer Institute; Lois rubbing elbows with Rudy Thoms; Lois's tell-all article about her wonderful cultural experiences and her love for her music students. Pearl was going to snip it out and pack it in my suitcase. What are friends for? She also gave me the inside info on a recent conversation with Jason Boudreau and his idea to surprise me with a visit. I hoped it was just idle talk.

"Tell Jason I'll be back on the mainland for good shortly," I said in closing. "It would be a wasted trip for him to come out here." Pearl just laughed.

To get my mind off the persnickety Lois and the persistent Jason, I threw myself into preparations for our afternoon tea. Tasha and I cooked and laughed in the kitchen, just like old times, except for the absence of decent mixing bowls and the glut of state-of-the-art appliances.

"Too bad we didn't have some of your homemade red-pepper jelly." Tasha gave the table a final examination.

"We're looking good." I leaned over and straightened a spoon on a napkin. "Pepperoni, cheese and crackers, finger sandwiches, Tasha's famous apple cookies."

"And Auntie's Hawaiian bread and gingerbread. Something

for everyone." Tasha popped a slice of pepperoni in her mouth.

"If they're as pleased with it as we are with ourselves, it ought to be a hit all around." I felt hopeful and happy. I prayed God would help me befriend Dot so we could get this squared away, as Scotty would say.

We ran upstairs to shower and change. I put on a floral challis skirt and pink silk blouse, moderately pleased with the results. I'd packed the outfit for church, in case we stayed over Sunday. What I'd wear Sunday, I didn't know, but I wanted to put my best foot forward today.

"Wow," Tasha said. "You're dressed to impress." She looked cool and casual in pinstripe capris and a pale-aqua, sleeveless blouse.

I wrinkled my nose as I gave the reflection in the full-length mirror one more look. "When you get older, you have to dress better," I said. "I need the camouflage for certain expanding body zones. I say, enjoy the freedom while you can."

"You wouldn't be dressing to impress a certain someone?"

"Certainly not." I slipped my feet into sandals. "Was that the doorbell?" I hustled out of the room and down the stairs, her low chuckle dogging my steps.

I was standing in the frontispiece, smoothing my skirt, when the chimes sounded for real and I opened the door to a disgruntled group. "Welcome." My voice sounded high and chirpy. "Thank you for coming."

Dr. Beckett nodded. Tasha came stumping to my side and grabbed my hand for moral support.

"I'm Gwen McPhail, and this is my niece, Natasha."

Dot Jones whisked past us with a scowl and turned toward the dining room. Trailing in her wake was the couple I'd seen the other day via the telescope. The stocky man dressed in short-sleeved sport shirt and chinos stopped in front of us and stuck out a hand. "Ron Jones." He took my hand in a rugged grip.

"And this is my w-wonderful fiancée, Laurel."

"Nice to meet you. Come in, come in." I shook hands and smiled, my lips aching to ask a few pointed questions. I thought of Scotty and his hat. *Where is he?* I'd need to be on my best behavior if I was going to win over Dot Jones.

Ron and Laurel seemed less reserved, already striking up a conversation with Tasha. "When are you getting married?" Tasha asked as the younger trio trooped into the dining room.

"It's a well guarded secret," Ron said, and the couple laughed.

"Dot is here under protest." Dr. Beckett claimed my arm and my attention.

"I noticed."

I started after the others, but he held back. "She's here as a favor to me. Tread lightly. There's a lot of water under the bridge; hopefully none of it from your bathtub, so don't get into any circling-the-drain subjects."

"I'll try not to," I agreed. "But I've never heard that statement before in my life. I don't know what it means, exactly, so I'm not sure about the drain issues."

He turned me to face him. "If I clear my throat, like this . . ." The gravel moved slowly and erupted into a fit of coughing. "Forget it. If you get into something you shouldn't, I'll start talking about church tomorrow, and you go with the change of subject."

"This is getting weirder than a skydiving moose in pajamas."

"Yes, it is." He grinned. "Just try to follow my lead." He tugged me along to the dining room.

The others were already seated, Tasha busy pouring iced tea and lemonade. "Would anyone prefer hot tea or coffee?" I asked.

"Herbal tea for me, if it's not too much trouble." The doctor sat down heavily next to Dot.

"Dot?" I asked. I'd debated on calling her Mrs. Jones, but that seemed stuffy and condescending.

"I'm fine with lemonade." The voice from the phone call? Lower, not at a manic pitch. I wasn't absolutely sure.

"Help yourselves to the food," I said to cover my spacey moment. I passed the sandwich platter to Ron. His mother glowered as he put two chicken salad rolls on his plate. I picked up the tea cozy and poured the doctor some raspberry tea. "Scotty planned to join us if he had the time. I understand he's your cousin." I smiled at Dot and purposely glanced at the doctor to make sure it was a medically approved topic, but the good doctor was tucking into the tea and Hawaiian bread.

"Ayuh, he's my first cousin once removed, but he's Vance's third cousin by marriage."

First cousin was all I could handle. I'd never been any good at that once-removed, second, third-buttonhole relation stuff. I tried to connect the dots of the family tree as Dot piled cheese and crackers on her plate.

"The Scotts have always been loyal to a fault."

Hackles up, the voice was a match. "It's a blessing to have a close family," I agreed. How had Dot known to call me? I didn't know that much about legalese, but didn't think the freedom of information act applied to people named in wills before they themselves were notified.

"Amen to that." Tasha gave me a wink.

"Would you excuse me, please?" Laurel scraped back her chair and rose in a hurry. "May I use your powder room?"

"Certainly." I stood.

"I can find my way." She brushed past me. The drape of dark hair partially hid her pale face, but her blue eyes shone.

I refreshed the drinks, then returned to my seat and my mental calculations. Mr. Blevins was as tight as Fort Knox. Who else could've gleaned the insider info about the will and my identity and spilled it to Dot?

"Wonderful tea." The doctor actually smiled. I couldn't say

the same for some of the other occupants. Ron was focused on the empty doorway, Dot on her inattentive son, I on eating questions I wanted to blurt out.

I diverted from my mental quest and took a polite detour, searching for a good segue topic to lead gently into the possible legalities of giving back their real estate. "I was looking through your library last night and found a wonderful volume of poetry by Robert P. Tristam Coffin. Your late husband must've loved good literature and poetry."

My comment was met with Ron's unbridled laughter. "Hah! Wouldn't Dad love you! He tried to whitewash his image so people would see him as some self-made Renaissance man." His white teeth gnashed together in a pitbull smile and his eyes turned cold as the gray Atlantic. "But I guess he *did* love you, didn't he?" His thick arm swept the room. "He gave you his castle."

I had my other voice match as his decibels rose. It wasn't a stretch to pin Ron as the background caller, his voice protective and angry, once again defending his mom. *So much for polite conversation.*

"No, it's not like that," Tasha argued.

I held up my hand to stop her defense. The Scotts weren't the only ones who still possessed clan loyalty. "I don't know why Vance left me his home."

Dot bolted from her seat, upsetting the silverware and jangling the crystal. "Come off it! I don't have to sit here and listen to this garbage. Vance was leaving me for you; admit it! The least you could do is be honest about your cheating, conniving ways."

I rose to my feet as the doctor said, "I hope you're coming to church tomorrow, Gwen. John Hersey is our guest pastor this summer; has a good way about him, and knows his way in the Bible."

"That's nice." I kept my eyes locked on Dot's black stare, sending up a desperate prayer. "I'm sorry for your loss and your troubles, but I'm not one of them." Dot swung toward the doorway. "Wait, please!" I gently touched her forearm. She shook it off but stopped. "I haven't seen Vance for forty-some-odd years. I knew your husband when I was four years old. He must've been in his early twenties back then, and he worked with my father for about a year and a half. They bought old sailboats that had been neglected or damaged. Not the little working boats, but ships that were quality built by the old craftsmen—with all the mahogany and brass. They refurbished and rebuilt them; my older brothers helped, too. Then they resold them for a profit. I really don't remember Vance very well, only that I called him 'Uncle Jonesy.' "

"Jonesy," Dot murmured, and the eyes that met mine went glassy, looking right through me.

"I'm sorry to say both my parents passed away a few years ago. I'm sure they could've told you more. I talked to my brothers when I got the news about Vance's will, but they weren't any help. They were eight, ten, and twelve years old back then, but they don't remember much more than I do about that time."

"Then why did my father leave you this property?" Ron paced in front of the floor-to-ceiling windows. "I mean, it absolutely makes no sense." He threw his arms wide then clapped both hands on top of his thinning brown hair.

"No it doesn't," I agreed. "Honestly, it was a shock to me. I can't for the life of me imagine why and how he pulled my name out of a hat all these years later."

"It's just like him." Dot's voice was thick and cold as January's molasses. "He'd give this to a stranger on the street just to spite us."

"Like I said, I didn't really know Vance, but he's gone now and it's up to us to straighten out this mess. I wanted to meet with you first before I called the lawyer to see what's involved in giving you back your inheritance."

"Never happen," Ron muttered.

"Yes, it can," I persisted. "We can make it happen."

"You say that now, but you've already got a taste for it." Dot picked up a silver spoon and flung it back on the table.

"Now, Dot." Dr. Beckett still sat in his seat, but his sagging face drooped like melted wax as he frowned at her. "Give Gwen a chance."

"I'll talk to the lawyer on Monday and see what he says," I promised.

Dot shook her head, looking up her nose at me.

"Daddy, wait!"

I jerked my head away from her disdain to the commotion in the next room. Laurel appeared in the doorway, clinging to the arm of a tall skeleton of a man.

"You!" The skin-and-bones intruder pointed a shaky finger at Ron, his jutting, lantern jaw trembling. Except for the waders and stained t-shirt, he could've doubled for the specter of Christmas future.

"Daddy, come on. Let's go home," Laurel begged.

"Frank." Ron and the doctor spoke in unison.

"Don't you talk to me!" Laurel's father turned on Dr. Beckett. "I trusted you, you two-faced quack! Look at all of you gluttons and winebibbers trying to corrupt my daughter! You haven't heard the last of this!"

"Get out of my home, Frank Shaunessy!" Dot rounded on him, vibrating with fury. "You think you and your daughter are such paragons of virtue—oh, how the mighty have fallen! Get out and don't come back!"

Laurel sobbed and backed away from all of us. "Mum!" Ron barged past Tasha's chair and wrapped his arm around Laurel's shoulder.

"You'd best leave, Frank." Scotty marched in and laid his hand on Frank's shoulder. "We don't want any trouble, and neither do you."

Frank's body went rigid as a telephone pole, his face sharp as a razor. "Stay away from my daughter or there'll be trouble; I guarantee it!" His eyes raked Ron, then froze out the rest of us. He backed out of the room; his gruff "Let's go," and something more I couldn't catch, was punctuated by the slamming door. The roar of an engine and squealing tires jogged us out of our shocked silence.

"That was weird," Tasha said.

"That's Frank; just like all the Shaunessys—used to be well off; now they're poor as church mice and pigheaded about it." Dot was almost friendly. "Think they're too good for the Joneses, well so be it! I don't care if—"

"Mum, stop it." Ron charged out of the room like a knight on a white steed and pulled Scotty with him. A moment later the whole door-slamming, engine-gunning scenario repeated. I looked up in surprise as Scotty reentered the dining room.

"Bad blood." Dr. Beckett rose and tossed his crumpled napkin on his plate. "There's no need of it. You could put an end to it, Dot."

"It's not up to me."

"This is like Romeo and Juliet." I couldn't stop the comment, and received a warning glare from Scotty and just a plain old glare from Dot.

"Ron and Laurel must be at least thirty-five," my niece joined in. Tasha takes after me; what can I say? "This is the twenty-first century. Surely they're old enough to do whatever they want."

"It's just like you people from away, coming here and sticking your noses into our business, trying to run everything. You don't know nothing." Dot swept past me, stopped to bend Scotty's ear, and went out. I hoped the door was rugged enough to withstand all the abuse of late.

"Hey, Doug, you want to take her home, or you want me to do it?" Scotty asked.

The doctor lurched forward and clutched at the table. Both Scotty and I reached for him, but he swatted at us as if we were pesky mosquitoes. "I'm fine; let me get my wind. I'll take her home, maybe throw some water on the fire; probably won't do any good." He swayed past me and put his heavy hand on my arm. "You tried," he said.

I watched the older man hobble from the room, feeling like someone had poked a pin in my balloon. "Don't look at me like that," Scotty muttered. "I'm just the hired help, not the high-society coordinator." He spun on his heel and left.

"That went well," I said, and it echoed in the cavernous room.

"At least the food was good." Tasha popped the last piece of pepperoni into her mouth.

Chapter Eight

Tasha and I walked down the driveway, not too far because of her ankle, but far enough to pass by Dot's place. My long-distance snooping was wasted. The small cape was as lovely as ever, but lonely, with no signs of life, except for one Purry Mason. The little cat followed us home, twining in and out of my legs. The fog came in and we hunkered down inside the mansion, indulged in Heavenly Hash ice cream and an old Deborah Kerr movie, then went to bed early.

I should've slept lousy after all the dining-room drama, but a baby wouldn't have dozed any better. We paid for our couch-potato evening, slept late, which I never do, and found it hard to get up and get going. I fussed with the Sunday-outfit-cum-tea-hostess threads, now returned to Sunday best. I shouldn't care that I'd already been seen in them, but I did.

I went to the upstairs bedroom window and gazed at the empty drive below. "Anybody out there?" Tasha asked.

"Not yet, but I'm sure Scotty'll be by to pick us up soon." I glanced at my wristwatch. "There's still plenty of time."

On my way downstairs, my straining ears picked up the sound of an engine. I smiled, relieved. I'd hoped he'd return last night, but I guess the drains and laundry concerns were fixed and, after all, it was Saturday and he did deserve a day off.

I floated to the door, my smile growing, and opened it to reveal Dr. Beckett's somber face. He was decked out in a pin-striped, beige summer suit. It hung off him like elephant pants on a scarecrow. His smile, tired but sweet, lifted the drooped, gray mustache. My feet immediately touched firmly on the ground. "How nice of you to come," I said. "We left it up in the air yesterday."

"There's a whole lot 'up in the air,' " the doctor agreed. "But 'This is the day that the Lord has made, I will rejoice and be glad in it.' There's nothing that prayer and a little help from a righteous man can't overcome."

"Amen," I said. "I thought maybe Scotty would be with you."

"Oh, no, not today. He picks up his grandfather. They've already been and gone."

"Hi, Dr. Beckett." Tasha breezed up behind me, already a master at her crutches.

"How's the ankle today?"

"Much better, thank you. It's stiff, but not nearly as sore. I was going to ask Sledge if I should put a little weight on it."

"Easy does it," the doctor said. "I'd give it another few days or so. Shall we, ladies?"

I don't know what I expected to find in the Coveside Community Church, but we walked in to the beautiful organ strains of "Two Prayers" (one of my favorite pieces) and a nearly packed house. The sanctuary was larger than my home church in Bookerton, but small when compared to a city church or the mega-churches across the country. It had the old-style wall lamps, dark, polished wooden pews with cranberry cushions, and the July sun pouring through the thick, stained-glass windows painted the air with rainbow hues.

"It's lovely," I murmured. Dr. Beckett gave a pleased grunt and ushered me down the center aisle to the second pew from the front. I covertly searched the congregation for Scotty and Old Stin, but saw no familiar faces until my gaze lit on Frank Shaunessy, his lean face furrowed with foxhole hostility. I quickly turned my attention to settling into the pew with Tasha and the doctor, and kept my focus on the service.

It was a nice worship, but I confess part of me was wandering in the far country, waiting for Scotty to put in an appearance, and worried he and Dot had stayed away because of yesterday's brouhaha. At the final *Amen,* the doctor threaded us through the clusters of parishioners, nodding to some, but never stopping to introduce us to anyone.

"I enjoyed your sermon." I shook Pastor Hersey's firm hand on the way out.

"I'm pleased you came, Ms. McPhail." John Hersey didn't relinquish my hand. My niece's bony elbow poked into my side.

"It's a beautiful church." The folks behind me were piling up. *Just say it!* "I thought I heard you ask Mr. Scott to read today. Is he ill?"

John Hersey laughed, patted my hand with his free one, and finally withdrew his clasp. My hand felt extraordinarily heavy as it dropped to my side. "I don't believe Scotty ever gets sick; no germ would have a fighting chance. He comes to the early service at the Island Church and teaches adult Bible study after."

"Oh." It came out jerky due to another prod from Tasha. "Well, thank you for inviting us to the service, Pastor."

"I hope you come again." John Hersey's comment followed us out into the sharp, clear light glinting off the water.

Tasha was buzzing in my ear like an island horsefly. "What gives, letting him call you *Ms.*? Don't tell me you're getting all modern-woman mellow on me."

I gave her my best stern eye that made even Johnny the kindergarten bully study his sneakers and promise to mend his mini-Mafioso ways. She had the audacity to laugh. "He likes you and you don't want him to. Ahhhh!" She held up her index finger when I opened my mouth. "You don't want to like him because—"

"Come along, Tasha, we don't want to keep Dr. Beckett waiting." I marched toward the car like the grand marshal of the Pasadena Rose Parade, ignoring the chuckle behind me.

I slipped into the passenger seat and turned toward the man hunched over the steering wheel. "Are you all right?" His face was the color of old ivory and his sunken eyes were dull. Throughout the service I'd noticed him slipping in cough drops nonstop.

"I should've taken you to the Island Church. I'm as bad as the rest of them, trying to pull people over to my side." His harsh breathing drowned out the voices and laughter filtering in from the congregation spilling out of the sanctuary.

"What do you mean?"

"My wife and I always went to the Coveside Church because it's close to our home, but it's the . . . uh—how should I put this?" A cough covered his hesitation.

"Upscale crowd?" Came the voice from the backseat.

"Thank you, Tasha." The doctor gave a tired smile.

"A bit like the country mouse and the city mouse," I said, understanding dawning.

"And we're country mice," Tasha added.

"No, no, it's not that; it's just that I wanted allies." The eyes I thought were dull a moment ago blazed into mine. "It's always been the Islanders and the Covers since before *my* time, anyway. They mingle, but they're always aware of their distinct identities. It creates a rift in our island. Sometimes it's a small one, like the city church and the country church; at other times, as you saw yesterday, it's a 'great gulf fixed.' I want to heal that fracture; I *must* heal that fracture before I—" He turned the key and lowered the windows. "Stuffy in here."

A pickup truck pulled alongside our spot on the curb and the driver cut the sputtering engine. " 'Mornin'." Old Stin's serrated smile hawked out the truck's passenger window. "Maybe I should say 'Afternoon.' Some folks can't get up before noon to go to church."

"It's good to see you again," I said. I focused on the older man, his white hair smartly combed back like an old Hollywood heartthrob, but I was acutely aware of the driver getting out of the other side and slamming the door.

"Don't know why Doug brought you to the Covers' church, but no matter. You're a visitor, so no harm done."

"If I'm visiting again some Sunday I'd like to come to the early service at the Island Church, but I didn't have a ride today." I glanced up in mock surprise as Scotty squeezed between the vehicles. Under my pointed stare he casually rested his rugged hand on the truck side mirror and calmly returned my gaze. He was still in a short-sleeved white shirt, but no tie. It was open at his tanned throat. I looked down at my clasped hands to get my mind off the scenery.

"Hope you do. Young Stin always takes me out to Sunday dinner," Old Stin said. "Sometimes it's no better than a hotdog, but it fills the belly." I looked over and grinned as the two Stinsons exchanged mirrored frowns.

"You eat red hotdogs for breakfast if you have them in your fridge," Young Stin said.

"Then why would I want to have a hotdog when I go out to eat?" the older gent replied.

"Fine," came the gruff drawl. "We'll go to the Pier today and have their scallop dinner."

"No use goin' to the Pier this time of year, what with all them summer people hoggin' the tables. Once they set down, they think they own the spot for the entire day. We wouldn't get served 'til Christmas." Old Stin grinned at me. " 'Course, if we're goin' someplace fancy, we oughtn't talk about it in front of Gwen, unless we're gonna invite 'em all along with us."

"Can't; they've got other plans today," Scotty said. "Just got a call at the house from the over-eager beaver." At my arched brow, Scotty lowered both of his. "The fiancé. He's headed back on the noon ferry with a bunch of folks from the mainland. He thought you'd like to know so Tasha could meet him at the landing." I looked at my watch.

"Oh." Tasha leaned in from the backseat. "Thank you, Scotty."

"My pleasure. Hey, Doc, you wanna come out to eat with Old Stin and me?"

"I could use some decent conversation and company," Old Stin remarked.

Scotty snorted.

"Tasha and I can walk to the landing," I said. "And I'm sure Dalton will have plenty of room to drive us back to Vance's place."

"Nonsense; can't leave you stranded. You have to take it easy on that ankle for awhile longer, young lady. I'll drive you to the landing and wait around just to make sure," Dr. Beckett announced. "Scotty, you can follow."

Douglas Beckett started the car and pulled away. I glanced in the side mirror to see Scotty sprinting around the truck before we dipped down the hill. A half-mile later, our chauffeur tooled down the middle of the road past the line of cars waiting for the ferry, and parked in the rock-rimmed lot overlooking the entrance to the harbor. He pointed through the windshield at the low-riding white ferry rounding the headland.

"I'm going to walk down to the landing." Tasha opened the back door. "Thanks for everything, Dr. Beckett."

"You're welcome."

We watched her swing away on her crutches. She smiled and waved. "Ah, youth," my companion mused. "She's a nice looking girl, and Sledge tells me she's a nurse. We could use a good nurse at the clinic. Flo had to get done. Family problems on the mainland."

"Oh." Since I didn't know Flo, I couldn't overtly sympathize.

"Well, Tasha's getting married in August, and neither she nor I have a place on the island."

The doctor leaned over and grabbed my hand. "I want to talk to you about that."

"Tasha getting married?"

"Don't be coy. I haven't the time nor the energy for it." His Adam's apple bobbed, gyrating the loose skin on his neck as he lapsed into a cough.

"I'm sorry."

"Apology accepted." Scotty's truck bumped into the lot and parked perpendicular to us, blocking our exit and that of the car parked beside us. "We'll talk later, away from the crowd." The doctor's mustache twitched and he released my hand. "Let's go." The ferry's short toot echoed his words.

Dr. Beckett climbed out of the car and laboriously made his way to Old Stin's side of the truck. He leaned on the bed and chatted with the old man like they hadn't seen each other in ages. The doctor surprised me. I sensed in him a kindred spirit and wondered if I dared ask him about the letter I'd found in Vance's book. Maybe when we were "away from the crowd" I'd find the perfect opening to talk about Vance's health and state of mind.

"You going to sit there all day, or go meet the in-laws?" Scotty's deep voice was laced with sarcasm. "I've heard you can't avoid them forever."

"You're right about that." He opened the door and held out his hand to help me from the vehicle. We stood together, leaning on the hood of the doctor's car, watching the ferry maneuver up to the landing. A teenaged girl I recognized from my recent crossing dodged through the parked cars on the open deck. She stopped at the side and threw the hawser to a man on the wharf, who whipped the rope around a cleat. They jogged toward the stern in tandem and repeated the process while oblivious passengers—some clambering into their vehicles, others, with bikes or backpacks, surging toward the bow—kept their eager eyes on the shore.

It was easy to spot Dalton and his mother, a petite ash blond (wouldn't you know it), chatting it up with an elegant couple. As I watched, Mrs. Madison hugged her yacht-club sister. They parted ways, the unidentified couple disappearing into a champagne luxury car, the Madisons swinging into Dalton's silver SUV. The sun glinted off the moving door just as I saw him.

I blinked away the glare, doing a double take when my eyes clapped on the familiar shiny dome circled with a horseshoe of barber-perfect, liver-colored hair. "Jason?" I whispered, just as he ducked into the backseat of the SUV.

"Something wrong?" Scotty asked.

"Oh, no," I chirped. "There's always room for one more."

"I'd say in Vance's place, you could conservatively say a hundred more."

"Bite your tongue, sir!"

He laughed and straightened from his lounging position on the car hood, only to stiffen as his eyes darted from my face to the far edge of the road. I turned and spied Ron Jones chasing Frank Shaunessy. Frank was obviously a man with a mission, striding swiftly toward the landing, but the stocky younger man caught up, grabbed his shoulder, and spun him around. The two men halted, facing off in the center of the shore road like a couple of sparring Bantam roosters.

"Davy Jones locker!" My companion spat out the words and took off.

"Let 'em duke it out!" Old Stin yelled after his grandson.

"I've taken it from my father all my life. I'm not going to take any—" Ron's voice cracked. It was high-wire taut, belligerent; only a twitch away from berserk. "Laurel's mine. We're not going to take any more of your abuse."

"Abuse?" Frank screeched. "You call a father's love for his only daughter abuse? What ails you?"

The throng of foot and bike passengers swarmed off the ferry and up the road like Boston Marathon diehards. Scotty stepped between Frank and Ron just as the fresh tide of humanity swelled around them. I could see Frank's lanky frame and Scotty's red head; the shorter Ron was swallowed up in the crowd.

"Auntie!" I slowly turned to acknowledge my niece's beckoning wave.

"I'll see you later," I called to Old Stin and Dr. Beckett, taking one more opportunity to glance at the confrontation behind us. The tidal wave of passengers had swept past, leaving the three men rooted to the spot.

"Auntie!" The cry came again, garbling Scotty's terse speech.

The first car off, a small, red convertible, clanked over the ferry ramp and putted up the hill. I jogged down to my niece and pasted a polite smile on my face. The champagne Mercedes crawled up the grade with hands waving from the sun roof. Tasha returned the wave. "The Ellingsfords," she said. "Friends of Dalton's."

I lifted my hand in a friendly gesture, but the car was already past. Dalton's SUV rolled up and stopped in front of us. I opened the door for the temporarily handicapped Tasha, then dashed over to the other side and jumped in. The SUV moved smoothly up the road as soon as I shut the door.

"Surprise!" Jason's eyes glowed. "I told Pearl I'd deliver your suitcase personally."

"How nice," I replied. The car stopped and I took my eyes off Jason and pinned them on the road ahead.

"Then I ran into Dalton and Hillary at the ferry terminal in Hanover's Point and they offered me a ride. No sense wasting money bringing two cars over on an island this size. Besides, there was a long line today; I'm not sure I would've made it over on this trip. I might've had to wait for the two o'clock crossing."

"Uh-huh." I smiled blankly in his direction.

"What's the holdup?" Jason stopped his monologue and joined the rest of us in gawking out the windshield.

"Some locals in the road blocking traffic," Dalton said. "Hey! I don't recognize the tall guy, but the other one's Ron Jones, and isn't that your maintenance man?"

I folded my hands in my lap to curb the urge to give my future snob-in-law a gentle slap to the back of the head. "Yes, I believe that's Mr. Scott."

Tasha reached across Jason and tweaked my shirt. Her face contorted in conflict and I was instantly sorry for my reverse snobbery.

"You haven't met Dalton's mom," she said, her voice forced and too cheerful. "This is Hillary. Hillary, this is my Aunt Gwen."

I took her cool hand in mine, surprised at the firm, honest shake.

"Natasha's second mother; I've heard so much about you," Hillary said. "It was nice of you to invite us over for the holiday."

"My pleasure." The car inched forward in line and crawled by Scotty and Ron, who were now standing in the parking lot talking. Frank had disappeared.

"My husband, Phillip, sends his apologies. He so wanted to come and meet you, but wasn't able to get away."

"We'll do it again another time," I said.

Dalton took over the conversation as official tour guide, ignoring Coveside's enchanting stone library, sturdy brown church, and old sea captains' homes with their gingerbread trim and widows' walks, in favor of a slow drive-by commentary of the Candle Island Yacht Company.

"Remember I said Royce Ellingsford's yacht came from here, Mother?"

"Oh, yes." Hillary had about as much enthusiasm for the information as I did, it seemed.

"I'm trying to convince Dad and Davis to go with a Candle Island design. Too bad Dad couldn't squeeze in an afternoon visit."

"He's got a lot on his plate right now."

"Sure, sure," Dalton agreed. "Before we go to the house, I thought I'd take you on a little drive out to Mulroon's Point."

"We need to eat first," Hillary said. "Is there a good restaurant you can recommend, Gwen?"

Barb's Lunch Box take-out trailer popped into my head immediately, followed by Old Stin's recent hotdog dissertation. The islanders may think they have an exclusive on the PFA (People From Away) issue, but it's pretty much universal, at least to those with rural roots. The slightly superior "from away" attitude that unconsciously condescends to the simple community life with its little mom-and-pop society, begs anyone with a whisker of pride to let them have a taste of the "We ain't got no cultcha" Cinderwench Act.

"I've heard the Pier is nice." I grinned. "What do you think, Tasha?"

"I liked it," she said. "What do you think, Dalton?"

"It was your typical on-the-wharf summer fare, but about the only game in town." Dalton detoured through the yacht yard and nosed the SUV back toward town.

A few minutes later, we pulled in across the road next to the cramped parking lot. "We can always eat at the house if there's a long wait here," I said, thinking again of Old Stin. Dalton was already out of his seat and hustling around the front to help his mother and Tasha exit.

"Oh, pshaw." Hillary waved a graceful, manicured hand. The

woman could be a hand model. I eyed her over the roof of the car when I got out. The hands fit with the whole package. She wore the kind of makeup that looked like she didn't have any makeup on; she was model thin, expertly toned and tanned, and she was beautifully casual in white, linen capris, pastel-pink espadrilles, a sleeveless, coral blouse, with matching lipstick and nails. I've always admired a woman who could wear white with confidence.

Jason took my arm, startling me, almost, but not quite, saving me from lapsing into feeling dowdy and old.

"I'm sure they can find us a table," Hillary said.

Jason escorted me across the shore road and onto the wharf. While Dalton talked to the hostess, a tall, cool blond dressed in black skirt, white blouse, and red sash, my eyes wandered over the outdoor tables. Old Stin caught my meandering gaze and flagged us over just as Dalton beckoned us to follow him.

I gave a noncommittal wave and allowed Jason to guide me to an inside table. In spite of the vintage ship's cabin décor and the wall of glass reflecting the harbor bustle of summertime Sunday sailors, it felt cramped and stuffy.

I sat through the small talk, the excellent tender, fresh scallop dinner, and the hot air, as Jason and Dalton regaled us with their considerable knowledge of all things nautical.

"I didn't realize you were such an avid boat enthusiast," I said in the odd moment when both men were chewing. Jason swallowed the mouthful of lobster and grinned like a first-grade boy showing off his bloody gap smile and waving his front baby tooth in his fingers.

"I took an Outward Bound sailing course, must be ten years ago now," my friend said. "That's an experience you never forget."

"I'm sure," Hillary murmured.

"Always wanted to get my own sailboat; nothing big, but

something with enough keel to make it out to the coastal islands, like this one," Jason continued. I nodded politely. "Of course, I'd need someone to crew with me." He glanced at me just as Tasha caught my eye and mouthed *burdocks.* If there hadn't been so many guest ankles under the table, she would've been in danger of re-injuring her sprain.

"Then you should go with me to Candle Island Yacht," Dalton said. "It's a sweet business they've got for themselves out here. Traditional craftsmen mixed with high-tech materials and design; it's a winning combination."

"Sounds interesting," Jason said.

I sat back and smiled at the sight of Dr. Beckett and Old Stin bearing down on our table like two old hawks dive-bombing big fish in a barrel-sized small pond. My smile widened to a grin at the convoluted thought, so much like the doctor's bathtub drain analogy at the recent tea party. Was I picking up on island ways so quickly, or simply so desperate to get out of this restaurant and conversation I was borderline delirious?

I bolted to my feet and made introductions all around. It had the desired effect of bringing our party out of its social stupor to at least a standing position. Scotty had managed to escape unseen, obviously a wise man when it came to stifling social situations. With Jason here his absence was for the best; still . . .

"You part of the weddin' party? A friend of the bride?" Old Stin leaned in, taking Jason's measure.

"A friend of the aunt of the bride." Jason put a proprietary hand on my shoulder.

"We work together," I clarified. "I teach kindergarten and Jason teaches sixth grade."

"They used to say, 'Them that can't do, teach,' " Old Stin said. "You put much stock in that, Gwen?"

I laughed, then tried to hold it in at Jason's wounded look. "Not in Jason's case," I said. "But in my own case, I'd say it's a definite probability." Old Stin's merry eyes met mine.

"Not at all," Jason said gallantly.

"It's nice to meet you folks." Dalton was back from paying the check. "I'm sure we'll be running into one another again on an island this size."

"A definite probability," Dr. Beckett agreed, earning Old Stin's snort of approval and an appreciative laugh from Hillary.

I glanced up at Dalton's mother, surprised at her genuine enjoyment of our visitors. "I look forward to it," she said.

"Gwen, I'll be in touch," Dr. Beckett promised in his low, gravel-laden voice, then louder, "Come on, Stinson. I've got a chessboard waiting at home with both our names on it." The island men nodded to us. "It's been a pleasure," the doctor added.

"Definitely interestin'." Old Stin wasn't one to leave without getting in the final word.

Chapter Nine

I usually look forward to Sunday summer afternoons—taking a long walk in the woods, picking flowers, and meditating on the Scripture lesson of the morning. Of course there were always those times when my nieces and nephews were visiting, or when all the siblings got together for a traditional Sunday dinner. Those were precious family times. This Sunday afternoon promised neither a relaxing spiritual meander nor family fun.

Once again sandwiched in the backseat between Jason and Tasha, I was hard-pressed to enjoy the interminable scenic drive. Dalton's sudden tour-guide obsession was akin to taking hostages. The curvy island roads, coupled with Jason's and Dalton's one-upmanship, filled the SUV with verbiage beyond belief and had me feeling queasy. It could've been the scallops, but one glance at Tasha wrinkling her nose like she used to do when sentenced to time-out made me know I wasn't alone. Besides, she'd had the haddock.

When Dalton swung the SUV onto a side road marked Bayside, I could only mentally beg for mercy that the small island would run out of road soon. We passed a garage, boat repair, and storage business, and a few houses before the road forked. Our chauffeur took the shore line drive and the road immediately narrowed further into a dirt track. I sincerely hoped we either didn't meet another car or Dalton was much better at three miles of backing up on this earthworm trail than I.

"I think we should let Royce and Joan settle in before we

descend on them like a hoard of locusts," Tasha said.

"We aren't going to stop by, Tash," Dalton stated. "I just wanted to take Mother on a trip down memory lane."

"Where are we?" I asked in a whisper.

"Mulroon's Point," Tasha responded.

Before she could elaborate, a map magically slipped onto my lap. "We're right about here." Jason's long finger traced the black line on a local chamber of commerce map. I nodded. "The wick of the candle, if you will," he added, chuckling.

"Thanks, Jason." I stared at the map, my eyes drifting down to a cupping of the candle wax marked Faraday's Mistake. In all our sightseeing, as far as I could tell, we hadn't made it to that particular spot on the island.

"This is the Ellingsford place." Dalton threw the information into the backseat, interrupting my mental travels, and just as well. I passed the map back to Jason with a nod as the car slowed to a crawl. "Joan and Royce are good friends of ours. We'll have to get together while they're here, won't we, Mother?"

"Actually, I think I told you Joan mentioned they want to throw you and Tasha a small dinner party." Hillary's voice held an odd note; not exasperation, exactly, and definitely not anticipation. I glanced at her profile—cool, sophisticated; her blond bob falling forward just enough to hide the set of her lips.

"That's right. Great!" Dalton had enough relish in that one word to top all the hotdogs sold at Barb's this summer. "Things are really coming together for us." He stopped in front of a wrought-iron gate set in Murdoch Island granite pillars. "Oceanview."

I looked past Tasha into the face of Young Stinson Scott. He set down a screwdriver and trudged over, a frown marring his tanned face. "Hi, folks." The slow drawl crawled in through Dalton's open window. "You looking for me?" Scotty pulled off his cap and rubbed his forehead with callused fingertips.

Dual nudges had me feeling like an accordion bellows, but they squeezed my focus onto my seat companions.

"You're smiling." Tasha gloated in my right ear.

"Who's the fisherman?" Jason's low voice cooled my smile as I turned toward him.

"We're just doing a little sightseeing." Dalton's reply delayed mine. "What's the problem here?"

Scotty lowered his brow but spoke without show of irritation. "Gate mechanism's acting up. Sometimes high-tech and island weather don't get along. I'll leave you to your reconnaissance. Good afternoon, all." He flicked his eyes past the driver's head and caught mine for the barest gleam before stepping away from the vehicle. He pulled on his cap, picked up the screwdriver, and went back to work, coolly oblivious to his audience.

"Who's he?" Jason repeated.

I was mentally urging Dalton to move along before I answered, but we weren't on the same wavelength. "He's the local maintenance guy for the island," Dalton said. A bullhorn wouldn't have been more effective at carrying to the mainland. I flinched but Scotty didn't. He continued to fiddle with whatever wires or buttons he was fixing. "Scotty looks after Gwen's place, too."

I couldn't keep still any longer. "Why don't we go back to the house?" I said through clenched teeth. "I don't know about the rest of you, but I need to stretch my legs."

"Sure, sure." Dalton proceeded to turn around in the end of the Ellingsfords' driveway, a space in which even a woolly bear caterpillar would have to execute a three-point turn. Dalton made it in six. I didn't look back, but I could almost feel Scotty's blue eyes glaring at our taillights.

I prayed for patience as we wound back toward Coveside, then turned and headed up to Blind Man's Bluff. I was doing well, convinced I could play hostess by appropriating God's grace, until we went by Dot's place. Mother and son were out in the yard. Dot glared in annoyance as we roared past the lovely cottage. By the time we reached Vance's mansion, I was mentally fidgeting again. It wasn't that I didn't want to schmooze with Tasha's new family; it was just that I needed to set some things straight about Vance's death.

I took Jason's hand and got out of the SUV, giving myself a silent dressing down. God brings individuals into one's life according to His plan and purpose, and I was a fool to squander His opportunity. I turned to my guests with a welcoming smile. Dalton gave his usual commentary, led the way into the house, and did a quick museum tour of the downstairs. When he finished, Jason looked at me and shook his head.

"It's a bit much," I agreed and he grinned.

"It's a lovely home," Hillary said. Her eyes held mine for only a fraction of a second before they roamed the throne room, lingering here, measuring there.

"Let me show you to the upstairs," I said. "Tasha and I have picked out a couple of rooms we thought were nice."

I started up the staircase; Hillary waited, speaking to Tasha. "Why don't you stay downstairs and rest your foot?"

"No, I'm fine," Tasha replied. "I'll help you get settled."

"Dalton, will you bring in my bags, please?" Hillary asked as she followed me, Tasha a few steps behind.

"Sure, sure."

I stopped at the second-floor landing in time to watch the men disappear out the frontispiece. I led the way down the hall and gestured past the room Tasha and I shared. "As you can see, there're plenty of views to choose from, so you're welcome to pick any room. I'd be happy to make up the bed for you."

"Anything's fine," Hillary said. "They're all lovely."

"Yes." I showed her into the room across the corridor from her son. I'd put Jason on the other side of Dalton.

Scotty's earlier cheeky comment that Vance's place had room for a hundred more came to mind as I watched Hillary stroll to the large double window. She observed the bird's-eye view of the landscape in silence. "Is it very windy here?" she finally asked.

"There seems to be a good breeze," I said, "but I'm only a visitor so I can't speak with any degree of authority." She nodded absently.

Tasha shifted her weight on her crutches and joined her future mother-in-law at the window. "There's a huge deck on the other side of the house. We can go down and hang out after you've unpacked," she said.

"That would be nice, Tasha." Hillary turned to me. "I look forward to it."

The afternoon went by pleasantly enough with polite conversation, never stilted. Hillary was agreeable company, if somewhat preoccupied with details. She and I took a short hike to the bluff, Jason tagging along while Tasha and Dalton lounged on the deck in the balmy July sun.

Jason stood on the cliff, hands on hips, drinking in the panorama of summer sailboats, diamond-backed wavelets, rocky green islands, and the smudge of the mainland on the horizon. I imagined Vance doing the same, surveying his private kingdom. How had he fallen from this perch? Given all I'd learned about his ego and personality, it made no sense.

"This is quite a view."

I gave myself a mental slap and turned my complete—well, almost complete—attention on my guests. "Like the cliffs of Acapulco," Jason continued. "But I wouldn't want to take a dive from here." He edged closer to the precipice.

I automatically placed a hand on his arm. "Be careful."

He turned his head and bathed me in the toasty glow of an amorous smile. He patted my hand, then let his rest on mine, towing us both closer to the edge and closer together. *Uh-oh!* I'd seen this coming for nearly two decades and, even though it had moved with the speed of an ice-age glacier, I wasn't ready.

I looked down at my sneakers. His soft, doting chuckle said my reaction was a mistake, but I barely registered his misconception. Beyond my toes, the cliff drop I'd thought was vertical jutted out in a shelf at least five feet wide before it sheered off to the sea. I stepped closer, forgetful of Jason attached to my arm.

"Now it's my turn," he whispered. "Be careful. I don't want to lose you."

"How far down do you think it is to that shelf?" I asked.

"About ten, maybe twelve, feet."

I glanced up in surprise. Hillary hovered nearby. She shrugged and grinned.

"I'd guesstimate closer to fifteen," Jason said.

"How wide do you guesstimate it is?" I asked.

Hillary's grin deepened, revealing a dimple in her right cheek. "At least five feet."

"Four at the narrow end, close to six right below us," Jason said. "What's so important about the cliff face? I wouldn't want to get stuck down there."

"I just never noticed it," I said, and stepped back.

"We ought to be heading back." Jason squeezed my hand. "I thought we might take in evening service together."

"Yes." I pulled away. His touch lingered before he let me go. I felt as if a ten-ton weight had lifted off my arm and settled on my heart. "Would you like to come with us?" I asked Dalton's mother. "It's a beautiful church."

"Thank you." Hillary's smile had jelled from genuine to polite. "I have a few phone calls to make, so I think I'll just stay here and soak up the peace and quiet. It's such a beautiful place."

"By all means," I said. "Make yourself at home."

Small talk took us through the tang of salt air and spruce, down the root-ribbed ledge path to Vance's house. Hillary's head was elsewhere, as was mine. Only Jason seemed to be fully committed to the conversation.

Inside, the clock was not my friend. I put in a call to the doctor, who gave me the time of evening service at the Island Church. He also informed me he wasn't feeling well. The news didn't surprise me. I hadn't thought him well from our first meeting. It did add a bit of shadow to the bright afternoon as I wondered and worried about the severity of his ailment.

Jason perceived none of my somber mood. I'd found Peter Pan's missing shadow, and it was Jason. Dalton and Tasha had taken off for the beach. Hillary sat on the deck, chatting on her cell, the richly appointed mansion a perfect foil for her.

It seemed rude to join her on the deck and intrude on her phone conversation. Wasn't I the one who'd done a Martha Stewart and told her to make herself at home? Did Martha Stewart invite complete strangers into her real house, or was that only on TV? I didn't know. I only knew I was a fish out of water—more like a fifty-cent guppy in a million-dollar aquarium.

And I was a prisoner, I realized as soon as I'd hung up the phone. With Dalton gone and Dr. Beckett ill, we were stuck here, swimming in circles in our brick-and-glass fishbowl. I thought about contacting Scotty for a ride, but dismissed the idea just before Jason asked, "What would you like to do now, Gwen?"

"Vance has an excellent library."

"We can read on winter nights. This is a moment to be shared and savored, like Tasha and Dalton. Is it very far to the beach?"

"Oh dear. I, uh, I think it's way on the other side of the island," I said. "Maybe another time. We have only an hour until we need to get ready for church. Perhaps we could check out the telescope in Vance's office."

"*Your* office now, Dear."

I mentally groaned. I didn't want to lead him on; yet the closer he got, the more I wanted to sprint in the opposite direction. We were friends, I reminded myself. Friends told each other the truth . . . later. *Chicken!*

"I think you'll enjoy it," I said in a rush, putting off the inevitable. "It's very high tech, too much so for me; some kind of computerized thing-a-ma-jig. Right up your alley."

"Let me at it." He grinned. "I can see I'm going to have to pull you into the twenty-first century."

"Kicking and screaming." I took off for the staircase. "I'm quite content in my twentieth-century world."

His "tsk-tsk!" spurred me up the stairs. "Comfort zones mire us all down. You'd probably be more content in the nineteenth century if you could manage it." He dogged my steps as we climbed. "But I have two words that I use in the classroom. Challenge yourself!"

"You first." I opened the door to the study and ushered him in before me.

"Just an old-fashioned girl." He chuckled and gave me a fond smile as he brushed by.

"The old part is correct," I muttered as he strode to the window. I felt old and sour in the face of his advances. *What is wrong with me?*

"Hey, anybody home?" The answer to my question came marching into the room like a gust of wind off the Atlantic, smelling of salt and fir and sunshine.

"Where is it?" Jason asked.

I stood transfixed for the blink of an eye between my past and my future. It wasn't one of those moments of total clarity yet; more of a twinge. Instead of the two men in the room with me, I had a mental flash of dear, sweet Mr. Blevins's earnest face telling me I'd already left my old life behind. He'd been confident with my "willow stubbornness," as he called it, that I'd find the right balance of old and new. I wished I shared his conviction.

"Mrs. Madison told me I'd find you inside," Scotty said.

"Yes." My mind was nowhere near my tongue and, even if it had been, it was like catching Zoey Gardner daydreaming out the window after snack. Those starstruck green eyes of hers always looked right through me when I called her back from the imaginary clouds of unicorns and princesses. In this moment I stood in Zoey's sparkly purple jellies, clueless, with no words. A buzzing fly filled the silence, knocking its brains out against the window. At least it had brains!

Jason was back at my side and thrust his hand out at our unexpected visitor. "Jason Boudreau, Gwen's, uh, friend." He gave Scotty's hand a hearty shake. I inwardly winced at the possessive pause, but Jason mushed onward. "I saw you earlier fixing the gate at Mulroon's Point."

"Scotty," came his clipped reply.

I glanced up in surprise at the ruddy features. What had happened to the slow, deep voice I enjoyed so much?

"Yes," Jason said. "Gwen's maintenance man."

I was torn between the desire to melt into the floorboards or bop Jason on the head. Scotty actually laughed, saving me from the temptation. He nodded. "I've been called worse." His eyes twinkled at me under raised brows. "I got a call from Doug. He said you might need a ride to the church service."

"That'd be nice." My voice was suddenly two octaves higher than usual.

Jason nodded. "We were just about to admire the scenery from Gwen's ivory tower." He dramatically spun toward the window, one arm sweeping out, encompassing the room and the view. "Where's this high-tech telescope I've heard so much about, Dear?"

I cringed and catapulted past him. The wall of glass stood stark, save for the frame of vintage sextant and antique globe, both displayed on ornate, brass stands.

"It was here earlier." I momentarily forgot my annoyance at Jason.

"It's not here now." Jason—ever the master of the obvious.

"Where could it have gone?" My eyes turned to Scotty. He met my inquisitive stare with a calm gaze, but his brow lowered slightly. "There was a laptop here that's disappeared, too. Do you know anything about it?" I asked, softly.

I instantly regretted ruminating aloud as Scotty's lids lowered. When they lifted, talk about icebergs! His eyes were Arctic Ocean–cold, his expression more guarded than a Brinks truck. "No, but I'll look into it."

I'm ashamed to say, evening service at the Island Church was more a flunked lesson in patience for me than the delightful worship it could have been.

CHAPTER TEN

After a wakeful, prayerful night, I rose early and baked doughnut muffins to go with the scrambled eggs and bacon I'd decided to fix. Not exactly Martha Stewart; more like plain old Granny Clampett fare with the slab equivalent of hog jowls. The muffins were swimming in butter, rolled in cinnamon and sugar, and, as I popped a steamy bite into my mouth, I jacked up my cholesterol and blood sugar a whopping hundred points. I closed my eyes and reveled in a moment of quiet indulgence as the piece of comfort food melted.

"Hey, my favorite!" My eyes flew open just in time to see Tasha following her aunt's wicked example. "Mmmmmm!" That non-word made the fog-shrouded morning bright. "Nobody cooks like you do, Auntie!"

"It's a good thing, or we'd all be in the ER under cardiac arrest."

"Morning, all. I love the way you always have a cheerful comment, Gwen, even on a gray day." Jason strolled into the kitchen looking brighter than a freshly minted penny. His brightness didn't affect his insights. "I'd heard the islands get a much higher percentage of foggy days than the coast this time of year, and the proof is in the pudding, as they say; or, in this case, in the pea soup."

"Good morning," I said. "I imagine it'll burn off in a few hours." I yanked open the refrigerator door and stood inside the cold locker as if it were a tank. I hurriedly amassed the scrambled-egg ingredients and, hands full, proceeded to the counter. God bless Tasha for pouring juice, making small talk, and accepting Jason's offer to set out the places on the bar. He really was a nice guy, but . . .

Last night I'd unpacked my suitcase, smiling at the catty note Pearl included. She'd tucked in the latest edition of the *Washington County Chronicle* so I could check out the continuing adventures of Lois Boyle. As I read Lois's glowing tales about Glastonburg and then perused the local news, I felt millions of miles away from good old Bookerton. The names of neighbors and exploits of former students were nice to see, but couldn't hold my interest. The old adage, "How're ya gonna keep her down on the farm now that she's seen Paree?" or, in this case—fog or no fog—Candle Island, rolled around in my mind, tiny pebbles recycled with each wave crashing in at the ferry landing. Just one of the many reasons I hadn't slept well. Two more, in the form of Hillary and Dalton, descended on the kitchen just as the eggs were ready, and took their places at the breakfast bar.

I asked Jason to say grace and caught the look that passed from mother to son as I bowed my head. Annoyance? Boredom? I tried to keep a positive outlook during the breakfast conversation.

"I thought we'd all go to the boatyard for a tour this morning," Dalton said. "I've arranged it with Les Bigelow, and he's even offered to take us out on Vance's private yacht for a short island-hopping cruise. The yacht's part of the shipyard's assets now, so they use it occasionally to schmooze clients. Sound good?"

I inwardly sighed but pasted on a smile as I caught the excited gleam in Jason's eyes and the anxious flicker in Tasha's.

"Sounds great," Jason said.

"Yes," I said. "I can't wait to see the island from the water."

"I'll have to take it in another time, Dalton," Hillary said. "I talked to Joan yesterday and offered to help her with the dinner party. She has a small staff of locals." She let the trailing insinuation drape over the table like smog; make that *snob.*

Tasha stepped in, in a hurry. "I'll be glad to help out, too. After all, she's going to all this trouble for Dalton and me; it's the least I can do."

"It's the least *we* can do," I amended, gathering up the dirty dishes.

"That's sweet of you, but I wouldn't dream of pulling you away from the island cruise," Hillary said, with the perfect pinch of regret. I wasn't fooled. Translation—we were no better than the "locals" when it came to recognizing sophistication and creating culinary chic. Okay, so we *are* the locals, and proud of it! I let my indignation smolder for just a second until I saw the pale under my niece's tan.

"We'd rather help you," Tasha persisted. *Family loyalty forever!*

I turned to the group pushing back from the breakfast bar. "By all means," I agreed. "We can catch a boat ride any time. I wouldn't miss this opportunity to spend time together, Hillary."

"I guess it's settled then." She caught my eye, gave me a rueful smile. "We'll get the men out of our hair and have an old-fashioned hen party."

I always figure if someone rubs me the wrong way there's a pretty good chance I affect them similarly. As for Hillary, I knew we'd get along well enough as polite acquaintances. We understood each other, and the knowledge deflated my puffed-up ego, leaving us, if not friends, at least sisters in respect. We'd always be continents apart when it came to lifestyle and, sadly, I suspected, we were worlds apart on the all-important issue of faith. Perhaps I'd nearly turned my reverse snobbery nose up at God's opportunity to share my faith with Tasha's new family.

I was jarred out of my thoughts by Jason at my elbow. He bent his lips to my ear, more for show than for privacy. Hillary was punching a number on her cell, and Dalton and Tash were holding their own discussion/face-off by the kitchen door.

"I'd be glad to help with prep for the party, too," he said in a low voice. "I only agreed to the boatyard tour because I thought you'd be coming along."

I yearned to take him by the hand, like Garrett Guyette when he arrived in my classroom halfway through the school year, and lead him out to the playground to play freeze tag with his new classmates. It proved a good way to thaw a child's reserve and, at least for Garrett, cement healthy new friendships.

Jason deserved better from me. "I know." I looked up into his pleading, brown eyes. "Things are a bit up in the air here, aren't they? If you don't mind, I think it would do Dalton a world of good to spend some time with you. He needs the influence and wisdom of a good Christian man."

The pestering suitor instantly transformed into a concerned brother in Christ, and I realized, once more, the privilege of his support and friendship. "You got it," he said.

I squeezed his forearm in response, just as Scotty came into the room clearing his throat as if the Queen Mary had run aground on his tonsils. I jerked up my head to meet his sharp, blue gaze. "Tasha let me in," he said.

"I'll see you later." This from Jason, who nodded to Scotty on his way out.

"I come bearing gifts, if you can call it that," Scotty continued. "I was out in the garage workroom getting the mower ready and who waltzes in but PM himself."

"PM?"

"Post Meridian."

"I know what *PM* stands for." I was at a loss to finish, but the discussion was putting a warm, teasing gleam in my sparring partner's eyes.

"The cat."

"Purry Mason."

"I refuse to degrade the old boy with that name," Scotty said.

"I've been looking for him. I called for him last night, but he never came." Reason number twenty-seven for my sleepless night—a roving, helpless pet.

"Well, he's back, but you'd better come take a look. Old Midnight's the epitome of 'Look what the cat dragged in.' "

I slipped past him and felt the steady gentle print of his hand on my back, guiding me to the outside door. Of course, our timing coincided perfectly with Jason and Dalton's departure.

"What's up?" Jason quizzed me during the bottleneck at the door.

"Just helping Gwen find her cat," Scotty supplied before I could get a word out. "It's under control."

Jason frowned into my strained smile. "Have a wonderful time, guys!" I threw out the platitude with a cheery wave, never breaking stride, nor did the man at my side. I was vaguely aware of the drone of the SUV engine departing as I stepped into the cavernous dance hall that doubled as a garage. "This is a garage? Who in their right mind would need a five-car garage?" At the sound of my voice, a plaintive meow echoed through the bays.

"That's Vance for you."

Purry picked his way around the tire of a dark-blue BMW. I scooched down, ignoring the twin gunshot cracks of my aging knees. Thankfully my companion did the same.

The cat rubbed against me, then feinted back. Where just yesterday he'd been lithe as a weasel, today his hip was puffed out, obviously sore. "Come here." I gingerly scooped up the pet.

"Probably an abscess from scrapping with Fluffy," Scotty said.

I stood and ran a gentle finger over the bulge. Scotty gave the gray head an affectionate scratch between the ears, kicking the cat's motor into high gear. "I'm afraid you're right," I said. "I'll have to see if I can get him to the vet."

"There's no permanent veterinarian on the island. A mobile vet comes by every three months."

"Oh, I hadn't thought about that." I sighed, hugging the warm creature closer. "Well, I'll just have to take him to the mainland and see if I can get an appointment with Dr. Averill in Bookerton."

"You *could* do that, but there's an easier solution."

"I'm all ears."

"Doc'll fix him up. I can take you over; I need to get some gas for the mower."

"Dr. Beckett?"

"The same. His granddad had a farm—Doug's early medical training. Gives new meaning to the term 'horse doctor,' eh?" He gave a snort, then pulled it back to a grin. "Just pulling your leg; he graduated top of his class from Johns Hopkins."

"Oh." I must confess I spent not a split second of regret on missing Hillary's hen party. "I wanted to look in on the doctor today anyway. Have you got a minute? I need to tell Tasha."

"My wish is your command."

At my frown, he laughed again. "Okay, no need to get huffy. I'll be sharpening the mower blade out back in the workroom. When you're ready, just let me know. Do you want me to keep an eye on Twilight."

"Ha. Ha. No, thanks; I'll take him with me."

Scotty nodded and walked away, but turned back in time to catch me looking. "Probably best to keep him away from food if he's going under the knife soon." It seemed to me both Purry Mason and Mr. Scott were rather pleased with themselves.

I clutched the little cat close and hurried over to the house.

Tasha was instantly sympathetic to the animal's plight and held him while I threw together a care package for Dr. Beckett.

"Joan's on her way," Hillary announced, parading into the room to marshal the troops. For someone who was on her way to work in the kitchen, she was dressed as usual in high-class casual chic. Perhaps she had a large apron in her canvas tote.

"I'm afraid I won't be able to come with you," I said. "The cat has an abscess and it needs to be taken care of for his own good, and for ours as well." I added the last part, lest she think I was a crazy old cat lady, although I knew I shouldn't care what she thought.

"Oh, that's a shame." Hillary stroked Purry's head as he lounged in Tasha's arms. "He certainly is a relaxed cat. I'm a dog person myself. We have two champion yellow Labs."

"Scout and Kip," Tasha supplied.

"I know whenever they have a problem, my husband makes sure they're seen right away," Hillary continued. "I sympathize and totally understand. I'm sure Joan would be glad to drive you to the vet's office."

"Thank you." I once again felt that gossamer strand of connection between us. "Mr. Scott's offered to drive us over."

"Oh, it's nice of Tasha to go with you."

"I meant the cat and me."

Hillary nodded and gave us a slow smile, completely unruffled. "That's fine," she said. "I'm not trying to get rid of you, honestly. I'm one who needs moral support when I go to the vet, so I just assume everyone is as spleeny as I."

Somehow I couldn't picture the cool blond standing before me as spleeny, but I'd never seen her sitting in the waiting room with a quaking, howling dog trying to crawl into her lap. It was a gracious out, either way, and Tasha took it. "I think I will go with Gwen, if it won't hurt your feelings."

"Not at all. You two do whatever needs doing; let Joan and I take care of the dinner party. There she is now."

"Thank you!" Tasha called after her future mother-in-law. "She's really nice, don't you think, Auntie?" Her voice carried the barest trace of the little girl I once knew asking me if I was sure there were no monsters under the bed.

"Yes, I think Hillary's a woman of her word." The sentiment surprised me, but as soon as I said it, I realized it rang true. Too bad I didn't feel the same about Dalton. "Let's go take care of Mr. Mason."

I shouldered my bag and took the cat from her arms so she could navigate on her crutches. Scotty was just pulling around with the truck and hopped out to help us into the cab. "Let's hope Afternoon is a good passenger." He handed me the cat and hustled around to the driver's seat.

Tasha gave me a puzzled look. "Don't ask." I shook my head, but I couldn't stop the smile from breaking out. Except for the quarter-inch dig marks in my legs, Purry stoically endured the ride to Coveside.

Dr. Beckett greeted us at the door, looking pale but pleased. "Come in, come in, ladies." He took in the animal patient with a knowing nod. "Easy enough to remedy, I should think."

"Do you want me to stay and help you out?" Scotty followed us into the cool, dark kitchen.

A huge horse-chestnut tree shaded the yard, and the room was fronted by a screened-in porch, cutting off the natural light. The strawberry wallpaper border and cream cupboards were comforting in an old, familiar way. I imagined the house had changed little in the last two decades. The vintage, worn, brick-pattern linoleum floor and the homemade, limp, gingham curtains spoke of a woman's touch in happier, simpler times.

"You go about your business. I'm sure the ladies can assist me," Doc said. At his gruff tone, I glanced up from my perusal of the tidy room.

Scotty nodded. "Call me if you need a ride."

"I'll take care of everything," the doctor persisted.

Scotty paused at the doorway. Did I imagine the dark look that flashed between the two men? He left without another word.

Dr. Beckett motioned us to the old Shaker chairs, picked up the phone, and dialed. "What're you doing this morning?" he asked into the receiver. "Fine. I got a job for you." Tasha and I waited in silence. Purry wasn't purring. He'd had enough, and I was doing my best to keep hold of him and keep him calm without appearing to manhandle the poor thing.

Dr. Beckett hung up the phone. "It'll only be a minute, Gwen. If you give Tasha the cat, maybe you can help me get the supplies."

"Sure thing." I placed the squirming pet in Tasha's waiting arms. "Good luck."

"Thanks a lot."

The doctor led me to a small, padlocked pantry next to the bathroom. "Never used to have to worry about this foolishness." He fiddled with the key. "Now you get folks sniffing around for ketamine to dope them out. It's a sick world out there, but I imagine you know that." He shook his head.

"The island seems a world unto itself." I wished I could lighten his load.

"That it is, but Candle Island has its own set of problems." He snapped open the lock and slipped the key inside a huge ceramic bee that sat on a knickknack shelf on the opposite wall. "You didn't see where I put that." His grin was back in place. "My wife used to do ceramics."

"I like it. Very lifelike in a gi-normous killer-bee way."

"It's not my cup of tea, but it's my favorite thing that she made me." He opened the door and handed me an array of operating instruments, syringes, and vials. "That should do it."

"Do you do this often?" I asked.

"Used to. The vet gives me a few supplies for emergencies. Nowadays I let Sledge do most of it. The boy has good hands and a good heart." He made his way back to the kitchen and took the cat from Tasha when a rap came at the door. "It's open!"

Sledge came in, a huge grin splitting his face at the sight of us.

"You ought to give him a snip in the pants while he's out," Dr. Beckett said. "Keep him out of trouble. Make him stick closer to home."

Sledge joined in the examination. "It'd actually be healthier for him in the long run. I can do it if you like. Only take a few minutes."

"Sure," I said.

Sledge got a plastic covering out of a nearby cupboard and spread it on the island at the far end of the kitchen. Dr. Beckett handed me Purry Mason and within a few minutes the cat was in a light sleep and in the process of being shaved by Sledge.

"Does anyone else think this is a little weird?" Tasha asked. "I mean, who operates on a cat in the middle of the kitchen table?"

As a higher ranking medical professional than I, she had the job of administering the little syringe of anesthesia. I mostly just hovered, since a kindergarten teacher has zero ranking in the medical profession.

"Welcome to the island," Sledge said. He was sure and quick with the scalpel, lancing and draining the abscess. Dr. Beckett observed the "boy with the good hands and a good heart." The older man leaned against the counter, drinking in a scene he must've participated in hundreds of times over the years. He lifted a bandana to his lips, hacking into it until his ears turned red and fuzzy. I seemed to be the only one in the room who noticed.

"You do good work, Doctor," Tasha teased.

"Thank you, Nurse. I have a good friend who's a vet; she taught me a thing or two."

"Oh." The news seemed to subdue my niece's playful spirit.

"She lives in North Carolina now." Sledge put the finishing touches on neutering the cat. "Just got engaged to a firefighter."

"Why don't you take Tasha back to the clinic," the old doctor suggested. "Check her ankle. Gwen and I'll keep an eye on the patient."

Sledge stripped off his gloves and gave the cat a shot of flocillin. "I'm agreeable; how about you?"

Tasha got the nod and removed the syringe of anesthesia, giving an automatic pinch to the vein. "That'd be great," she said. "I'm getting tired of limping around."

Sledge placed Purry in a box on the porch just as the sun burst through the fog, drawing the trailing tendrils of moisture up into the deep-blue sky. "A perfect day." He held the door open for Tasha. I think everyone but my niece knew he wasn't referring to the weather.

We watched them go with a quick wave before the doctor pulled me back to the kitchen. The tea kettle was already set to boiling and he gestured toward an old-fashioned corner china cupboard. I took out fragile, gold-rimmed, floral tea cups, my fingertips caressing the cool bone china.

"My wife, Muriel, loved her tea," the doctor said. "Taught me to love it, too."

"She has a beautiful collection."

"Yes. Wherever we went, that's the only thing she wanted for a keepsake. I'd say, 'Muriel, you already have enough cups to serve tea to all our friends,' and she'd say, 'Just one more cup for one more friend.' She must've meant you."

"Thank you." I blinked back tears. "You and Muriel supply the cups and the hospitality, and I'll contribute the tea and crumpets, if you'll allow me," I said briskly to lighten the mood.

Dr. Beckett gave me a toothy grin. "Crumpets. How Muriel would take to you! I love a woman who's not afraid to be one in this day and age of 'I don't cook or keep house because I'm not one of *those* women.' " His large fingers sketched in air quotes.

I laughed. "You're so modern. I'm glad you got over your initial revulsion towards me."

"Oh!" He shook his head, flapping the fleshy jowls of his emaciated face. "I apologize for that foolishness. The older I get, the more senile I become; honestly!"

I rummaged in my bag for the care package, pulled out the leftover doughnut muffins and arranged them on a plate. "May I?" I gestured toward the microwave.

He nodded, and puttered with the sugar and creamer set. I zapped two muffins for twenty seconds, feeling completely at home.

When we sat down at the little maple table, my companion closed his eyes and drank in the fragrance. "I don't have much of an appetite anymore," he confessed. "In fact, this is one of the rare times that food smells good to me. Your food at the tea on Saturday was some of the best I've had in a while."

I offered him a muffin with a sad smile. "I know it's none of my business, but I'm sorry for your ill health. Is there anything I can do to help you? Even if it's not talking about it, I can do that."

The doctor gave a tired nod and took a bite of muffin. "This is addictive."

"And totally bad for you." I stepped back from the sensitive subject to safer conversational ground.

"I don't know as that's true." He sipped his tea and again closed his eyes for a moment. "This must be good for me. I'm feeling better already." He reached across the table and clutched my hand. "I'm glad you came, Gwen. You're an answer to prayer."

I held on tight to his large, bony hand. "How so?"

"I need a friend who's not entangled with island bloodlines, feuds, or politics."

"Okay."

"I'm dying." The words softly delivered made me tighten my grip on this fragile friendship. "I have lung cancer. I'm too old and decrepit to have surgery. I've seen what the treatments do, and I'm no fool. I'd rather have three months of life than a year of torture."

"I hear you," I said. "My dad died of mesothelioma a few years ago, and he and Mom didn't go the standard surgery/chemo/radiation route. To this day, I know they made the right decision. Quality of life is a choice, and when you know this life will be swallowed up in immortality, it makes the time here precious, and the time hereafter a gift we can anticipate and take comfort in every day."

"Amen to that! I know my Muriel's up there with your dad and our Lord and Savior, waiting for me. I'm looking forward to joining them." The sentiment was punctuated by a feeble, dry cough.

"So what can I do for you here and now?"

"You can help me straighten out this idiotic Jones–Shaunessy feud business." He glowered at the topic.

"I don't know exactly what I can do," I said. "I'm from the mainland, a stranger Dot already mistrusts, but that reminds me. Could I use your phone to call the lawyer's office? I want to get the attorneys ferreting out the whys and wherefores of returning Dot's inheritance to her."

"You really think you can?"

"I do, and I've got a feeling if anyone can tackle it, Mr.

Blevins can. He seems a thoughtful and valiant man for a lawyer."

"If he impressed you, I have no doubt this Mr. Blevins and you and God can bring it to fruition."

"We'll give it our best."

"You're welcome to use my phone, but what's the matter with the phones up at your place?" He finally released my hand and settled back in his chair.

My hand felt cold and powerless without the shared grip. "Nothing. I, uh—"

"Oh, stop pussyfooting around, Gwen! I've just told you I'm dying, and you can't tell me why—" The sentence disintegrated in a coughing spasm.

"Okay, point taken. There're some odd happenings up at Vance's house. Things are disappearing." I bit my bottom lip, then pressed on. "The other night I was reading a book of poetry in Vance's library and found the letter you sent to him tucked inside the pages."

"Ah, I should invoke doctor–client privilege, but that's a bunch of hogwash in this case. But what I say goes no further than this room." His words came out in a rush. I nodded, but he didn't pause. "Vance, Frank Shaunessy, and I hit the trifecta, you might say. We were all diagnosed with terminal cancer. In different forms, of course, but no less deadly. Vance was diagnosed with pancreatic cancer; I made the discovery myself on a routine checkup. No one on the island knew. He didn't even tell Dot."

"Why not? I mean, she was his wife. I would think he'd want her to share 'in sickness and in health.' "

"You'd think," the doctor agreed, "but Vance wasn't like that. He took the news hard. Didn't want anyone to think he was less than the Superman image he presented to the world and especially to the island."

"Do you think he changed his will because of the diagnosis?"

"You mean in favor of you?" Douglas Beckett shook his head. "No, I imagine he had you in mind for a good long while, and I'm glad he did. It's an instance of God using the devil's craftiness and turning it into His good."

"The devil? Surely not." I took a sip of raspberry tea to help process the information and calm my whirling thoughts. I didn't want to be a part of Vance's hurtful schemes. I refused to be a party to them any longer.

"Okay, so Vance wasn't the devil, but he had more than a passing acquaintance with Lucifer." The doctor frowned. "You didn't know him. Some of the things he did to his neighbors, to his own family, I'll never understand. I know he was simply a mortal man, a sinner like all the rest of us, but he never saw his need for a Savior."

I opened my mouth and he held out his hand to silence me. "I'm not speaking ill of the dead." His voice was gruff, the same tone he'd used with Scotty earlier. I listened to the thread of frustration, weariness, and queer desperation wrap itself around my own nerves and squeeze. Why was my friend so anguished about Vance? "I tried witnessing, coaxing, and shaming that man over the years, and he purposely turned a deaf ear and a blind eye to the love of God."

He hung his head, scrubbing his palms over his face. I got up and gently rubbed his hunched shoulders. "I'm sure you did all you could. It wasn't your fault Vance got cancer. You were simply the messenger."

The eyes he raised to mine blazed with anger. "No!" A fit of coughing interrupted his tirade but not his train of thought. As soon as he could gain a breath he was off again. "I knew Vance was a proud man. I knew he couldn't face the prospect of wasting away, of having others see his weakness and his need. He took the diagnosis all wrong. It wasn't supposed to be this way.

I thought I knew him so well. I should've seen it."

His shoulders rose in a choking sob, head bowed in defeat. This was more than remorse for a lost soul.

"You're not responsible for Vance's fall. You couldn't know." This time the eyes that met mine were washed of anger and shimmered with torment. "Vance didn't fall, did he?" I said slowly. "He jumped."

The doctor's bony hand clamped onto mine. "There's no proof."

I nodded. There was no sense putting Dot and Ron through the wringer of suicide. They were still going through a rough time. "You're right," I said. "No one but God and Vance can know what really happened up on Blind Man's Bluff."

"Thank you," Dr. Beckett whispered. "Not much of a tea party. I'm sorry."

"Not at all." I turned to the stove and grabbed the simmering kettle. As I refreshed our cups, I smiled. "There's nothing that prayer, tea, and friendship can't make better." The doctor took a sip of tea and nodded. I was pleased to see the deep lines on his face relax into a contented smile.

"Anybody home?" We both started at the intrusion, turning guilty eyes to Ron Jones. "Oh, sorry, Doc. I didn't know you had company."

"Not at all. Come in, Ron. Come right in."

I was surprised at the hearty tone and watched in admiration as the doctor concealed his frailty in the offer of a quick handshake.

Ron winced at the friendly gesture. "That's why I'm here," he said. In a gesture I'd seen hundreds of times, like a hurting little boy, he presented his wrist to the older man. "I got into it with Frank yesterday; messed up my arm. I didn't hit him or nothin'. I wouldn't do that, even if he was out of line. He grabbed me, but I walked away. You don't disrespect the father.

I thought I could walk it off."

"I'll go out and check on the cat." They didn't seem to notice when I left the room.

Chapter Eleven

By late morning, I'd accomplished my phone call to Mr. Blevins, who thoughtfully processed my request but cautioned that he'd look, first and foremost, after what he considered "my best interests." I couldn't get into it with him as much as I would've liked, simply because I suspected the ears in the next room were pressed to water glasses against the wall, drinking in every word of my side of the conversation.

When I hung up and stepped into the doctor's kitchen, the grins on Ron's and Doug's faces proved me right. I'd have to stop in for a face-to-face with Mr. Blevins after the holiday. The reality of going back to my life on the mainland at the end of the week, coupled with the doctor's dire health, had me feeling blue. The ringing phone forced me out of my mental doldrums as Dr. Beckett stepped into his tiny home office and left Ron and me alone.

I was wracking my brain for a benign topic, but I needn't have bothered. Ron Jones wasn't one for chit-chat. He jumped into life with both feet. "So you're really going to do it."

"Yes." I didn't want to promise anything Mr. Blevins couldn't deliver. "The lawyer said it might take some time."

His eyes narrowed. "Dad's lawyers!" He spit it out like a kid force-fed Brussels sprouts.

"No, this lawyer assured me he works for me, not you or your dad, and I believe him. We'll work it out no matter how long it takes."

He nodded and leaned back in the chair. "Okay. Good enough. Doc says you're on the level. I guess I believe him."

"I don't know all the whys and wherefores, but if there's no stipulation in your father's will forbidding it, I don't see any reason why you and your mother can't move back into the mansion."

"Ha! Are you kidding?" Ron was on his feet, wearing out the faded linoleum floor between the porch door and the old cast-iron sink. "Dad's will might as well be a human lobster trap for me. He's tied my hands so I can't run the boatyard. I'm sure he's fouled up any chance of Mum and Laurel and I ever living in the big house."

I smiled at the "big house" reference as Vance's place seemed very much like a prison to me. "Like I said, I'm sure we can work something out."

"Where would you live?" Ron stopped in mid-pace and spun around to face me.

"I have a home in Bookerton. I teach kindergarten there."

"Really?" He swallowed the news in a gulp that made his eyes bug out.

"Yes. I've been a teacher for years and years. I thought everyone knew." Obviously the island grapevine wasn't nearly as entwined as I was led to believe by one Mr. Scott. I felt a warm glow knowing Scotty was a man who padlocked his lips. It cooled instantly as I thought about his stonewall silence to all my questions.

Ron shrugged. "I didn't. Huh! I wonder if Mum knows. Laurel's a teacher, too. She taught kindergarten, first, and transitional second. Seven students. She loves kids."

"Taught?" The word pricked my ears.

"She's . . . um . . . she's thinking of taking some time off." Ron was instantly on the defensive.

"Teaching's a tough job."

"She says I'm a natural teacher." His hands moved as he spoke, shaping the words and sentences in the air like a tai chi exercise in communication. I saw the sketch of a dory in his hands before he delivered the sentence. "I taught some of the guys at the yard how to lay a keel and I want to—" His hands and his tongue stopped.

Despite his rugged build and thinning hair, Ron Jones was a big kid, in some ways still struggling with kindergarten issues of self-esteem and fair play, by no means alone in his Gen-X of those searching for purpose.

"Can you still work at the boatyard?"

He nodded, his face sullen. "Just hired help."

Dr. Beckett lumbered into the room, coughing. "Sledge is stuck at the clinic and Tasha's helping out. I'll give you a lift home." He wheezed and gasped and I sprang from my seat. I clutched his arm and helped him to a chair.

"Are you all right, Doc?" Ron was instantly by the man's side.

"Just a touch of a summer cold." The doctor looked at Ron but squeezed my hand until it hurt.

"Maybe Ron wouldn't mind giving me a ride back to his house," I suggested. "I could walk the rest of the way." Both men looked at me as if I'd divulged a secret desire to run off and join the circus as the human cannonball. "I'm harmless . . . mostly."

The doctor's laugh developed into a cough, ending my moment of attempted humor.

"Okay," Ron said.

"I'll be in touch," I promised Douglas Beckett, and gave him a quick peck on the cheek.

"Another tea," he said.

"Definitely."

He ponderously rose from the chair, his weight crushing my

support. The morning had tired him tremendously.

"Thank you for everything," I said as we made it out to the porch. A big-eyed, baleful Purry Mason glared up at me from the confines of his box.

"Take the box; Sledge or Ron can bring it back to me."

"I'll be back later on," Ron said, favoring his wrapped wrist. He brushed aside my help and picked up the box. "Thanks, Doc."

"Bring Laurel with you. I should have a look at her."

"I'll try." Ron ushered me out the screen door.

"You can do it. If you have trouble, send Frank to me."

I slipped into Ron's pickup, trying to sort out his relationship with the doctor. It went beyond doctor–patient; beyond friendship.

The truck was brand new, Red Sox–red with *Candle Island Yachts: Vance Jones & Son* scripted in black on the doors. "Nice wheels," I said as he started the engine.

"Dad liked to ride in style." Ron pulled out of the yard. "The trucks were one of the last things we agreed on." He shot me a ghoulish grin. "Make that one of the few things Dad and I ever agreed on, period. Mum used to say we were like fire and water, total opposites."

"You were the water?" I ventured, my pulse picking up the tempo of the big tires on the narrow, broken, tarred road. I felt almost breathless in the spacious cab. It might have been the lingering new-car smell, but I sensed it had more to do with unexplored territory.

He snorted and yanked the wheel around a switchback. "I'm the fire! I was constantly after Dad to branch out, but noooo, he always had to do things the Vance Jones way."

"Ah, he liked to rain on your parade." I needn't have spoken. I watched his hands leave the wheel and cut the air like ASL karate. I was glad we were only going forty mph, but the road was narrow and my eyes widened as he literally steered the truck around a sharp bend with just his knees. I was obviously in the presence of a professional.

"Money and power; all he ever cared about was catering to the wealthy yacht crowd. His rich friends were all he talked about. You would've thought he was from *away.*" Ron's rage built. "He brought in craftsmen from outside for all the skilled jobs, as if the islanders weren't good enough for him anymore. A bunch of clam diggers, he used to call them. That wasn't right!"

His hands dropped to the steering wheel and the truck stopped dead in the road at the turn off to Blind Man's Bluff. He killed the engine and swiveled to face me, his charcoal eyes burning. "Can I ask you something?" He didn't wait for a reply. "Do you think I have enough smarts to start an apprenticeship boatbuilding school? I want to give the islanders, and maybe a few of the coastal natives, a chance to get back some of their self-respect. The way Washington keeps slashing the fishing season and slapping regulations on everything, custom-built boats is about the only safe way to make a living these days. So what do you think?"

"It sounds like a great idea," I said, my words as slow as Scotty's, my teacher brain buzzing. "With your background and resources, I imagine you'd be able to manage quite nicely. The secret to success in any venture is to surround yourself with wise and experienced people who can help you."

"Yes!" He snapped up the encouragement, his eyes staring through me with an almost psychotic glow. "That's exactly what I thought. I wish you'd been here to talk to Dad. That's just what he needed to hear. He would've listened to you."

"I don't know about that."

"He would've; you know what you're talking about. That was important to him. He didn't like people who couldn't speak up for themselves." Ron nodded, his eyes sharply focused on mine once more. "Maybe you could help me find a way around the hangman's noose so I can take over the boatyard."

"What seems to be the problem?" Purry let out a yowl and we both reached into the box to stroke him, our hands brushing each other. Ron kept his hand steady on the cat's back, unabashed by the contact. I wasn't sure what to make of this boy/man, but my heart ached for the boy who couldn't speak up for himself, and the man who still walked in his father's shadow. How many times growing up had he tried to talk to his father and become tongue-tied?

I was already knee deep in his problems and I wanted to grip his hand and wade in the rest of the way. He deserved the opportunity to live out his ideals and achieve his dreams. Perhaps Ron was the reason God had brought me to Candle Island.

"Dad fixed it so I can't inherit the boat works unless I give up Laurel." At his petulant tone I glanced up from the cat, half expecting to see his full lower lip thrust out in a five-year-old pout, but his eyes were sparkling with tears and his lip was caught between white teeth.

"Your fiancée?"

"My wife. We eloped to the mainland three months ago." He gripped my hand, pulling it up from the cat. "Nobody knows except Doc. Not even Mum."

"Whyever not?"

Ron held up his injured wrist.

I squeezed his hand. "Life is short." I thought of Frank Shaunessy's diagnosis. Ron's father was already gone. Surely Laurel's father would find it reassuring to know his daughter was happy. "You know, other people, even our parents, don't have the right to control our adult lives. You and Laurel are already married. You made that adult decision together. That's good. This should be a joyful time for both of your families." His features rippled from sad to dreamy to worried, like a pond reflecting the racing clouds in the sky. "Are you happy she's your wife?"

"I'm the proudest man on Candle Island."

I smiled. His were the words of a good man who'd found his treasure and was smart enough to know it. "Then you might want to let the world know," I said. "You can keep it a secret and worry about her father's anger and your father's will, but that won't help any of your problems. You might want to talk with Laurel and discuss the possibilities of publicly sharing the joy of your marriage and moving into the big house as husband and wife."

"You think her dad would let us?"

I could see the idea spreading like a sunrise over his big face. "It's your decision, both you *and* Laurel."

"Yes, that's right!" He grinned. "Thanks, Gwen." He let go of my hand and cranked the key, then whipped his gray, earnest eyes back to my face. "You won't tell anyone, will you? The last time I did it was . . . hmmm." He lowered his head and shook it. When he lifted his head, his eyes sparkled with tears. Who had he told? Dr. Beckett, of course. "But you won't let it out, I mean, not until I . . ."

My smile deepened. "This is your story to tell. You and Laurel are the only ones who have the right to share it. My lips are sealed."

His face once again went from sorrow to sublime joy in a blink. "Thank you!"

I thought it would be a promise easily kept, but it turned out to be more difficult than I imagined.

We spun up the gravel road at joyride speed, skidding to an abrupt halt when we encountered Scotty's truck, hood raised, bisecting the narrow road. Scotty's body was hunched over the exposed engine. Ron was out of the truck, driver's door left open, engine still running. I kept a quieting hand on the suddenly vocal Purry Mason.

"What's up?" Ron's chipper call brought Scotty's head up in a flash.

"Just quit when I was backing into your driveway. The choke's been acting up and flooding her." The blue eyes looked over Ron's head and squinted when they met mine through the windshield. "Do you need to get by? This'll only take a second." His blue cap bent down again and his hands disappeared inside the engine.

"No. Would you mind taking Gwen home? I've got some business that won't keep."

"Sure thing."

Ron hustled back to the truck.

"Scotty'll take you up the hill, soon as he gets his truck going." His words tumbled over each other. "You don't mind, do you? I want to get to Laurel's place. The tide's low so Frank's probably out clamming. Could be a good time to go over to Doc's and, well, you know."

"Sure, I'll be fine. And so will you," I added just before the door opened. Scotty was there, palm outstretched, waiting to help me out of the vehicle. His blue eyes raked us both with a sharp gleam. Let him wonder what Ron and I were discussing. *See how you like being stonewalled.*

"Thanks, Gwen," Ron said.

"I'll see you later." I took Scotty's hand and stepped out into the road.

"I'll let you know how I make out," Ron said as Scotty reached down and lifted the box with the recuperating Purry Mason inside.

I held up a hand; Ron nodded in response and floored the red truck backward down the road.

"I see you've made a new friend."

Scotty's comment had just enough barb to hook my pride

and reel it up to the surface of my tongue. "He certainly drives well." I never took my eyes from the retreating truck. "He drives better backwards than I do forward."

"Well, Twilight looks none the worse for wear." There's nothing worse than someone ignoring the fact that you're ignoring them. "Shall I put him in my cab for safekeeping while he sleeps it off?" He turned toward his disabled truck.

"I can carry him back to Vance's." I put my hand on the box.

He stopped mid-step. "He may be a runt, but combined with Doc's Fort Knox apple crate, Old Eleventh Hour's on the heavy side." Scotty made no move to relinquish the box.

How long we would've stood there in our silly little stand-off was thankfully cut short by the arrival of Dot charging out from around her house, a small, compact ship under full sail. "What is *she* doing here?"

"Just in the neighborhood," Scotty said, a calm eye in this hurricane.

"Good morning, Dot," I said. Scotty clamped a hand on my arm and trawled us over to his truck.

"If you know what's good for both of us, you won't mention Ron," he muttered, and opened the door, depositing the cat-in-the-box on the seat. He rolled up the window halfway and slammed the door.

I flicked my gaze away from his scowl and saw the shingle bundles in the truck bed. "I'd be glad to lend a hand shingling," I said. Dot's scowl joined Scotty's. "I've done a bit of it over the years and I don't mind climbing."

"I was waiting for Ron," Dot said.

"He probably got tied up with business somewhere," Scotty said.

"I'll call the boatyard." Dot glowered at me before presenting her back and trudging indoors.

"Here." Scotty thrust a rag into my hand. "I got some grease on your hand, sorry."

"I didn't notice." I wiped the dirty smear on my palm.

"I know. You took my hand without hesitation. You shouldn't do that, you know."

"Thanks for the warning." I smiled; he didn't. "I meant what I said about helping." In spite of his unreadable mood, I didn't want to go back to Vance's place.

"Okay. I can't speak for Dot, but I could use a hand. Hop in the cab." He opened the door for me and held out his hand. This time I made a quick show of staring at the grimy fingers, gave him my best school-teacher "you can't fool me" look before putting my hand in his. He shook his head and handed me into the truck. "Pump the gas pedal twice before you turn the key. I'll tell you when." He closed the door and ducked under the hood.

His head popped out a second later. "It's a standard."

"I figured that out. Three pedals. Don't worry; I won't run you over."

"Good enough." He was gone again. Some clanking and muttering followed. "Give her a try!"

I pumped twice and turned the key. When the engine spluttered to life, the ear splitting grin on my face was sickening. But it was like the tide; I couldn't stop it, especially when Scotty slammed down the hood and I saw an exact replica on his lean face.

"Want to back her down?"

I didn't really want to; the end of Dot's driveway was steep. But I guess whatever Ron had was catching. I nodded, said a prayer for guidance for giddy old fools, and slipped it into reverse. I rolled the old truck back slowly, stopping at his shout.

"A girl who can drive a rattletrap standard pickup!" Scotty opened the driver's door. "Better not let *that* get out. Heads will turn."

"He wasn't at the boatyard."

I jerked my gaze from Scotty's and felt my cheeks burn as I met Dot's disapproval. "She's still here?"

"Might as well give her a hammer and put her to work," Scotty said. His blue eyes twinkled, but his face and tone were grave. "Could have a thunder shower tonight." He squinted up at the milky summer sky. "Good chance of it, I'd say, so we ought to get the roof tight ASAP."

"Fine!" Dot folded her arms under her ample bosom. "She can work until Ron gets here, but make sure she knows what she's doing. Any fool can brag about climbing a ladder."

Or backing up a truck, I silently added, my head out of the clouds in the face of her hatred. "Kill her with kindness," I muttered a few moments later as I climbed the ladder, laden with carpenter's apron, hammer, measuring tape, and chalk line. Scotty followed, shouldering a bundle of shingles and chuckling.

The sun radiated heat waves into my knees, but the puffs of sea breeze sent a chill down my spine. I set to work with a will, intent on forcing Dot to address me as something other than "she" and "her" by the end of the day.

My determination wasn't lost on my companion. "She's not as trusting as Ron, but she'll come around." He laughed. "Eventually . . . possibly . . . maybe."

"Thanks for the vote of confidence; I think."

We worked side by side, squaring the shingle to the chalk line and each pounding in three nails. "You must've done this more than a time or two."

"I live in a fixer-upper. And that's being polite. It was my grandparents' old cottage, which I've been converting into a year-round house."

"Sort of like this one."

"No, nothing like this. I'm on the twenty-year fix-it plan, and I'm not keeping up with the decay." I plunked down on the sloping roof, legs spread in front of me, giving my stiff knees a rest. The ocean danced in a whitecap ballet. The blue and pink lupines drowsed under the July sun. The sturdy home beneath me felt as warm and solid as the Rock of Gibraltar. I glanced up from drinking in the mini panorama to meet my companion's eyes watching me. "This baby makes my place look like, well, a handywoman's nightmare."

"You like this place." His words were low and murmured, as if he were talking to himself.

"It's a thrifty little Cape Cod," I answered briskly, not comfortable with the lowered red brows directed at me.

"You should see the inside," he said. "It must be time for lunch; come on."

He held out that square, calloused hand again. Mine itched to take it, but instead I levered myself onto my knees with the grace of an overturned turtle. I got up slowly on stiff, shaky legs. The helping hand that I'd refused came to rest in solid gentleness on my back.

"Feel better now?" he whispered in my ear.

"Much. Wasn't it you who warned me about holding hands?"

Before the taunt was out of my lips, his other hand came up to grasp mine. "I should've known better," he murmured.

I let him guide me to the roof's edge and assist me to the ladder.

Dot was waiting at the foot of the ladder, hands on hips. Though her pink crocs were planted firmly on the grass, I had the sensation of hearing her foot tapping impatiently as she silently kicked me off her property with her scathing stare.

I gimped over to the truck, trying to work the kinks out of my body. I peeped in at Purry, laid out in the box, looking dead except for the slow rise and fall of his shiny, gray fur.

"Three-quarters finished." Scotty's voice was hearty and more cheerful than his usual mien. "That Gwen's a worker."

"If it leaks, I'll know who to blame," Dot said.

I kept my back to them, untied my carpenter's apron, and set it in the truck.

Scotty kept up his cheerful chatter. "How about some lunch? We can finish the job in another couple of hours this afternoon."

"For someone who was so worried about a thundershower, you seem content to lollygag around all of a sudden." Dot's voice was a carbon copy of Ron's earlier petulance.

"It'll get done in time; don't you worry." Scotty strode over to the truck as he spoke. "I work better on a full stomach and, as I recall, someone promised me a crabmeat roll for dinner. After all, the workmen and women are worthy of their hire."

"It's all ready," Dot griped, still peevish. "Didn't know I was gonna have to feed an army. Wipe your feet."

"Dot's the best crabmeat picker on the island," Scotty said, loud enough to chase his surly cousin across the ledge-cropped lawn and into the house. He dropped his tools in the truck bed.

"I should go home," I said.

"Not on your life." Again, the gentle strength of his hand rested on the small of my back. "I fought hard for this one and we're not retreating now." Together we strolled to the back door. My heart tripped faster than our feet as I stepped onto the huge, flat fieldstone that served as a back stoop. I couldn't deny the shiver of anticipation at entering the snug island home and getting a peek at a daydream.

Dot's dour face couldn't dim the sunshine spilling in from the picture windows facing the shore. The light glittered off the incoming tide and speckled the beamed ceiling with afternoon firefly flecks, and the old-fashioned wainscoting mellowed to rich, golden tones.

"Gwen . . . Miss McPhail." I started at Scotty's hand on my elbow. "I lost you there for a few minutes."

"Oh, uh, sorry." He steered me past the airy living room and into a compact kitchen.

"You can wash up here." Dot pointed to an old slate sink. "I'm renovating the bathroom, so I hope you don't need to use it."

"I'm fine." My response sounded vague, even to my own ears, but my mind was drawn outside the kitchen window to the cascade of flowers rioting over the banking, set off by the rippling, emerald backdrop of dark spruce topping the ledges. "Beautiful perennials." I could imagine myself on hands and knees weeding those gorgeous King Arthur delphiniums, clipping the rugosa roses.

Dot clicked her tongue, snapping me out of my fantasy. Not my garden, *her* garden; though her waspish tone made me feel sorry for her. "A bunch of overgrown weeds, mostly. Vance's mother used to get slips from everybody on the island and half her relatives on the mainland. Everywhere she went she was always digging roots or snapping off twigs and carrying them back here in her pockets."

"My kind of girl."

"Waste of time, if you ask me. Speaking of wasted time, sit down."

Scotty held out a chair and Dot made a beeline for it. I slipped unaided into the seat opposite her. "We always say grace at this table." Dot compressed her lips in disapproval at me before nodding to Scotty.

I bowed my head and when I lifted it after the short, sweet prayer, my eye snagged on the lines of a telescope. I leaned forward in my seat to get a clearer view of Vance's high-tech telescope in the far end of a small corner sun porch.

Pretending to adjust my chair, I sat back and took a quick bite of crab roll to prevent the questions from tumbling out. The implication frosted my heart, killing the tiny feelings that had sprouted there. I fiercely swallowed the tasteless food, and my sudden melancholy with it. How dare I give in to the foolish prickle of tears like a moonstruck teenager!

"You don't like it?" Dot's Spanish Inquisition tone yanked my eyes back into focus, meeting Scotty's raised brows and exaggerated smile.

I responded by pasting on my best Miss America–smile and, ignoring Scotty's suddenly eclipsed teeth and pained expression, I turned to Dot. "Oh yes, it's wonderful." I vomited out the words to hide the sick feeling in my stomach. "You never get a crabmeat roll like this at a restaurant. It's the best I've ever eaten."

Dot's beetle-browed glare remained, but her frowning lips reverted to a straight line. I was beginning to see the cousinly resemblance. I'm ashamed to say I finished the meal chattering away like an old gray squirrel, covering up my heartfelt questions with verbal drivel. It was one of the first times in my life I truly meant it when I said no to a slice of homemade chocolate cake. "I wish I had room." I passed the plate to Scotty. "But that lunch was so good and so filling. I feel like I ate Ron's crabmeat, so I won't be guilty of gobbling up his cake and, hopefully, he'll forgive me."

"I made a whole cake just for him," Dot retorted.

I knew if I stayed in here another minute I'd likely say something I'd regret, so I scooted back my chair and stood. "You're such a good mother," I said, and, on that parting shot, I turned to leave.

I hadn't counted on Dot bolting from the table and blocking my dignified exit. "Come out to the porch and I'll show you Ron's drawings."

"We really ought to get back to work, Dot." Scotty was on his feet, too.

I tried to do a little two-step around the shorter woman, but she crowded me into the porch and, short of giving her a football linebacker block, I could do nothing but step out ahead of her and be herded into the sunny alcove, like a sheep to the slaughter. I could feel her silent prodding and Scotty's looming presence behind, so I did what any woman would do. I made a beeline for the telescope. "You must get some wonderful views of the smaller islands from here," I said, gesturing toward the contraband scope.

"Oh, yes!" Her smile flashed a brilliant weapon more cutting than a dagger. Her dark eyes gleamed in triumph.

I love speed chess, McPhail family rules, of course, but this wasn't the type of game I enjoyed and I refused to play. "I recall one just like this in Vance's office yesterday." I wondered what she'd do if I called her on the carpet for the phone threat.

"Looks like clouds sitting out there on Silver Key. Could be bubbling up into a storm. We'd better get the rest of those shingles on in a hurry. Come on, Gwen." Scotty's usual slow speech pattern was quick and sharp as a dog's bark. He slipped past his cousin, took my elbow, and spirited me out of the room. The last thing I saw was Dot's mouth yawning open, but we were out before her protest hit the air.

We didn't stop until we reached his truck. "I don't see any clouds on the horizon." I put the truck bed between us.

"Oh, but you did. Metaphorically speaking, they were thunderheads." His blue eyes, sharper than lightning, struck mine and held fast.

"So this was a rescue?"

"In a manner of speaking." He ran a hand through his rusty hair.

"Hers or mine?" I had to say it. He knew it. I knew it. "How did the telescope get here?" I held my breath.

"I can't say." The words were slow, lazy, and deep as the summer ocean.

"You can't say." It came out in a murmur of a released sigh.

He looked away, squinting out to sea. Little Brian Orr always looked at the flag when I caught him in a lie or, as he liked to call it, a "flab." I'd joked to my fellow teachers that with his patriotism he was bound to be a soldier or a politician. I always asked him to look me in the eye and tell the truth. I had no heart to ask for the truth today.

Sun bounced off a hood, hitting me in the eye. Ron's red truck swung down the driveway, stopping an inch from the front bumper of Scotty's pickup. I silently thanked God for His perfect timing and rushed toward the new arrival. "Ron, would you mind giving me a lift up the hill? The cat needs to get out of here." *And so do I.*

"Gwen." Scotty joined me at Ron's open window.

"I don't mind." Ron was all smiles. "I'll take her up, then come back and give you a hand finishing up; okay, Scotty?"

"Yeah, okay." Scotty went back to his truck and retrieved the patient. I hurried over and opened the passenger door of Ron's cab. I stepped back, giving man and cat a wide berth.

"Looks like you don't need me anymore," I chirped as he slid the box onto the seat and the cat yowled.

"Easy there, Buenos Noches." Scotty straightened and gave me a grim smile. He camped in the way and held out his hand. I sidled by and felt the gentle strength on my back for an instant before I hitched up into the cab. He closed the door, his hand resting on the open window. "This isn't over."

Ron chose that moment to throw it into reverse. I was growing to love this boy more with each passing second.

"Good news!" he crowed, as soon as we gained the dirt road. "Laurel thinks you're right. We're going to tell her parents soon; we haven't decided exactly when yet."

I nodded and smiled. "That *is* good news."

"But you haven't heard the best news!" He waited until I looked at him; both hands were off the wheel and he pumped his fists up and thumped the roof of the cab. "Laurel's going to have a baby!"

"A baby? Congratulations!"

"Yeah. It's a dream come true. When Doc encouraged us to get married because we wanted to start a family, I wasn't sure." Ron grasped my hand. "Now it's all coming together."

I was happy for him, even though my world was falling apart.

Chapter Twelve

My house guests were first rate at going through more clean towels than Ted's Barbershop on a Double-Cut-for-Cut-Rate-Price Saturday, and for almost keeping my mind off Scotty's duplicity—almost. While throwing in a load of laundry early the next morning, I heard the water from the hose strike the cellar window. I caught a glimpse of his sneakers as he moved back and forth watering the shrubs. I hustled upstairs to the kitchen and soon saw water squirt past onto the cluster of rhododendrons outside the window. Since there'd been a thundershower last night, I thought his appearance in the yard transparent as the plastic wrap I was putting over a cut half of grapefruit.

Before I could stop myself, I wondered if Dot's roof had leaked. Should I go out and talk to him and put an end to our . . . ? That was just it. An end to what? A friendship that might've become something more? The wondering of: what was he thinking? The why of: why hadn't he just asked me if he could take the computer and telescope and who knows what else?

I'd used all night to figure out the big why—family loyalty. It didn't take all night to come to that rocket scientist conclusion, but since I was awake for hours it kept running around in my head like Lenny the kindergarten gerbil on his infinity wheel.

I felt lonely, as if I didn't matter. I wasn't part of the island family. I was an outsider. I could see Dot sitting at the tea on Saturday, her black eyes small and hostile. Her querulous boast echoed in my head, blending with the sudden whine of a weed whacker under the kitchen window. "The Scotts have always been loyal to a fault." I had a feeling my house guests would fault this loyal Scott for working on a holiday.

I set down my tea cup and, on weary, bare feet, hurried to the French doors just as the engine cut out. I opened the door to silence. Purry Mason came bounding toward his freedom and I slammed the door in his face. "Sorry. You can't go out today." I gently scooped up the little cat. He purred, but his yellow eyes were reproachful.

"Hey, I hope you don't mind, but I told Scotty to take the day off." Jason appeared behind me and put his hands on my shoulders.

"I was just about to do that, in a manner of speaking," I said. "Thank you."

"What would you like to do today?" he asked. "It's Independence Day; shall we cut loose and go off on our own, leave the others to their own devices for awhile?"

"Oh my." I cleared the morning webs and mounting claustrophobia out of my throat. "Let's get some breakfast and discuss our options." I slipped away from his near embrace and double-timed it into the kitchen. I gave Purry his breakfast before raiding the refrigerator for people food.

By the time Jason and I got omelets going, the rest of the company had joined us. I glanced at Tasha, no longer using her crutches but looking as heavy-eyed as I felt. She'd come in last night at a decent hour, but her constantly creaking bed joined symphony with mine into the wee hours. Dalton's next words enlightened me. "We're all going out on Royce Ellingsford's yacht today. I asked him to put her through her paces for me sometime, and last night he suggested we all come along today."

"Isn't that a bit much?" Tasha said. "I mean, we're spending the evening with them at the dinner party."

"You'd rather hang out with that mechanic down at that glorified two-car garage they call a hospital?" He gulped down his first mug of coffee.

"He's a doctor, thank you very much; a professional colleague; nothing more, nothing less." Tasha on her high horse did her only-blood-aunt proud, pausing and jutting out her chin for maximum dramatic effect. *Bravo!* "And, for your information, it's a medical clinic, a very modern one, and, obviously, closed today, as it's Independence Day."

"Whatever." Dalton made a beeline for the pot and poured another cup. He lounged on the counter by my elbow. I thought about giving him a poke in the ribs with my spatula before I turned the final omelet, but his mother saved him.

"Tasha's right. Joan needs time to get ready for the party, but she did say she was hoping we could join them for awhile on the boat. I understand there are some sort of boat races this morning and we can watch from the water." Hillary handed me a plate as I scooped up the fluffy, lightly browned egg concoction.

"That's exactly right, Mother. The island's annual lobster-boat races." Dalton took the plate from his mother and carried it over to the table, stooping to give Tasha a kiss. "It'll be fun and relaxing for those of us who should stay off our feet."

"These look excellent, Gwen. I feel guilty having you cook for all of us, but I never really took to the kitchen. Even peanut butter and jelly was a struggle for me. It's a wonder Dalton grew so tall." Hillary helped me ferry over the juice and toast.

"Gwen's a wonder." This from Jason, who followed at my heels with the cream and sugar.

"Cook never let us starve, Mother." Dalton ignored Jason and the rest of us in favor of guzzling his coffee. Around the table, grace was said with no askance looks from the Madisons, I'm pleased to report.

In spite of my antsy thoughts, the morning boat excursion went well, two parts cruise-ship luxury, one part windjammer tourist schooner, and one part Gilligan's *Minnow* cruise. I confess the *Minnow* encounter, make that the *Sea Lemon* encounter, was the highlight of my morning on the water. While anchored out beyond the lobster-boat race course, a jalopy boat spluttered up beside us, spewing black smoke from its stack.

"Oh, come off it! Isn't there some sort of rule of the sea that the larger vessel has the right of way?" Dalton's head snapped up turtle fashion from his relaxed seat in the row of deck chairs.

"Only if we're moving," Royce answered.

"You've got to be kidding me!" Dalton's loud complaint was punctuated by a hail from the approaching crew.

"Gwen! Hey, Gwen, is that you?"

I nodded to Hillary, Joan, and the others, and scooted out of the lineup of chairs. Hanging over the shiny brass rail, I perched my sunglasses on top of my floppy hat brim and looked down into the saw-toothed grin of Old Stin. "Hi, there!" I called.

The doctor sat on the plank bench in the stern of the small boat and gave a tired wave. Old Stin crowded close to the side of the boat, propping one foot up on the gunwale. "Don't fall overboard." The old man frowned at my nursemaid tone. I smiled. "Sorry! Sometimes I'm such a kindergarten teacher, I can't stop myself."

"Apology accepted, this time. I been on the water since I was knee-high to nothin'." His sneering smile was back in place. "What're you doin' on that fancy barge?"

I glanced at Royce Ellingsford out of the corner of my eye. His white captain's hat with gold braid sat atop a styled mane of silver as impressive as Old Stin's. The large, flushed face told of a more opulent lifestyle, but the merry, blue eyes and the suave Thurston Howell III grin spoke of a common-law-of-the-sea brotherhood. "She's just slumming." Royce rose from his deck chair with a chuckle and took his place beside me. "That's a nice design you've got there," the captain of *El's Folly* stated.

Old Stin nodded, his long thatch sticking out scarecrow style under his faded cap. "My grandson and I built 'er ourselves. She can move, too. Got a Chevy V8 engine we hauled out o' my old truck."

Royce nodded. "Are you going to be in one of these upcoming lobster-boat races?"

"Naw!" Old Stin frowned. "Those young fellas spend all their time and money soupin' up them engines. It's a bunch of pride an' foolishness. This is a workin' boat, not meant for nonsense."

"And it'd fall apart if you revved her over two miles per hour," Dr. Beckett scoffed. "It's a tub." He laughed and I could hear the effort it took. "But a nice tub."

I looked past the small American flags fluttering from the rail to the shadowed interior of the pilothouse. I could make out a familiar figure standing with his back to us, one hand resting on the wheel, the other on the throttle. As I watched, the square, rugged hand eased the throttle up a smidgen to compensate for the running tide. The small boat remained steady at a constant distance from the sailing yacht.

"Looks like they took the old two-by-fours off your porch and nailed a lean-to on a dory, then stuck in a steering wheel as an afterthought." Jason's low voice buzzed in my ear, as irritating as a mosquito. I immediately reprimanded myself for the uncharitable thought.

I took my eyes off Scotty and focused on my companion and longtime friend. "Hopefully it's much more sturdy than my porch," I said, and Jason grinned.

"Never did tell me what you're doin' out here, Gwen!" Old Stin hollered.

"Watching the races with friends." I turned back to the sailors.

"Don't suppose we could kidnap you," Doug said.

"We're goin' for a picnic on Brass Key; nice little island," Old Stin added. "And doin' a little handlinin'."

"Are you having red hotdogs?" I couldn't stop myself.

"Of course!" Scotty's voice carried over the water, sending vibrations up my spine. I took a peek under the Jason-described lean-to. Scotty's back was still to us, but obviously his ears were tuned in this direction.

"Sure could use some of your cooking, Gwen," the doctor said. "I might starve with these pirates in charge."

"Oh, quit your bellyachin', Doug." This from Old Stin. "I brought some clams to steam and you know it."

"So, do you want to jump ship?" Royce Ellingsford asked. "It sounds tempting."

"I'll take a raincheck," I said, loud enough for all to hear.

"I'll hold you to it," Old Stin called just before the engine roared and the boat chugged off.

"Did you see the name on the stern?" Jason asked with a chuckle. "*Sea Lemon.* At least the old gent's got a good sense of humor."

"He's got more than that." Royce's gaze lingered on the departing vessel's wake. "He's got a working boat." My eyes raked his face to detect any sign of snobbery, but there was none. "That old seadog's got it good and he knows it. He can come and go without all this high-tech, high-priced folderol. Just a bunch of guys going fishing."

"The old man and the sea," I murmured.

"Exactly," Royce said, the word smacking on his lips like a sweet chocolate bar.

"Royce is right." Jason ushered me back to the deck chairs. "This would be the life for a few weeks in the summer, wouldn't it? I mean, it's like a fairy tale—no work, just sun and fun."

"I think they work here." I settled into my seat.

"I know," Jason said, "but it's not like it is on the mainland.

Everything runs at a much slower pace. I can't imagine spending the winter out here with nothing to do. I'd be bored stiff."

Tea parties, roof shingling, island hikes—I couldn't summon up one boring moment, and I was sure no matter the season, life here would be full and rich. But it wasn't meant to be my life, I reminded myself as I watched the lead lobster boat, *April May,* speed past.

The morning passed into early afternoon, pleasantly bobbing in the harbor, eating chicken salad sandwiches and shrimp with cocktail sauce. With each bite I thought of red hotdogs and steamed clams.

By the time we arrived back at Vance's mansion, I was sick and tired: sick of my wayward thoughts, and tired of Dalton's and Jason's constant comments. While the others drowsed on the deck, talked on their cells, or napped in their rooms, I slipped away to Blind Man's Bluff.

I sat on the sun-warmed ledge, part of my mind in prayer while part of it picked at the edges of my troubles. Scotty's theft and dishonesty, the doctor's cancer, Ron's secret marriage, Dot's hatred, Tasha's upcoming wedding to an apparent unbeliever, Vance's will, Mr. Blevins's promise to do whatever was in my best interests, Jason's escalating attentions, Vance's death.

No matter how long the line of problems, it always came back to Vance standing here, alive one minute, plunging to his death the next. I closed my eyes and visualized the proud man I'd seen in the framed photo on his desk, standing on this cliff, feet spread apart like a king surveying his domain. The iron man in the photos was untouchable by his arrogance and his ego. Had he been so despondent over the news in Dr. Beckett's letter that he'd committed suicide?

I thought of Douglas weeping in his homey little kitchen over a lost soul. He'd called Vance a man with a Superman image. I shook my head, opened my eyes, and gazed out over the sun-gilded Atlantic. Why would a self-proclaimed Superman commit suicide? It made no sense.

From what I'd learned of Vance's domineering personality, from the overwhelming accumulation of personal trophies, he seemed the type to fight his disease with everything his money could buy: the newest treatment, the best doctors.

My thoughts hit a brick wall. Of course Iron Man Vance would go for a second opinion, somewhere ultra high-tech on the mainland—Portland? Boston? When there were MRIs and genome therapies, he wouldn't trust an old country doctor's say-so. And why had Dr. Beckett sent him that letter if Doug had already shown him the test results and talked to him in person?

He took the diagnosis all wrong. It wasn't supposed to be this way. I thought I knew him so well. I should've seen it. Douglas's tortured voice sobbed in my memory.

How was anyone supposed to take such a devastating diagnosis? At the time, I thought my friend was weeping over the news driving Vance to suicide, but I was the one who'd jumped to that conclusion. Doug Beckett never mentioned suicide. He'd said, "There's no proof." An odd comment to make, unless he was protecting someone.

Ron Jones instantly popped into my mind. His secretive closeness with Doug; Doug's protective, lion-hearted care for the boy/man, his adopted cub. There were no father/son photos in the mansion, no proud dad's odd collection of an only son's battered baseball, blue ribbon for winning the school spelling bee, plastic trophy for peewee basketball, or a hundred other little mementos of love. Ron Jones was still a neglected, lonely, hurting ten-year-old in an adult carrying case.

Maybe Dot's phone accusation had less to do with me being the perceived "other woman" and everything to do with an obsessive mother finding excuses for her child's mistake. If you could call murder a mistake.

Had Ron's immaturity, indecisiveness, and his thirty-five years of resentment of his father combined and erupted in one violent act? Was this the reason for Douglas's remorse, or was I letting my imagination and curiosity get the better of me? It was clear the doctor was tortured by Vance's death and he wanted me to help him find peace. I prayed God would grant me wisdom to meet the task and give my new friend a measure of solace in his last days.

"Hey, I've been looking for you."

I turned from my sightless study of the sparkling waves, bright halos dancing in front of my eyes and around my niece's honey-colored head. I laughed.

"What's up?" Tasha asked.

"You look like an angel."

"Oh, sure I do. I look like a raccoon. I took a nap this afternoon, but it wasn't enough to make up for last night. By the way, what was keeping you up, Auntie? A certain school chum, or the ruggedly handsome-but-aloof caretaker?"

"Ha. Ha. I plead the fifth. How about you?" She'd had a good teacher when it came to heckling. I gave as good as I got.

"There's nothing so eloquent as silence." Her haughty tone ended in a giggle. "Like Auntie, like niece."

"Fair enough. Did you have a good time today?"

She shrugged. "It was okay. The picnic on Gilligan's Island sounded like more fun. You should've gone with them."

"There's plenty of time for that later. I want to spend time with you and Dalton. Hillary seems nice."

"I guess."

"Try not to gush." I put my arm around her young, strong shoulders. We were nearly the same height, but she had my old body, slender and passably athletic. I just had an old body.

"I'm keyed up about tonight. It's a big deal for Dalton that we make a lasting impression." I could feel the deep sigh leave her body.

"I wouldn't worry about it. From what I saw today, Joan and Royce enjoy your company and genuinely like you."

We began walking back toward the house. "We're not worried about their friendship; we want to impress them with our intellect and vision as one of the up-and-coming generation of movers and shakers."

"Ah." I nodded. "Just be your unshakable self."

"I knew you'd say that."

I stopped on the edge of the lawn and faced her. "Tasha, I see you struggling with self-esteem issues, and I can't for the life of me understand it. Where's the girl I knew who worked two jobs and still got a 4.0 GPA in college; and who dared to go on that short-term mission trip to Honduras, even though it freaked out your mom? Dalton may be a 'mover and a shaker,' but you've got so much more to offer him, starting with your faith. It's the only place to start before you get—"

Tasha held up both palms like a traffic cop in front of an eighteen wheeler. "I know," she cut in. "Dalton's a good man. He doesn't mind if I'm a Christian, and sooner or later he'll see that he wants it, too. You always told us one of the greatest ways to witness is through your everyday life."

"Well, yes."

Tasha linked elbows with me and set off at a sprinter's pace across the grass. "It's time to get ready for the dinner party. We'll show those old-money Ellingsfords that the new-money McPhails can hold our own in high-falooting society circles." Her voice matched her step, fast and high. Dalton's carefully tousled, dark head poked out the door and I knew enough to hold my tongue, for the time being.

The conversation with Tasha put me in a somber state of

mind while dressing for the upcoming shindig. *The new-money McPhails.* That could only be Dalton talking, but I'd have no opportunity to say anything more to my niece. Tasha was incommunicado, hiding out first in the shower, then in the bathroom.

I put on my periwinkle-blue floral dress; out of fashion by almost a decade, I still loved its lightly fitted bodice with a jewel neckline, puffed short sleeves, and gathered skirt. Hey, maybe it was in fashion again by now, who knew? I twirled in front of Vance's full-length mirror, pleased with the flattering lines of the dress and the style's camouflage of my little extra around the middle.

I liked the feel of the dress and always got compliments when I wore it to special school functions. I'd instructed Pearl to pack this one and my version of the quintessential LBD. I'd intended to wear the black tonight—it's always slimming—but after my little upset with Tasha, I put on what I had designated as next Sunday's dress.

Tasha and I had a bond with this outfit, one I hoped she'd remember. On a long ago school vacation, I'd sewn this dress while she used the extra fabric to make a skirt, one she'd worn to many high-school functions thereafter. It had been one of many special times for us, and I sincerely hoped and prayed the memory of it would keep us close tonight.

I slipped on sandals, a simple, gold-chain bracelet, and an Austrian crystal angel necklace, one of the last gifts my mother gave me. "Passable," I muttered as I exited the room and progressed down the stairs.

Jason stood in the throne room, lost in thought, staring out the window. At the sound of my descent, he slowly turned and gave a low whistle. He came to take my hand and escort me off the final step. "You look gorgeous! Forget about Dalton and Old Royce; I'm the richest man in the world tonight."

"Thanks." The compliment boosted my spirits and calmed

the rising jitters in my stomach. Purry added his approval by weaving soft, furred figure eights around my bare ankles. I hadn't realized I was facing tonight with a tickle of apprehension until now. I silently blamed Tasha for the unwelcome butterflies as she and Dalton came down the staircase deep in conversation.

Tasha's hair was piled up, her sun-kissed natural beauty complemented by Dalton's dark, rough looks. He'd used his razor tonight and they looked like the poster couple for the Academy Awards red carpet: young, hip, and not totally happy.

Tasha met my eyes and hers started to glow as a genuine smile spread across her face, as wide and full of glory as the island sunrise. "Look at you! What a total glam girl!"

"Right back at you!" The shadow lifted off my heart.

"Hah! I should've worn my matching skirt."

"You still have it?"

"Of course; timeless fashion knows no expiration date. Besides, I'm going to give it to my daughter one day." She gazed up at Dalton and the couple exchanged a private look.

On the way to the Ellingsford house, I tried to picture the young pair as parents, but I couldn't get the image to gel. Then Ron's jubilant face and waving hands came to mind. His excitement over starting a family was contagious. Would I want anything less for my beloved niece?

Jason opened the SUV door for me, interrupting my musings. Dalton was eagerly leading the way over a dappled, sunlit, cobblestone walkway with his fiancée on one arm, his mother on the other. The house was as big as Vance's, but looked like the old-fashioned summer homes of the Roosevelt-era rich and famous. It had its modern accouterments but, in spite of its size, it had a pleasing, welcoming sprawl about it.

The door opened before we rang the bell. A tanned, blond, Swedish super model greeted us with a TV-commercial smile.

"Hillary. Dalt!" The voice was low, and sultry as a tropical night. The woman and Hillary air kissed, then she moved on to "Dalt," giving him a warm hug and a kiss on the cheek. She took Tasha's hand and gave her an impish grin. "You must be Natasha. You've got your hands full with this one."

"Your mother didn't mention you were going to be here, Sondra." I thought Hillary's tone registered barely thirty-two degrees on the human-warmth conversational thermometer.

She'd become detached from her son's arm during the hug escapade and beckoned Jason and me forward. "This is Royce and Joan's daughter, Sondra." During the introductions, I watched the facial byplay and body language. These three had a history, not all of it pleasant. Sondra sizzled, obviously enjoying Hillary's wary reserve. Dalton, oh, excuse me, "Dalt," was harder to read. If he was uncomfortable, he didn't show it. As we shuffled into the richly carpeted living room, he put his arm around Tasha's shoulders and swept her along like a conquering prince.

The Ellingsfords were congenial, but more reserved than they'd been on the boat earlier. They had cocktails. Jason and I had ginger ale. I listened as the talk was mostly about their friends and club acquaintances, spurred on by Sondra and Joan. I was mentally fidgeting, hoping dinner would soon begin so we'd at least be able to make a comment on the food, when a musical series of notes chimed, bringing a smile to my face.

"You like that?" Royce asked.

"Very much."

"It has a little bit of history—island mystique, if you will—surrounding it. Seems a young man name of Lemuel McMahan, black sheep of an old island family, ran off when he was branded a thief. Spent his whole life on the sea, but as an old man, he came back secretly to this island and ran aground on the Three Sisters, a bunch of rocks out here." He gestured out the window with his tumbler. "They're a navigational hazard at low tide. My grandfather helped him out and he made the door harp in payment for our family's kindness and secrecy. I've never heard another one like it."

I smiled at the mention of Lemuel, my erstwhile forefather, according to Old Stin. If he could produce this type of music, he couldn't have been all bad. "It's beautiful."

"You'll have to forgive Father. He's a Candle Island history buff." Sondra flashed him a smile to take the sting out of her slightly bored tone.

"Hey, is the party started?" All heads turned as two more couples entered. "Sorry we're late. I got hung up at the yard." The man was a hulk with coarse features. Salt and pepper curls clung to his large head, reminding me of a dissipated Roman ruler.

"It's a holiday; you'd think Les could take one day off, but you know how that goes, Joan." The woman with him was dressed to the nines. Her face was plain, in a gentle way, and, despite her smile, her eyes were haunted. Her husband ignored her and her comment, and made a beeline toward Royce and the liquor.

Again introductions were made: Les and Marjie Bigelow, who were bringing out the sycophant in my future nephew-in-law. Dalton pounced on the Candle Island Yacht designer, talking over Joan's introduction of their summer social-set friends, Mark and Kitty Simcock. The Simcocks were my idea of understated elegance, a nicely matched genteel couple, a good decade or more older than Joan and Royce.

Joan left to check on the dinner. Jason and I people watched. I'd fooled myself into thinking we were all alike inside. The past couple of days, I'd purposely focused on the little connections, the similarities between Hillary and me.

I'd hoped to feel more positive about Tasha's new family and her choice of a husband. Now, seeing her future mother-in-law and Dalton socializing with their peers, I realized how differently we approached life. I struggled with the distasteful feeling that in this room superficiality and artifice reigned supreme. It was the social order of the day, and, most likely, every day.

"A bit out of our league here," I whispered to Jason. Hillary nudged my shoulder. I looked up to find her standing behind our sofa and I instantly colored. "I apologize," I said too quickly.

She didn't smile but nodded, leaned over between us and said, "Maybe *we're* the ones out of *your* league."

I swallowed hard. The last thing I wanted to do was put my Christianity on a pedestal and taint my witness with reverse snobbery. "It's nice of you to invite us along," I said. "I've truly enjoyed your company and your wit but, after all, I *am* just an aunt."

Hilary laughed and sat beside me. "You were never 'just an aunt.' That would describe my and Phillip's nieces and nephew. You're closer to Tasha than I've ever been to my own children. Closer than I thought blood relations could be."

Did she mean *should* be? A second ago I'd been concerned over the superficiality of the company, and now I was plunged in over my head, nearly drowning in a subject that went straight to the heart. I sent up a prayer to guard my tongue and tried to lighten the topic. "Well, boys are different, you know. Trust me—I have several in my class each year; always lovable, but always a challenge."

"A challenge," she murmured. "What do you think Tasha's chances are of meeting that challenge?" She clasped my wrist, her heavy bracelet pinning my simple costume chain to my forearm. Her less-than-gentle squeeze pulled my gaze away from my fascination with the crown jewels circling her wrist and directed my eyes across the room to where Dalton was schmoozing Les and Royce. Sondra was at his side laughing, drink in one hand, touching his arm with the other.

They looked like a magazine couple, perfectly groomed, socially elite, and much too intimate for my liking. I scanned the room for Tasha and caught Mark and Marjie standing companionably by the windows overlooking the shore. Tasha wasn't a part of the mirthful group. I finally picked up her sun-streaked hair—*naturally* sun streaked, take *that,* Sondra, with your over-processed highlights—nodding at something Kitty Simcock was saying. The two of them sat together on the sofa in front of the massive stone fireplace, chatting like magpies. As I watched, the petite, older woman leaned closer, touched her head to Tasha's, and they laughed together like co-conspirators.

I quickly looked up and met Hillary's sharp gaze. "Exactly," she said.

I wasn't exactly sure what she meant by that. "She's always had a good way with people," I said carefully.

The tension in her grip never eased. I wondered if she was going for a pin in arm wrestling and was ready to shake off the contact when I felt Jason's gentle pressure on my other arm in support. "She's a charmer, just like her aunt," he piped up.

I knew he was only trying to help. "I pray she and Dalton will find their way." I was tiptoeing through the minefield of my true feelings about her son and the wedding. "It's their life and they must make their own decisions."

"That's always been my viewpoint since Dalton was a toddler." Hillary finally released my wrist. "But I thought you'd have a different outlook on the matter." The group stood as Joan announced dinner.

"I didn't have that view when Tasha was a toddler, but I like to think both she and I have grown into it," I said. "I did my best, along with many others, to guide her as a child. Now she's matured into a thoughtful, responsible adult capable of making her own decisions."

"We'll see." The words, and a subtle expensive scent, trailed after her as Jason and I followed Hillary and the other guests into the dining room.

Jason hung back at the doorway. "You might want to watch your step," he murmured in my ear.

"What do you mean?" I knew what he meant.

"You sometimes tend to get . . ." He paused and hummed in his throat, a tic he'd possessed ever since I'd known him. It was also a tell that preceded a time of indecision and nerves to those who knew him well. "How should I say this? Overly zealous when it comes to defending your students and, uh, any of your kids, especially your nieces and nephews."

"Point taken." I marched in to take the chair opposite Hillary. I smiled across the table, feeling more in tune with her than with my long-time friend.

Chapter Thirteen

The salad, grilled veggies, rolls, scalloped oysters, and spicy swordfish steaks with some sort of cucumber-cumin concoction, combined with the fine china and crystal, made for an opulent meal. I spent my time chewing each bite twenty-seven times so I wouldn't be tempted to speak without thinking. I had a feeling Hillary was practicing the same restraint, although I wasn't sure she was actively using silent prayer as I was. One thing was obvious: Dalton didn't share his mother's reticence. He was alternately complimenting his hostess on everything from the Americana wallpaper to the zucchini, while talking yachts with the men, including Jason. I had to hand it to him: the young man was good at juggling several conversations at once.

I hazarded a few sidelong glances down the table at Tasha. She still seemed most involved conversationally with Kitty Simcock, but once I caught her responding to something Sondra had said. By dessert I'd begun to relax. Royce toasted the engaged couple with sincere words for their future happiness together. The meal was over and everyone pushed back from the table; I'd kept my comments isolated to the food, the Ellingsfords' beautiful summer home, and the island. I was feeling good about myself, always a danger.

"Why don't we retire to the patio?" Joan said. "The fireworks should be starting soon." Truer words were never spoken.

An oblivious Jason, engrossed in boat talk with Les, trailed out of the room with the men. Hillary, Marjie, Mark, and the Ellingsfords followed. Dalton grabbed Tasha's hand and they slipped quickly past me.

A tentative hand on my sleeve stopped me when I would've followed. I turned and faced the graceful, serene presence of Kitty. Her white hair framed her cheerful face in a thick, elegant pageboy, making her appear more like a garden sprite than a socialite. "Gwen." Her voice was low and raspy. I bent closer, suddenly understanding my niece's attentive posture. "Your Tasha is such a delightful young woman. I just wanted to let you know how much I've enjoyed her company tonight."

"Thank you." I felt warmed by this tiny woman's personality.

"I understand she's a nurse. What a lovely choice she's made; a perfect fit for her compassionate nature. I thank you for sharing her with me tonight. I've had a wonderful time, and I hope to see you both again." As she spoke, her husband returned with a sweater and gently draped it around his wife's shoulders. "Fireworks are for the young."

"And young at heart." I smiled.

"Yes," Kitty agreed. "But my heart's had more than enough excitement for one night. This'll wear me out for two or three days, but I'll bounce back. If you're down this way again, you and Tasha drop in and see us."

"You'd be more than welcome," Mark added. "Good night, now."

I watched him support her weight as they slowly left the room, stopping at the door to say their farewells to Joan and Royce. I slipped out of the dining room and wandered toward the back of the house, my head in a small cloud of wistful euphoria spilt over from the elderly couple's ordinary act of devotion.

I entered a sort of day room/library and suddenly realized I hadn't a clue where I was going. I hadn't been aware the rambling house was so large. I decided to wait a moment before I returned to the living room to give the Simcocks time to take their leave.

The old oak paneling and cranberry-flecked wallpaper could have made for a dark room, save for two spacious, old-fashioned bay windows complete with window seats. I couldn't stop from tiptoeing in and testing out the cushioned bench. I closed my eyes for a moment, tucked in the corner, the drape partially blocking the real world. I imagined the luxury of the rain drumming down the window pane as I sat inside reading a can't-put-down novel while savoring the bittersweet of dark chocolate melting on my tongue.

"What are you doing?" My eyes snapped open at Dalton's low, belligerent voice. "I could get more support from your aunt's stray cat."

"What do you mean?" Tasha's voice wasn't angry, but it was defensive.

I glanced toward the open door. I could see the outline of Dalton's head and hand as he leaned against the door frame backlit by the hall light. His shadow lightly fell onto the Oriental carpet before blending with the dimness of the room. I couldn't see Tasha, but I could tell from his posture that she faced him across the open doorway. Like armed guards, they blocked my escape.

"Come off it, you know what I mean! You spent all your time talking with that old woman. I didn't bring you here to practice geriatric nursing!"

"I was just being nice."

"Polite is one thing. Hiding in the corner like a mouse is another. You want to be an Old Maid like your aunt, be my guest. You want to be Mrs. Dalton Madison, start acting like it."

My jaw dropped open and I nearly bolted to my feet, but Tasha's wheedling tone stopped me. "I'm sorry. I wasn't thinking. What should I do?"

I grabbed the drape and strangled the life out of the heavy material.

"Try to act like an intelligent woman. Show some class, like Sondra."

"Okay."

"I know you can do it, Babe. I'm sorry if I came down as a heavy. I'm just . . . well . . . you know." He leaned across and, in the sucking silence, kissed my niece. "This is a big deal for me; for us."

"I won't spoil it; I promise," Tasha whispered, and I strained to catch the words.

"I know you won't, Babe. I'm counting on you to make Old Royce's head spin. He likes you already. All you have to do is chat him up and follow my lead. He'll see us as a can't-lose, young professional team." He chuckled low in his throat.

"I won't let you down. I'm going to the ladies' room to freshen up. I'll meet you on the patio."

"Don't be long." Another kiss and the brute was gone.

Tasha stepped inside the room and let out a shuddering sigh. This was none of my business. At best, I was an unintentional eavesdropper. At worst, I could become an interfering, nosy relative.

I didn't think twice; I chose the worst. "Tasha?" I stepped out from the shadowed seat.

"Auntie?" Tasha sniffed and sucked the waver out of her voice. "What are you doing in here?"

"I honestly lost my way and I overheard you."

"It's not what you think."

"No; I'm sure it's not." I should've left it at that and left, minding my own beeswax, but I couldn't. "Are you all right?"

"Why wouldn't I be? Dalton just wants what's best for us."

"What's best for Dalton, you mean." I said it as gently as

anyone could when delivering the equivalent of a sledgehammer comment.

"Aunt Gwen, that's just like you! You're . . . well, you're you, and I'm not! Don't expect me to be!"

She bolted into the hall but I caught her arm; there seemed to be a lot of that going on here tonight. "I only want you to be happy," I argued. "Not just for this moment, but happily ever after."

"No, you don't," she said. "You want me to be just like you, just like Dalton said. Stay out of it. Leave Dalton *and* me alone!"

My hand fell away from her as if she'd chopped it off. Blinking back tears, I silently skirted past her and rushed out to the bright lights of the living room. The Simcocks were still there with Joan and Royce. I sent up a sigh of gratitude and joined them. "I've had a wonderful time," I said. "But I wonder if I might hitch a ride with you to Coveside. I've developed a monster headache."

"Oh." Joan was instantly sympathetic.

"It happens sometimes. I just need to lie down in the dark. I don't want to ruin the festivities for the rest of you." It was the absolute truth. The dammed-up tears were pounding in my brain. I needed to be alone, to blubber and pray and hurt.

"We'd be glad to take you home, Gwen," Kitty offered.

"Thank you so much."

The blanket comment and my ailment made for an easy escape. On the quiet ride to town, I felt a twinge of guilt at abandoning ship like a rat. When the lights of Coveside came into view, the guilty conscience had superseded the headache. As Mark pulled up to the stop sign, I spied the doctor's house, the soft glow of his kitchen light spilling out golden into the dark night. I needed a friend and a listening ear.

"I'll get out here," I said.

"Oh, no," Mark said. "We're happy to take you all the way home."

"It's not out of our way," Kitty agreed.

"You're too kind." I attempted a laugh. "No one lives on Blind Man's Bluff."

"We actually live down on Faraday's Mistake," Mark said. At the name, my ears pricked up like a dog hearing the refrigerator door open. Another sad note in my recent relationship blues of friends and relatives.

"I appreciate your generosity, but I'd like to stop in and see Dr. Beckett. He's a good friend, and I feel he might have something that would help me."

"Doug's salt of the earth." Mark eased the car through the intersection and pulled up beside the doctor's house.

"Would you like us to wait for you, dear?" Kitty asked.

"No; I'll be fine, but thank you for everything. I hope we can get together again sometime."

"We'll be good friends. You and me and Tasha. The sisterhood. Three generations of women of faith and substance."

I was getting out of the backseat and I stared at the small, white-haired, gentle woman, her head haloed in the car light. Mark laughed and patted his wife's shoulder. "Kitty's got a sense about these things."

"And we'll let Mark join us once in awhile," Kitty said. "If he behaves himself."

"Definitely," I agreed. "I look forward to it. Good night, and thanks again."

I stood at the edge of the doctor's lawn and waved as they drove away, feeling a tiny bubble of joy lift my sagging spirits. As their taillights disappeared around the corner, the light behind me winked out.

I turned toward the dark house and chuckled. *So much for my plans.* ". . . 'If the Lord will, we shall live, and do this, or that,' "

I murmured as I slowly walked down the road. My feet took me toward the ferry landing. I couldn't for the life of me say why I was wandering the streets of Coveside at nine thirty at night. I would've been better engaged in putting some mileage under my sandals on the long trek up to Vance's house. Then I heard it—music, rough and lilting, rolling in with the waves, calling me forward.

I detoured toward the sound, and the strains of *God Bless America* grew with each step. I crossed the boulder-rimmed parking lot and saw sparks shooting up just as the first pink-and-green burst of roman candles exploded over my head. With the booming echoes over the water, I flicked a glance at the fireworks display before picking my way down to the bonfire on the beach.

When I hit the narrow band of sand, I kicked off my sandals and, as I stooped to pick them up, a familiar voice hailed me. "Gwen!" Sledge left his driftwood log seat by the fire and hurried over.

"Was that you playing?" I inclined my head toward the guitar propped against the circle of logs.

He nodded, grinning sheepishly. "Don't quit my day job, huh?" He looked as much a part of the atmosphere as the beach under his bare feet. Sledge Knox, the doctor's protégé and a good man with no need to impress others or to pretend to be anyone but himself. If only Dalton . . .

I buried the thought and focused on the perfect surprise God had prepared for me this moment. "Are you kidding? I thought it sounded great, but I just got here. Is the show over?"

"It's only begun." He pointed at the golden burst flowering over the water.

"I meant the singing."

"I know." He shrugged. "I usually put a lid on it while the fireworks are going; give them center stage. After all, it's their night and a once-a-year celebration." He nodded toward the group of folks standing at the water's edge, gawking at the night sky. He took my hand and walked me to the bonfire. Still favoring the Hawaiian shirt and khaki shorts, his blond hair and tan fit so naturally with the island night. But I saw the strength of character shining in his steady, hazel gaze and felt the rock-solid steadfastness emanating from his gentle touch.

The wind came off the water, carrying a damp nip and the promise of fog. The snap of the flames and the heat felt good, radiating through my chilled arms, but not enough to banish the chill that had settled in my heart.

Like a gentleman of the first order, Sledge offered me a seat next to the guitar. He sat down beside me with a low whistle. "You're dressed for the party."

"Oh, yeah."

"You look beautiful," he said. "How'd it go? Is Tasha with you?" I smiled at his compliment as his eyes darted back toward the landing.

"I took off early with a headache."

"Oh, I'm sorry. Would you like me to take you home?"

"No; actually I think you just cured it." He grinned, his teeth gleaming in the firelight. "As for Tasha, she's . . ."

"Hanging out with Dalton and his crowd," Sledge supplied without censure. "She's . . ."

My turn. "Making a big mistake."

"I was going to say 'fantastic,' " he said. "But you said what I was thinking. I guess you should know I'm falling for her. I know it's a head-over-heels thing and doesn't make any sense. She's taken. I've only known her a few days. At least that's what I tell myself a hundred million times a day, but I guess my head's too thick. I'm not getting through, because I can't stop thinking about her. I don't want to sound like a home wrecker, but I'm praying it's not too late."

"I'll say Amen to that," I said. "With both of us praying for her, I'm feeling better by the second."

"Really?" His voice held a trace of Ron's uncertainty. "Feel like singing?" He reached over and retrieved the guitar. "Tasha said you have a great voice."

"Ha! She's been known to exaggerate." I hoped my argument with my niece was Tasha's exaggeration of stress and not the blurting of heartfelt truth.

Sledge didn't give me time to sink back into melancholy. He plucked the strings as the fireworks exploded, drawing my sadness out and letting it wander its way into the mellow joy of this moment.

Oh Danny boy, the pipes, the pipes are calling, from glen to glen and down the mountainside. Our voices blended as if we'd sung together for a lifetime. Sledge's baritone, poignant and healing, wrapped us in our own private world. For me, that cozy world was my parents' crowded living room where I'd gathered around the piano singing gospel with Mom, Dad, my brothers, and, later, expanding to include my sisters-in-law, nieces, and nephews. The slosh of the waves, the crackle of the fire, and the island pulse under the soles of my feet buried in the sand vibrated a rhythm of home into my soul.

I was vaguely aware of others migrating back to the circle of light, of the hush, of the stars above as bright as Christmas lights now that the fireworks had ceased. As the last note died, I felt a longing and a belonging. I shook my head at my muddled thoughts. Obviously if I felt like I belonged here, why would I feel a longing to belong?

I looked through the fire and Scotty's eyes met mine through the wavering light. I swallowed hard, my throat that had been filled with liquid notes now clogged with emotional sand. The connection shattered as Dot appeared beside him. He turned away, leading his cousin a short distance down the beach. They stopped, heads nearly touching. Dot's hands thrust out like an air-traffic controller and I thought of Ron.

Sledge struck a chord and the crowd began to sing a patriotic standard.

"Rather hear you than this howlin' bunch of coyotes." Old Stin glowered down at the young doctor, his sharp, weathered features giving him the fierce appearance of a proud, disgruntled eagle.

Sledge grinned and rose, still strumming, and made way for the older man. I held out a hand to help him down. He ignored it and remained standing. I got to my feet and grabbed his hand. "Hello," I said. "Did you have a nice picnic?"

"Can't hear you with all this caterwaulin'." We threaded through the gathering and meandered down to the water. The damp of the ocean goose-bumped my arms.

I looked at my companion in his sweatshirt and cap, wind ruffling his shaggy mop. His bony hand was warm in mine. "Did you have a nice picnic?" I asked.

"Naw. Doug needed to get back home so we cut it short. Say!" He looked me up and down with a keen eye. "We're goin' out on the boat tomorrow. I told Doug we'd try again and do a little handlinin'; you wanna come?"

"I don't know."

"You told me you'd take a raincheck. What's the matter with tomorrow? You goin' on that fancy barge again?"

"No; I don't imagine I'll be going on that fancy barge anytime soon."

"Made you walk the plank, did they?" He let out a bark of laughter.

"Something like that."

He squeezed my hand and his next words were filled with a gruff kindness that brought tears to my eyes. "Well, no matter. They ain't worth a grain of sand on this beach. I could tell just by lookin'. Doug and I'll show you the *real* island, includin' the Scotts' secret fishin' hole, but I'll have to swear you to complete and utter secrecy first. Deal?"

"Mum's the word." I was rewarded by another quick squeeze of the hand.

"Hope I'm not interrupting." Scotty's slow, deep voice at our backs startled us both, sending warm shivers up my chilled arms.

"No, you don't," Old Stin retorted. "Looks as if the fun's over 'til tomorrow, Gwen."

"Did I miss something?" Young Stin came and stood beside me. I could see only one side of his face in the darkness. The flickering firelight played over the severe planes, capturing a manufactured innocent air. The man could be a Shakespearean actor.

"Time to go home," Old Stin announced. "I got a big day tomorrow."

"Fine; can we give you a lift, Miss McPhail?" Scotty asked.

I was tempted to refuse, but the old man holding my hand tempered my need for an argument. "I'd appreciate that."

"Good; you ride in the middle." Old Stin towed me up the beach to the parking lot. "That way I won't hafta listen to Young Stin's lecture."

We rode down narrow, twisting roads, something I was getting more comfortable with as each day passed. I wondered if I was developing Dalton's affliction as I knew the urge to drive over every little dirt lane and learn the lay of the island by heart. Tonight the excursion ended after winding along the dark shore and taking three turnoffs before stopping in front of a little red cape. The truck lights picked up the fresh paint job and the Spartan yard. "You wanna come in for a cuppa coffee?" Old Stin asked.

I felt the man at the wheel stiffen, though he wasn't touching me. It was more of a tightening of the atmosphere in the cab. "Maybe some other time. I need to get to bed so I can be sharp tomorrow."

Old Stin snorted. "Another raincheck. I'll send Doug for you 'bout nine. We'll catch the tide." Scotty had gotten out and held the door open for his grandfather. "Ever notice how some people are in a awful hurry to get nowhere?" the old man said. "No need to deck yourself out tomorrow, but I sure do appreciate the view tonight. Tomorrow's just friends fishin,' nothin' fancy."

"I'm looking forward to it. Good night."

Old and Young Stin exchanged a few gruff words on their way to the house. The inside light switched on and Scotty was back in the cab, reversing without a word. The silence lengthened over the distance to Blind Man's Bluff. I saw Dot's kitchen light was on as we rode past her house, Ron's truck in the driveway.

"I guess Dot found a ride home," I said.

"Ron came to the bonfire with Laurel, said they needed to talk to her; it couldn't wait. He was more worked up than usual, and that's saying something because Ron's always in a state."

"Ah."

He sped up the hill, drove the truck to the backside of the garage, and cut the spluttering engine. "What's that supposed to mean?"

"Nothing. I hope it all works out." I said a quick prayer for Ron.

"You know something." His voice and gaze were sharp as a first-day-back-to-school number-two pencil. "What happened?"

I slid over to the door, suddenly embarrassed that I hadn't thought to do so as soon as we dropped off Old Stin. "I'd better call it a night."

"Oh, no, you don't," he said. "You accuse me of stealing—"

"I never—"

"I was indicted by your looks. I didn't even get a chance to take the witness stand in my own defense. Your eyes sentenced me to at least fifteen-to-twenty, maybe life, for a telescope. No jury, no trial, no parole."

"I didn't!"

"Oh, yes, you did. And you and Doug Beckett got something going on. He was itching to conspire with you so bad he kicked me out of his place like a stray dog with fleas."

"I didn't notice."

"Oh, yeah, right, and I'm supposed to believe that, Miss Nose? You notice everything. You and the doctor plotting together—not a good idea. Whatever you've concocted, it's got bad weather written all over it. Ron brings you back from the doctor's acting weirder than a gull at a crow convention. I don't know what you're up to, but we're going to sit here all night until I find out."

"Is this the moment of truth, then? Or is it the moment before the moment of truth?" My voice got smaller. The humor I'd intended fell flat at the import of what might happen next. I wanted to forget about my suspicions, but he had his own. The cab was thick with unspoken questions and it was time to clear the air or suffocate.

"You tell me."

"Okay." I was tired. Tired of skirting the issue, tired of secrets and sorrow and sickness, but I couldn't break my promise to Ron. I went back to the one problem that affected all the others. "How do you know Vance fell off the cliff?"

"This isn't what I had in mind."

"I know, but I need to understand."

"Why is it important, especially to you? You didn't even know him." He leaned toward me in the cab, his voice terse and commanding. "Vance is dead, period. Leave it be."

"I can't. Before I even knew you, or anybody on Candle Island, I was a part of this. I got a midnight phone call one night. Dot accusing me of all sorts of evil doings."

"What?"

"Nothing. I wouldn't be here if Vance wasn't dead." I sighed. How could I make him understand without betraying confidences? "And we need the truth in order to set things right."

"You mean *you* need the truth. Everyone else is fine. He's buried. It's over."

"No, it isn't over. People are suffering because they don't know what really happened. They need to know."

"Okay, you asked for the moment of truth. Only God knows the truth. This is the moment after that moment. I found his body. Is that what you need to know? One man is dead, good or bad, only God can judge. Don't poke around and ruin all the other good lives on this island. Stay out of it!" He sat back, the cab stuffy with his suppressed frustration and my trampled feelings.

First Tasha, now Scotty. "Go back where I belong, to my old life on the mainland."

"You were the one who insisted on giving Dot back her house. You came in here like Amelia Earhart—"

"What?"

"You made it pretty clear you were just passing through; you weren't here for the long haul. It's for the best, really. You have a home. A life. A family. You've got Jason what's-his-name." His voice sounded as weary as I felt.

"Boudreau."

"Whatever. The point is, a few days of vacation on the Titanic isn't any reason to go down with the ship. Get in the lifeboat while you can."

Chapter Fourteen

I rose early feeling like I'd spent all night bailing on the sinking Titanic. Tasha was on the back deck, huddled in Dalton's fleece pullover, watching the sun peep over the ocean. Tiny threads of fog rising off the trees caught the golden gleam as they spiraled upward to disappear in the lightening sky.

I quietly let myself and a crazed Purry Mason out of the house. The cat bolted across the lawn, insanely happy to be free. I slipped over beside my niece and pretended to watch the sunrise. "Pretty," I murmured. She didn't move.

We were too much alike, and part of that was my fault. Over the years I'd encouraged her to be a strong, independent-minded woman. She didn't need my approval or my condemnation; she needed my love and understanding. I thought of Kitty and her comment about us being women of substance and faith. The memory brought a smile. "I'm sorry about last night."

"You don't look sorry." Tasha's voice was barely above a whisper.

"I am. I was just thinking of Kitty. I hitched a ride with the Simcocks. They're such extraordinary people. I fell in love with them."

"Me, too." A trace of a smile graced Tasha's solemn face.

"It's mutual, you know. Kitty loves you."

Tasha nodded and I saw the glitter of unshed tears in her eyes. "Do you think Dalton and I will be like them?"

I chewed on my upper lip, praying for wisdom. "I think once

you set your mind to something you can make it work, and that definitely includes your marriage to Dalton."

"You didn't answer the question."

She gripped my wrist, nothing like Hillary's arm-wrestling technique. It reminded me of the time we were hiking the Beehive and she clung to me, afraid of falling. I was able to assure her back when she was nine, but now? "I don't know," I said. "You could have fifty wonderful years together and be more in love at seventy-six than you are now. Only God knows that." I paused, battling all my natural instincts.

"Say it."

"You can't be responsible for anyone else's happiness; not mine, not Dalton's, not Hillary's. You can't make people change, or even expect them to change. It's not fair to them or to you."

She nodded and her grip slackened. She threaded her fingers through mine and held on to my hand, her grip warm and steady. "I know. I'm sorry for what I said last night. I didn't mean it."

"Thank you, but I understand. You were right. You're an adult, more than capable of making your own decisions. I don't want to be an interfering busybody old biddy you constantly avoid. I want us to stay close, and I want you to be happy. It's your life."

"Yes, it is. And last night I was ready to leave Candle Island. I thought I could slide back into my old life, you know? I thought if I could just focus on preparing for the wedding, period, not bother to look ahead . . ."

"Ostrich-head-in-the-sand moment? I've been there, except for the preparing for the wedding part," I confessed.

"What about Jason?"

I sighed. "Right now I seem to have the problem of looking too far ahead, straining to see the future. I don't see myself with him in that way, ever."

"It's this island." Tasha lightly thumped the rail of the deck with our clasped fist. "It's—I don't know how to describe it, but I can't shake the feeling God brought me here to shake me up, and now I know I can't go back to how things used to be. I'm going to talk to Dalton this morning. I'm not sure what'll happen."

"Well, I'll be praying for you, and you can pray for me. I guess I need to talk with Jason."

"No need."

I dropped Tasha's hand and spun around, mouth agape, eyes glazed like a dead fish. "Jason!"

"It's all right, Gwen. I got the hint when you left the Ellingsfords last night without telling me." Tasha slipped down the steps and disappeared around the corner of the mansion.

"I'm so sorry. Tasha and I had an argument. I didn't think."

His puppy-dog brown eyes were filled with soft reproach. "That's just it. You don't think of 'us.' " He air quoted the pronoun. "You're too used to doing everything on your own."

"You're absolutely right. I'm too set in my ways. I *am* sorry," I said. "You're a dear friend, but I know that's not what you want from me. I didn't mean to lead you on."

"You've always kept me at arm's length," he said, his voice bitter. "I thought it would be different here. I guess I was wrong. Would you mind giving me a ride to the ferry? I was going to ask Dalton, but it seems he has similar problems."

I nodded. "Let's have some breakfast and talk. We've always been good friends who could talk about anything."

His thin lips compressed until they disappeared into a white line. "Some other time, if you don't mind. When you come back to Bookerton, we'll talk. Right now I'd just like to go home."

I appropriated Dalton's SUV without permission and endured the awkward ride with Jason to the ferry landing. With that behind me and concern over Tasha's talk with Dalton hovering over me, I wasn't in the best frame of mind when I returned to the kitchen to find Hillary at the counter sectioning grapefruit.

"Headache better?" she asked.

"Somewhat." The morning's stress was already pounding and my guest's question added to the hammering. "It was a lovely dinner. I'm sorry I had to cut it short, but I didn't want to ruin the celebration."

"That's what Joan said." She fixed me with a pin-your-ears-back truth-or-dare stare.

"You would've made a good teacher." I smiled.

"Please! Two of my own was plenty. I'd never want to take on any others."

"Meaning Tasha." In the morning light Hillary was still a fine-looking woman, much finer than I'd be when I reached her age. She stood before me without makeup, showing the slight lines of worry around her mouth, the beginning stripe of gray at the part of her professionally sun-streaked hair, and the slight crow's-feet from years of laughter, tears, and vigilance—her badge of motherhood.

"Tasha." She shook her head. "I admire her. She's extremely bright, committed, and selfless. I thought she'd be perfect for Dalton, so much more substance than the Sondra Ellingsfords he's attached himself to in the past. He *is* a good man, you know, basically."

"I'm sure."

"No you're not. You never have been. You and I can be honest with each other, Gwen. We see the same thing, only from different vantage points."

She was being tactful, but I could see the strain it exacted in the way she slashed through the grapefruit rind.

"Perhaps," I agreed. "But ultimately it's their decision."

"If I told you I can see Tasha ten years from now, compromising her principles a little more each year because Dalton will expect her to conform to his lifestyle and she'll never quite measure up in his world, what would you do? She won't have the privileged background or the conditioning of private school to help her. And she doesn't have the desire for social position that's necessary for her self-preservation. I know. I've been Tasha."

"I'll pray for both of them," I said. The shutters came down over her beseeching eyes and her face took on a bored facade. "I know what you're saying, and last night I felt like you do now. In fact, Tasha and I had a few words. This morning I think the future looks brighter for both of our children. I wouldn't worry, Hillary."

"You got all this calm from a prayer?"

"Yes, and Tasha talked with me this morning. She'd basically come to the same conclusion you and I have."

Hillary dropped the knife with a clatter, turned, and leaned against the counter, her arms folded across her chest. Her eyes were bright, no longer wary.

"She's going to have a talk with Dalton. I'm not sure what'll transpire, but I know Tasha. She'll stick with it until they get it thrashed out."

"I'm glad I got to know you, Gwen. I would've enjoyed hanging out with you at family functions, had their marriage worked out, but this is for the best."

"You don't know that they'll split up," I said. "They may come to an understanding." But my brain wondered why I was voicing dissent.

"Dalton wants his own way, period. He can be, and has been, manipulated by conniving women, but Tasha is neither conniving nor manipulative; simply honest. Honesty is something my son has trouble facing in anyone, particularly himself. He's not mature enough to handle any real emotional issues."

I raised my brows at her brutal assessment of her youngest child.

She laughed. "What kind of mother would I be if I didn't know my own children? Trust me; it's for the best."

Her words echoed Scotty's and stayed with me through the polite breakfast table talk. Dalton and Tasha were no-shows, but we heard the frontispiece door click shut, and a few minutes later the SUV left.

Hillary was more than content to be left on her own with her cell as I hustled into jeans, pink t-shirt, and a yellow Candle Island cap I'd found hanging in the closet. I couldn't bear the confines of Vance's house any longer. I felt like the cooped up Purry Mason as I busted out of the mansion and trotted down the road. Ironically, I met the doctor creeping along just as I fast-walked past Dot's house.

The driveway was empty and Doug's car turned in. I jumped out of its path, then scrambled in, but he just sat there, engine idling. "Shouldn't we be going?" I glanced at the snug house. A curtain moved at the window. "We don't want to keep Old Stin waiting."

"He's been up since four; he can wait a little longer. Since when are you such a Nervous Nellie?"

"I don't think Dot would appreciate us lurking in her driveway. She and I haven't exactly become best friends yet."

My companion let out a gravel-choked chuckle and backed into the road without looking. I swiveled my head around enough for both of us. There was no traffic on the private road, but I kept a sharp eye out for a certain dark-blue beater truck or a shiny SUV with a needy niece inside.

After the holiday festivities of last night, the island folk appeared to have gone into hiding. We passed only a handful of cars as we swung onto a road Dalton had missed on his island tour the other day. Doug slowed the car to a dying snail's pace, rested his arms on the wheel, and turned to face me. "I guess Ron told you the good news."

"About his marriage? Yes." I was careful not to betray any confidences.

"No, about Laurel's pregnancy."

"Ah, yes; I'm happy for them."

"Let's hope you're not the only one."

"Surely Dot will be happy. I mean, Ron is her only son."

"And she wants him all to herself." The doctor turned down a steep dirt road without taking his eyes off me.

I glued my eyes to the windshield for him; I thought one of us should. The front wheels slid on the gravel and the old, heavy sedan picked up speed. The ocean loomed over the hood of the car, stealing away the import of his words over more pressing life-and-death concerns. "I hope your brakes are good!" My eyes bugged out.

The doctor scowled at me, ignoring the water world in front of us. "I feel responsible. When Ron came to me for advice, I encouraged them to get married. They wanted to start a family; it was only right. But, wouldn't you know it, they went ahead and eloped just when Old Vance got it in his head to fire Frank from the boatyard. Never met a boy who had worse timing than Ron."

He yanked the wheel to the left and my noggin snapped like a bobble-head doll as he stomped on the brakes and killed the engine. Suddenly gawking at a bunch of spruce and rocks, terra firma, I could once again breathe and focus on listening. The doctor continued the conversation without missing a beat. "I was surprised he hired Frank in the first place, with all that bad blood between them. Did it just so he could cut him off at the knees six months later, if you ask me. Vance called it a work slowdown—last-hired, first-fired—except he kept on Tinn Jones.

Tinn'd only been working there a month, so that didn't hold water."

"So Ron and Laurel didn't tell anyone?" I tried to bring him back to the subject of interest.

"Not a soul, until you came along. I advised them to hold off and not tell Vance or Frank until things cooled off, but Vance and Ron got into it over Laurel." He hesitated, pulled on his chin. "Only time Ron stood up to Vance in his life. Usually the boy would get so frustrated he'd tie his tongue in a double knot and that's all Vance would need to bring him down another peg."

I nodded. "What happened?"

"Vance lost it; disowned him."

A sharp rap tattooed on the window next to my ear. I jumped a mile, or at least enough for my hat to brush the ceiling of the car. I cranked my head around to see Old Stin's face leering in at me, his raucous laugh steaming the glass. He opened the door and, reminiscent of his grandson, extended his hand to help me from the vehicle; probably a good idea, considering the whiplash I'd suffered from the drive over.

"Whatcha doin' in there, recitin' the Constitution of the United States?"

"Just chewing the fat." Doug stopped by my side. He'd obviously gotten out and around the car in a flash. I blinked at his sudden burst of energy. He shot me a quelling look. "Talking about church and whatnot, weren't we, Gwen."

All that was missing was the wink on the sly. I smiled; the doctor was a dear, but not a natural when it came to subterfuge. "I was just thinking about how much I enjoyed the bonfire last night, and how much I'm looking forward to this morning's boat ride." I was rewarded by both men's grins.

They each took an arm and we paraded down to the town wharf. I felt a little overwhelmed by the gentlemanly attention, praying that neither of my older companions would fall into the drink while helping me aboard.

Doug cast off while Old Stin started the engine and pulled us away from the roiling clouds of black smoke. The doctor sat down heavily on the stern seat as we chugged out of the cove. "Are you all right?" I asked.

"Just the smoke getting to me. Engine'll warm up and I'll be fine in a few minutes."

"Gwen, come up here!" Old Stin demanded. I stepped into the pilothouse and he beckoned me to the wheel. "You ever driven a boat before?"

"Only toy ships and sailboats, canoes, rowboats, and kayaks on lakes," I said. "I've never driven a real ocean-going craft."

He gave a pleased chuckle. "Well, come on, then. You can take us out around the island."

"I don't know if that's a good idea, if you value your boat. What if I bottom out on a rock at low tide?"

"I won't let ya. Besides, it's near high tide now. Give 'er a go. You'll like it."

I raised my eyebrows but let him guide my hand placement on the ship's wheel. He stood beside me like a proud, vigilant parent, but it was clear he wasn't the hovering type. "That's it. Give yourself time to get the feel of 'er. We're in deep water here, nothin' to navigate 'til we round McMahan Point, named for one of your great-great-grandfathers." He nudged my arm and pointed at the approaching headland.

I smiled. "Careful, you'll knock me off course and next thing you know we'll be landing in Normandy. How's your French?"

Old Stin let out a snort of laughter. "Never happen with you at the helm. Told you before: it's in your island blood."

We rounded a beautiful point, dark spruce meandering down to huge ledges shining gray, bits of yellow lichen catching the morning sun. As I watched, an eagle soared by and perched in the crown of a tree, its head glistening white against the evergreen backdrop.

I took a deep breath, savoring the essence of sky, sea, and the old salt beside me. Island life—I wasn't sure it was in my blood, as Old Stin maintained, but I sure felt it settling in my bones, warming my spirit. It wouldn't hurt to give in to the peaceful comfort of belonging, just for a few hours.

"Give 'er a bit more throttle," my captain directed. "She can take it. Not much wash on the lee side today." I put my left hand on the stick and felt the throb of the engine. "Ease 'er up, nice and steady. That's it."

Around the point, I cruised into calmer water, the mouth of a cove; a couple of boats sat at anchor. "Faraday's Mistake," Old Stin announced, and my eyes sharpened, scanning the shoreline; a nice pebbled beach. Across the road a large weathered house with a glassed-in porch sunk into the scruffy landscape, the yard cluttered with equipment. Definitely not his style.

Old Stin pointed off toward the next headland, capturing my stray attention. "There's some sly rocks called The Notches over that way, but I'll getcha around 'em safe and sound."

"Maybe you ought to drive."

"Naw, you'll never earn first-mate status if you only take the wheel in a bathtub. We'll swing plenty wide." One of his gnarled hands rested on a spoke of the ship's wheel and he guided me firmly out to deeper water. I kept one eye on the splash of white water barely covering one of the Notches. With the other I checked out the shore, finally spotting a neat, gray-shingled, modified saltbox at the far end of the cove.

"That's Young Stin's place." He pointed an arthritic finger. "Fair amount of land, but no good moorin'. 'Course he could anchor in the cove with his neighbors, but he prefers the town dock. Just keeps a little sailboat here."

I drank in the small, pistachio-green meadow; the swaying,

ivory birches; and the alabaster gulls hollering and swooping over the ledges as the sturdy engine chugged us around another headland. "Best let me handle 'er around Mulroon."

I stepped aside. "I haven't graduated from bathtub sailor yet, huh?"

He laughed. "The tide gets a little tricky here unless you go out around Emerson Rock. We'll take the shortcut today. Don't know how long Doug's gonna last. He's lookin' white as mother's sheets on the clothesline."

"I'll go sit with him."

Old Stin nodded. "Thought you might."

A breeze caught us as we crossed the narrow gut to the other side of the island and I staggered slightly on my way to the stern. Little whitecaps kicked up, racing toward the bow and frilling the side of the boat with liquid lace. "How are you doing?" I slipped in beside the doctor.

"I'm hanging in there." He clenched his teeth.

"Why don't we head back?"

He gripped my wrist in a vise tighter than Tasha had earlier. "No; I want you to see it."

"I've seen enough of the island. We can go boating another time. Let's go back to your place and have a tea party."

My fingers went numb from his grasp. I scanned his face, now paler than mother's bleached linens, but his eyes burned with desperate fire. "We'll have our party on our own time." I bent my head closer to hear the ragged words. "Look there. Stin'll show you." He stood on unsteady legs, bringing me with him. We lurched across the slight pitch of the deck into the wheelhouse.

"This it is," Old Stin chortled.

The small boat was riding between a rock and a towering cliff. I felt like a teeny cork bobbing next to Gibraltar with the walls closing in on us. Taking his sweet time, Old Stin turned the wheel and took us past the huge rock. I gazed up, suddenly aware of my surroundings. "This is Vance's place." I craned my neck.

"Blind Man's Bluff," the captain verified. "Best fishin' is right here, just past the bulk o' that rock, but only when the tide's right. No one else knows about it."

"No one else is fool enough to come in here," the doctor said.

"Bunch o' fair-weather, fancy-pants bathtub sailors. Don't know nothin' 'bout the water, let alone navigatin'."

"That may be," Doug argued. "But you're going to run us aground if you don't back out of here."

"Can't you just go forward?" I glanced back at the narrow alley of rough water astern.

"Naw! My grandson'll do it, but it's risky. See that crevice in the cliff over there?" Old Stin took his hands off the wheel and gestured. I put out a hand to stop the wheel from spinning and he let out a bark of laughter. "I got 'er, mate. Rest easy." His hand came down on mine, strong and sure. "As I was sayin', that hole over there causes a rip in the current; not always consistent, though. Depends on the tide, the weather, the season, and the Atlantic. She always has a mind of 'er own. Never the same two times in a row. Can reach up from below and smash your boat into the cliff, or spin you around willy-nilly so you run aground on the rocks."

Rocks or cliff, it was all the same to me, and I was thankful Doug felt the same way. "You gonna show us the truth of it by crashing this tub, or what?" he asked.

"Naw; I got it all under control as usual, Doug." Old Stin put it in reverse, angled the wheel, and I let go. The boat chugged and pitched fiercely in the chop.

My hand itched to crank the throttle full out, but the old salt never touched the stick, even when the *Sea Lemon* was being sucked forward into the crevice of Blind Man's Bluff. "Doesn't look like you're in control." The doctor laughed. "It's not like we have Young Stin here to rescue us this time."

I glanced up into his tired face, wondering at the smile that had lifted the sagging jowls and momentarily erased the pain. "This time? That doesn't sound good." I tried to keep my voice light. No need to worry about their fears; both men laughed even as the boat shuddered and inched backwards. I couldn't look.

"Young Stin was in air-sea rescue, one of the best," his grandfather said. " 'Course he had a natural advantage growin' up here and navigatin' the island waters."

"Yeah, yeah, we know. You taught him everything he knows," Doug teased.

"He's still got a lot to learn," Old Stin scoffed. The edge of the Rock of Gibraltar caught my peripheral vision and, much to my amazement and answered prayer, I realized we were moving and maneuvering back out into open water. "But he *is* a decent mariner; proved it, too, with Vance, didn't he!"

"That he did." The doctor instantly sobered.

"Scotty retrieved Vance's body from here?" I'd known the bare facts, but not the rough reality of water, wind, and tide. "How could he?"

"By God's grace," Doug muttered, but Old Stin didn't hear. He had the boat backed clear into the open water and leaned back to face us in his glory as he launched into his take on the story.

"It's a wonder, all right. He was put in the right place at the right time. If he hadn'ta been here to see Vance fall, likely as not the body might'a never been found. As it was, Young Stin risked his life to pull him outta that hole, even tried to revive him, but he was broke up so bad there was no savin' him."

"Terrible sad business," the doctor murmured.

"Still, for the life of me, can't figure how Vance got down here." Old Stin gunned the throttle and pulled the boat out further, then idled it down. "Didn't jump like some folks say; not Vance. If he'da jumped, he'da done it on the upper edge and sure wouldn'ta landed here."

"What do you mean?" The old man's thoughts echoed my own.

"See that ledge up there?" He pointed near the top of the cliff face, nothing I hadn't noticed myself. "Don't look like too much from this distance, but it sticks out plenty, more'n enough to catch a jumper. Don't make sense, but don't tell Young Stin that. He don't like to talk about it. I 'magine it's 'cause he couldn't save him."

I studied the rocks, the rough striations making dark, shadowed streaks in the cliff. At the top a movement caught my eye and I stared. A man stood on the ledges, unrecognizable at this distance, or so I thought.

Old Stin ducked out of the pilothouse and waved. "Young Stin watchin' out for us."

"It's hard to tell if it's him." I wondered exactly what Scotty had seen the day Vance died. I had a sickening feeling it was more than just a body falling into the water.

"Naw; I'd recognize that stance anywhere," Old Stin said.

"Yeah; me, too." The doctor seemed to shrivel in front of my eyes. "I need to go in, Stin."

"Not a good day for handlinin' anyhow, Doug. You can tell by the direction of the wind. Sorry 'bout that, Gwen. Never can tell 'til you get out here."

"It's fine. I've enjoyed steering the boat. We'll fish another day. Come on." I took Doug's arm. "Let's sit down and enjoy the sun."

The doctor was quiet to the point of brooding on the trip to the dock. Old Stin skillfully maneuvered his craft on the direct route for our return, mindful of his friend's fragile state. Douglas Beckett might delude himself that no one realized his ailment, but he was willingly blind. His friends might not know the exact diagnosis, but they knew he was in trouble. As his newest friend, I felt it acutely, and I sensed his sorrow and stress had nothing to do with his terminal cancer. "Are you all right?" I asked.

"No," he said. "I'll never be all right."

I took his cold hand in mine and clung to it, absorbing the tremors that passed from his soul to mine. I had to help this man find peace, but first I was called to mate status to help Old Stin tie up the boat. We disembarked a shaky trio.

"Let me drive you home," I offered, and Doug nodded, dropping heavily like a sack of bones into the passenger's seat. By the time we made it to Coveside, he was grayer than a gull's wing. "Shall I call Sledge?" His dead weight crushed me as we tottered up the walk to his house.

"No; just let me rest. I'll be fine."

"I'll stay with you."

"No; you take the car and go. Come back later this afternoon with tea." He was gasping; the sound filled the small kitchen with the harsh truth.

"I can't go." My spine bowed as we progressed, one eternal, painful step at a time, to his bedroom.

I eased him onto the bed as gently as I could and removed his sneakers. Pulling a quilt over his chilled body, I sat on the edge of the bed. "That's good," he rasped. "I'll be okay in a few hours, but I won't sleep until you leave. Now go!" He gripped my hand. "And bring me back some good news and some raspberry tea." The ghost of his smile gave me the strength to stand on my rubber-made legs and trudge to the car.

Chapter Fifteen

I felt like I'd inherited the doctor's dubious driving skills, or maybe it was just the old boat of a car, but I spun gravel out of his driveway as I raced to the clinic. Sledge saw me immediately—one more treasure of island life that had disappeared from the rest of the medical world.

"So, what do you think?" I asked after spilling my concerns like an overturned rain barrel.

Sledge nodded and scratched his blond hair, looking like sleepy Michael Bodour who constantly raised his hand, then, when I called on him, invariably scratched his head waiting for the answer to surface. I had a feeling this young man had been wide awake twenty-four/seven from the obstetrician's first slap. "I know he's fighting a losing battle, but there's no medical help for him. He's in the best place spiritually, and he's ready to go."

"Maybe. I mean, I know he's prepared to be with the Lord, but he's not at peace. I think it has something to do with Vance's death. I want to help him."

Sledge nodded again. My liking for this kind man, who was slow to speak and quick to listen, deepened. "I don't know if this is a violation of doctor/patient confidentiality, but I need to ask. Was Vance seeking any off-island treatment for his cancer?"

Intelligent eyes locked onto mine, their granite intensity as solid as the island cliffs. The light gaze narrowed and his broad brow furrowed. "What makes you think he had cancer?"

"Quid pro quo, eh?" I quipped. Unlike the young doctor,

when I should keep my mouth shut, I usually babble while my brain scrambles for the right answer. "I found something personal to that effect in a book he'd been reading." I clamped my lips shut, unable to say more.

To my surprise Sledge smiled and nodded. "It makes sense. He came to my house about a week before he died, pounding on the door, demanding an immediate and complete physical, then and there. No clinic visit, no paperwork. He wanted me to submit the blood work under my name."

"Did you do it?"

Sledge sighed. "I gave him the physical, yes, but I put the blood work under his own name. I wasn't about to go behind anyone's back."

"When did he get the test results?"

"The day before he died," Sledge admitted. "You think the timing has something to do with his death; what is it?"

"I can't say right now." The facts buzzed around in my head like angry bees and I didn't like how they were swarming.

Obviously Sledge was busy doing the math, too. "Understood." There was that solid and steady character again, supporting without trying to control or interfere. Truly a man of grace. I smiled at the small anchor of peace God had provided in the maelstrom of my suspicions. "What do you need from me?"

"Two things," I said. "Could you check in on Dr. Beckett and make it seem like a coincidence?"

"Sure thing. I need to ask his opinion on a tricky diagnosis anyway." He grinned. "I imagine the second thing might be more difficult."

"Not at all. Just one question. Purely hypothetical."

"Ach! Those are the worst kind, but I'll do what I can; fire away."

"If I were Iron Man Vance Jones and had just gotten a clean

bill of health, would I go jump off a cliff?"

Those steady eyes never blinked, and his face was as grave as Mount Rushmore. "It would surprise me if you did."

I nodded sadly. "Thanks. I'd better go so you can check on Doug."

"Okay." His large hand clasped mine. "No matter what it is, God'll work it out. I'll talk to you later."

I drove the big car slowly down the narrow island roads, creeping toward the truth. I passed Dot's place. She, Ron, and Laurel were sitting in the peeling, green Adirondack chairs on the side lawn. For once Ron was sitting still, holding Laurel's hand; with the other he gave a casual island wave as I went by. They looked like the average family relaxing together on a carefree summer day. How long would it last? Having just found their peace, I felt sick at the thought I was the one who could shatter their fragile family very soon.

I took my foot off the gas to stall the moment of truth, but the big V8 crawled up the final hill under its own steam. The driveway was still empty, but I couldn't worry about Tasha and Dalton. I needed to do this, I reminded myself as I trudged to the garage.

Purry Mason met me and twirled ecstatically around my ankles. I picked up the lithe, gray cat and rubbed my cheek against his warm fur. So many good things had happened to me here. *Why does it have to end so badly?*

The cat climbed to my shoulders and we set off together, back to where it all began. With each step toward Blind Man's Bluff, I prayed for those I now thought of as my island family. When I broke out of the winding spruce trail, I saw him standing, resolute as a rock cairn, staring out to sea. I stopped beside him and we stared together at the horizon. It was a long time before I could speak. "Have you been here all this time?"

"Yeah. I saw the boat and knew you'd come eventually. I've

known this was coming since the day you arrived."

"I don't believe that." I looked up at his profile.

I was rewarded with a quirk of his cheek muscle signaling half of a small grin. "Let's just say I recognized the iceberg and Titanic inevitability when you wore my hat that first day." He took off that cap now and ran a weary hand through his cropped, rusty hair. "You figured it out, didn't you?"

"The lesson of the tides finally sunk in, I guess. You saw what happened on the cliff, didn't you? You had to be right down there in perfect position, or the body would've been pulled out on the tide."

"Been talking to Old Stin, I see." He put the cap back in place and faced me, his blue eyes narrowed to slits under the shade of the cupped brim. "I witnessed a death."

"Who was there with Vance?"

"I can't say for sure, and that's the truth." His voice was so unlike him—fast, and it rasped in his throat as if each word had thorns that ripped and tore. He gripped both my hands tightly, but I barely noticed the pressure, holding onto his strength for all I was worth. "When I looked up, Vance was on the ledge. I might not have seen anything, but the breeze was right and I heard him hollering a blue streak. Nothing new there. He was chewing somebody out big time."

"Ron." I whispered the name that had lain heavy on my heart.

"Not likely." The words were spit out like an inhaled black fly.

"But it fits, don't you see? Vance had always belittled him and he couldn't take it anymore. Look, I don't want to see him hurt anymore than you do, but you forget: I saw all of you—Ron, Laurel, and you—throwing something off this very cliff. It had to be evidence of the murder."

"No." Scotty's grip grew painful, but he wasn't aware of his increased force. "I didn't witness a murder. I saw Vance trying to climb up. He slipped, lost his balance, and fell. Ron had no more reason than usual to be at odds with his father that day."

"But the evidence."

"The little chest they threw over?" He laughed a harsh, scornful bray. "Only Vance's stash of papers on all of Ron's misdeeds. I can't imagine Ron ever did anything worthy of his father's permanent demerits." He shook his head. "Okay, I'll admit Ron sneaked into your house a few times and helped himself to the laptop, the telescope, and whatnot. That was my fault. I put in the new code for the security system, but he rewired it. Pretty smart kid, but I had a talk with him and he was going to come clean with you."

"Never mind that. Borrowing a telescope is one thing; murder is another."

"No. He's a Boy Scout. He'd never hurt his father, because it would kill his mom and, despite everything, both Dot and Ron loved Vance. Ron seemed to think Vance had hired a private investigator to, in his words, 'spy' on him and Laurel. Supposedly that was in the chest. I never saw it."

"So if there was nothing incriminating in there, why get rid of it so long after Vance's death?"

"I think it had something to do with a stranger coming and taking over the house."

"Oh."

Purry got up from his mink-stole pose and dropped to the ledge at our feet. At the same moment, Scotty released my hands. He and I both looked down at the mottled flesh. "Sorry. I didn't mean to hurt you." He gently rubbed my hands.

Looking down at his hands, I saw Ron's hands gripping mine and my heart ripped open. A son wouldn't hurt his father, but would a father kill to protect his son? "Who?" I whispered, unaware I'd spoken aloud until Scotty spoke so low I strained to hear him.

"Someone was on their knees, looking down at him. I couldn't see who it was, and God didn't put me here to be another man's conscience."

I bit my bottom lip and spun away, running back along the pathway. My side ached by the time I got inside the doctor's car. "Gwen, wait!" I heard Scotty call, but I cranked up the engine and shot down the road, not touching the brakes until I reached Doug's house.

I slipped in the door without a thought to knocking, not knowing what I'd do or what I'd find. Dr. Beckett sat hunched at his kitchen table, his hands clasped in prayer. "You know, don't you?" he whispered. "I'm glad. I wish it'd been me that went over that cliff."

"You were there when Vance died."

"Yes." He raised dark, owl-like eyes to mine. "I killed him."

"No. Scotty said he saw Vance fall from the ledge."

"I killed him," he repeated dully. "I didn't intend to."

I drew up a chair, sat next to him, and put my arm around his sagging, emaciated shoulders. "It's all right," I crooned. "You were protecting Ron."

My guess made his shoulders straighten. "Ron came here in tears, ready to leave Laurel and leave the island, all because of Vance. I couldn't let him ruin Ron's marriage. I went to talk with him, and there he was, out on the cliff surveying his domain. He never gave me a chance to open my mouth." Doug buried his face in his hands.

"Vance found out about Ron's secret marriage and about his bogus cancer diagnosis," I said softly. "He was angry at you."

He swallowed hard and raised his head. "He was crazy. Said he was suing for malpractice and he pushed me down. I got up and he laughed when I came at him. He stumbled and went over the cliff."

"But he landed on the outcropping. You didn't kill him."

"He was down there screaming and cursing. Have you ever tried to fight sin with sin, Gwen?" He turned haunted eyes to search my face. "I got down on my knees, but I wanted to make Vance promise to give Ron and Laurel his blessing before I helped him up."

An image of the ledge flashed through my mind. "You couldn't have reached down that far."

"I know. I was going to get help after he promised, but he wouldn't have any of it. He just kept ranting. He was so stubborn, so much of a Superman; he was climbing the rock face on his own when he missed a handhold, hit the outcropping, and fell."

He sobbed and I held him close.

"I wanted to confess, but I knew what it would do to Ron."

"Don't you worry, Doc."

I jerked my head up when Scotty's hand came to rest gently, half on Doug's shoulder, half on my supporting arm. "We'll walk through the inquest together."

"It'll be okay," I said. "I'll be there, too."

"I knew it." Scotty's voice was slow and sure, calm as a sleepy ocean; but he winked at me. "Gwen's settling in for a long stay."

"I hope so." Doug looked at me, his mouth trembling.

"Oh, count on it," Scotty continued. "I knew it the minute she rescued scrawny Buenos Noches. That cat'd never survive on the mainland; he's island born and bred. And then there's her crusade for justice. She's got to get Dot back in the Big House. And don't forget all those promises she's made. She has to go handlining with Old Stin."

"And we still need our tea party." I swallowed past the lump of sudden joy in my throat.

"That's right, and don't forget you owe us a picnic on Brass Key." The doctor's voice sounded stronger.

"She's going to be right out straight. Don't know as the island can take it."

"We'll see," I said.

"At this moment we only see the tip of the iceberg, Miss McPhail. There's so much more." Scotty shot me a genuine grin. Just like him to have the last word. I decided to let him, this time.

Dear Reader,

Thank you for taking the trip to Candle Island with us. We hope you enjoyed Gwen's story and plan to join us for more misadventure, miscreants, and mystery in the future.

Obviously, Candle Island and its inhabitants exist in a world of fiction, but we tried to wrap our love of the islands and their people in the pages of this book. Every summer/fall, the Cuffe sisters board a ferry, a mail boat, or cross a bridge, to one of the beautiful islands scattered like diamonds along the Atlantic coast. We've biked, hiked, backpacked, camped, and been stranded a time or two, on these wild, extraordinary shores.

Like Gwen, we believe our hearts shouldn't grow old unless we choose to "pack it in" and lose interest in seizing the opportunities of today. So to all the Gwen-age heroes and sheroes out there, we celebrate the road wear on our bodies, knowing this is the trip of a lifetime and we've gained the wit and hard-won wisdom to relish each step of the way.

You can find us on our Facebook page (: http://tinyurl.com/9cflp7w), and check out our blog, other books and recipes, and some facts and factoids on our website.

Best regards,

Sadie & Sophie Cuffe (real-life sisters forever!)

RECIPES

Gwen's Yummy Donut Muffins

Mix together and set aside:

1 1/2 cups flour
1/4 tsp baking powder
1 tsp nutmeg
dash salt (optional)

Cream together in mixing bowl:

1 cup sugar
1/3 cup shortening

Add one egg and beat well.

Alternately add dry ingredients with 1/2 cup milk.

Bake in greased muffin tins (makes 12) 20-25 minutes.

While muffins are baking mix together:

1 cup sugar
1 tsp cinnamon

Melt 1 stick of butter.

When muffins are done, remove from tins and brush all over with melted butter, then roll in cinnamon/sugar mix.

Best when served warm; easily reheated in microwave for a few seconds.

Gwen's Flatbread

Ingredients:

1 cup milk, scalded
1 tsp salt
1/4 cup warm water
1 package dry yeast (or 2 1/4 tsp)
1/4 cup honey
1/4 cup butter
1 egg
1 tsp sugar
4 cups flour

Instructions:

Place scalded milk in large bowl with honey, butter, and salt. Stir until butter is melted. Let cool.

In a small bowl, combine sugar, dry yeast, warm water. Yeast should bubble.

To milk mixture, add the egg and 1 1/2 cups flour. Mix well.

Add the yeast mixture, followed by 2 1/2 cups flour. Mix until dough is sticky. Knead on a floured surface until smooth.

Place dough in greased bowl, flipping so top is greased as well. Cover and let rise until double (about 1 hour).

Punch down dough and cut into 16 pieces. Form each piece into a ball, then roll to 1/8″ thick, about 8-10″ round.

In large heated skillet (lightly greased), cook for 15 seconds, flip, and cook other side 15 seconds. Bread should be lightly browned.

This flatbread goes well with any filling, but Gwen prefers chicken salad with just a hint of finely chopped onion.

ABOUT THE AUTHORS

The Cuffe sisters live on the edge of the Atlantic, where the sunrise first touches the shores of the USA. They know rural and island life and the unique flavor of Yankee characters—tough and salty as their wave-pounded rockbound coast, and just as solid and unpredictable. Privileged to be raised in a large extended natural and spiritual family, much of their childhood was spent in the churches of Five Islands and Georgetown. The rural church remains a major force in their lives.

They run a small farm Downeast and bring Jane-of-all-trades know-how to their novels, writing squarely to the hearts of real women who aren't twenty-something, who don't wear a size two, and who prefer boots and flannel to high heels and the LBD.

To learn more, visit www.cuffesisters.com.